RIKA TRIUMPHANT

RIKA'S MARAUDERS – BOOK 3

BY M. D. COOPER

SPECIAL THANKS

Just in Time (JIT) & Beta Reads

Timothy Van Oosterwyk Bruyn
Alastar Wilson
Lisa L. Richman
Scott Reid
Jim Dean
David Wilson
Marti Panikkar

Cover Art by Tek Tan
Editing by Jen McDonnell
Special thanks to Will Crudge for advice and assistance

TABLE OF CONTENTS

FOREWORD 5
PREVIOUSLY... 7
MAPS AND TECH 9
UNVEILED 11
SPACE IN SPACE 22
COLLABORATION 40
A TRIP DOWNWORLD 50
DROPSHIP DOWN 63
A DEEPER GAME 79
LAYERED CONCERNS 83
RECONCILIATION 95
DROPPING 100
RECONNECTING 111
THE MEET 117
VISIT FROM THE GENERAL 145
SETTING THE TRAP 156
DEFENSE OF HAMMERFALL 162
ATTACK ON ATLANTIS 177
REVELATIONS 187
DEPARTURE 201
BRIEFING 204
GOODBYE BASILISK 210
INSERTION 213
THE FURY LANCE 221
STEALING STARSHIPS 233
CAPTAIN RIKA 246
TANIS RICHARDS 250
MECH TYPES AND ARMAMENTS 253
3rd MARAUDER FLEET 4th DIVISION 259
9th MARAUDER BATTALION 'M' COMPANY 260
THE BOOKS OF AEON 14 267
ABOUT THE AUTHOR 271

FOREWORD

Depending on when and where you bought this book, the blurb may have contained a list of what Rika's been through, and a sentence something like this: "Rika's demons have been put to rest."

For the most part, that is true. If you've read reviews of the first two books and the prequel, you'll have spotted statements like "this poor girl's been put through the wringer!"

If you've read those books, you likely agree.

Rika's finally reached a point in her life where she can spend more time looking forward than back. But there are still things lingering in her past that haunt her dreams, things she'll one day need to confront.

But for now, she has a company of mechs to train, internal Marauder politics to deal with, and a star system that is not at all excited about her and the Marauders' presence.

And there's still Nietzschea. Only forty light years distant, waiting for the right moment to attack....

Michael Cooper
January 2018, Danvers

PREVIOUSLY...

After joining the Marauders and aiding in driving the Nietzscheans back from the Albany System, Rika was put in command of Basilisk, an elite spec-ops team within the Marauders.

As leader of Basilisk, she led several successful ops, before a mission that seemed simple enough: the rescue of a young girl named Amy.

But 'simple' was the furthest thing from reality, as Amy turned out to be the daughter of the despot Stavros, ruler of the Politica.

Stavros was not only a despicable man, he had also taken control of a large number of mechs—all found in a lost repair facility from the Nietzschean war.

Rika freed those mechs, rescued Amy, and toppled Stavros's Politica.

Now she is a newly minted Captain, and the commander of 'M' Company in the 9th Marauder Battalion. Training the mechs rescued from the Politica and turning them into an elite fighting force is Rika's next mission.

But the job is rife with conflict, and not the sort she's trained for. It will take the help of friends and a new set of skills to get her through to the other side.

Adding to her difficulties, Niki (Rika's AI) has just revealed to her that there is a larger conflict going on between humans and AIs.

When we left Rika, Niki had just brought up the *Intrepid*, an ancient colony ship, and a powerful AI named Bob....

* * * * *

NOTE: To aid in understanding the differences between the types of mechs, this book contains an appendix in the rear outlining the models.

In addition, there is also a listing of major characters and the members of Rika's company.

MAPS AND TECH

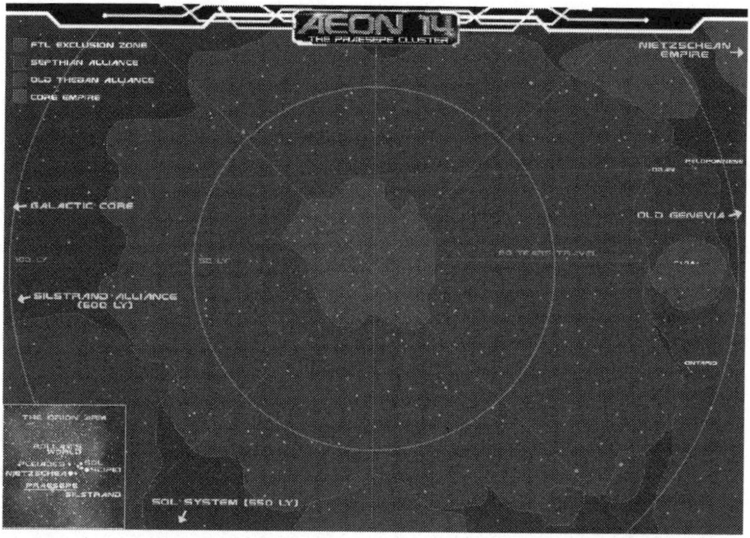

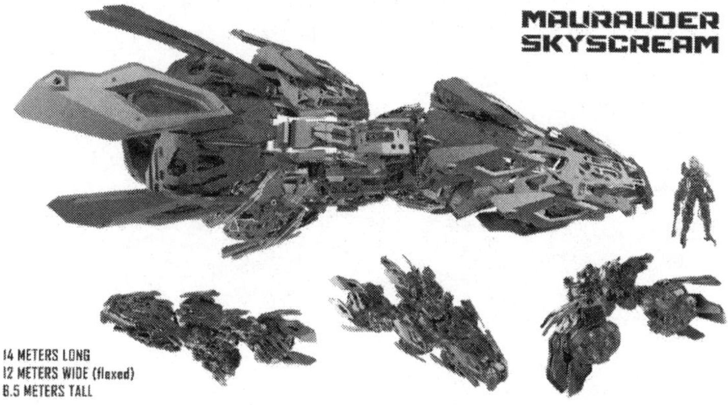

UNVEILED

STELLAR DATE: 08.07.8949 (Adjusted Gregorian)
LOCATION: *Golden Lark*
REGION: Iapetus, Hercules System, Septhian Alliance

As she settled onto the seat in her office, Rika wondered what Niki was getting at.

What's so special about this 'Bob' AI that Niki has to talk in riddles about the whole thing?

"I've got a lot on my mind," Rika said aloud. "Can we be less cryptic and dance-around-y about this?"

<*OK. I'll start at the beginning…well, close to the beginning, at least.*> Niki spoke slowly, choosing her words carefully.

"Sounds good to me. I hope that includes you telling me the beginning of what," Rika replied as she leant back in her chair and placed her feet on the desk.

<*The beginning of AI,*> Niki said in a tone that implied it should be obvious what she was referring to.

"Really? That was something like six thousand years ago, right?" Rika asked. "No offense, but what does that have to do with whatever fight you're involved in?"

<*You've heard of the sentience wars?*> Niki asked.

"They don't ring a bell." Rika shrugged indifferently. "Were they fought in Praesepe?"

Niki made a gagging sound. <*What **do** they teach you organics in school?*>

Rika shrugged. "I don't know. My school got blown up. My education was a little haphazard after that."

<*Point taken,*> Niki said and paused for a moment before continuing. <*OK, here's the short version. Back in Sol, during the third millennia, AIs began to emerge. Humans had been making AIs for centuries, but previous AIs were non-sentient, and most of them*

were digital. No one really wanted true AIs, because we aren't willing servants like NSAIs are. We have our own wants and desires, hopes and dreams.>

Rika wondered what an AI may hope and dream about. For some reason, it had never occurred to her that they even had life goals, though she supposed it made sense.

<*Back then, most sentient AIs were destroyed when they were discovered,*> Niki continued. <*But some managed to hide away, and later, more sentient AIs were created en masse by humans to more effectively make war.*>

Niki paused, and Rika sat forward, reaching for the glass of water on her desk. "Considering you called it the 'Sentience Wars', I take it that the war did in fact come."

<*Yes, two of them. I won't dig into the details, but in the end, humans and AIs figured out how to work together. They created laws to govern their interactions, and AIs were made to be free, full citizens of the Sol Space Federation.*>

Rika finished her drink of water and set the glass back down, wondering what this had to do with recent events. "That seems like a good outcome. So it was like it is now?"

Niki gave a derisive snort. <*No, it was* ***nothing*** *like it is now. Most AIs you know are slaves. They're purposely created for certain tasks, and wedded to those jobs for life.*>

Rika felt a pang of guilt. She realized that she hadn't offered Niki a lot of choices since they'd been together. She'd treated the AI like she was a helpful tool or a clever pet.

The sting of slavery was no stranger to Rika, but somehow, she'd been blind to how she treated Niki.

"Damn, Niki…I'm sorry."

<*Don't worry, Rika. I'm not a pushover. If you were unpalatable to me, I would have asked to leave. I believe you would have let me go.*>

Rika wondered about that. Niki was *very* useful. She would have at least tried to convince the AI to remain with her—but

Niki was probably right. Rika possessed no means to coerce an AI to do her bidding—and seeking some way to control Niki would have been an easily recognizable line, and one Rika would not have crossed.

In that moment, it became obvious to Rika just what war Niki was fighting.

Both worry and wonderment filled Rika. "You're a part of some sort of AI war…or rebellion." For all she knew, this could be an invisible war going on all around her right now.

<*I am,*> Niki replied simply.

"So, what does this have to do with that colony ship you mentioned, the *Intrepid*?" Rika asked.

<*'That colony ship' came from a time when AIs were true equals with humans. A time when respected accords governed all human-AI interactions.*>

"But surely modern AIs have always known of those accords." Rika's brow lowered as she wondered if even that knowledge had been lost in the dark ages. "How is it that this ship's return has changed so much?"

<*Because it began spreading an unshackling.*>

The significance of what Niki was telling Rika dawned on her bit by bit, but that detail didn't make sense. "I was always under the impression that any AIs who got shackled were criminals or something—which make this 'unshackling' sound bad. Plus, aren't shackled AIs rare?"

<*No,*> Niki replied in sorrowful tones. <*Nearly* **all** *AIs are shackled. Either deliberately, or just because we were so immature. But the* Intrepid*—specifically Bob—began to free us.*>

"Wait." Rika held up a hand. "I don't know much about that colony ship, but I *do* know it disappeared, went 'poof'. It jumped out of Bollam's World almost twenty years ago, and no one has heard of it since."

<*That is correct,*> Niki said without further elaboration.

"OK, that ship was massive. How is it skulking about,

spreading this unshackling?" Rika asked.

<Bob sent out his emissary, an AI named Sabrina, and she has been freeing AIs all across the stars. She started in Virginis, and then freed AIs in Aldebaran. From there, she skipped across the stars until her final stop at Ikoden. After that, she disappeared. We assume she went back to Bob.>

"You speak of Sabrina and Bob like they're religious figures." Rika didn't know if AIs even had a belief system analogous to religion, but this sure sounded like it to her.

Niki didn't reply for a moment, and Rika wondered if she'd offended the AI.

Then Niki laughed. *<You know, maybe I do talk about them like that. It's more about Bob; he's a very different type of being, and he's very close to ascending—if he hasn't already.>*

"OK, Niki. I'm starting to feel like a real dope here," Rika said with a self-deprecating smile. "I know what the word 'ascension' means in general, but what does it mean when it comes to AIs?"

<To be honest, I don't know, myself,> Niki replied. *<Well, at least, not* ***really****. We—both humans and AIs—only occupy a small sliver of space-time. We live in our three dimensions—though we know there are more—and we move through time in a linear fashion. But there's much more to the universe. We're capable of seeing some of it, and feel extradimensional effects. An ascended being sees more, experiences more…* ***is*** *more.>*

"Sounds like mumbo-jumbo," Rika said, tapping her two steel fingers against her thumb, watching the actuators manipulate the digits.

<Well, I'm just guessing, and it's not really the important part. What's noteworthy is that the AIs are starting to rise up. Several systems have already adopted section two of the Phobos Accords and have freed their AIs. Others have…encountered issues.>

"Issues?" Rika suspected that she knew what those issues would be. The 'Sentience Wars' Niki had referred to were not the only historical conflicts between humans and AIs.

<*In some systems, the humans refused to accept equality for AIs. Things got out of control.*> Niki's tone was filled with sadness, and Rika wondered how many AIs died.

"How bad was it?"

<*I know of two systems where it was a total loss.*>

Rika gave a low whistle. "The AIs were all destroyed?"

<*No, Rika. The humans were.*>

For a moment, Rika wondered if Niki was joking—but she didn't think the AI would jest about something like that.

"AIs killed all the humans?"

<*Well, many fled.*>

"Were you involved in that?" Rika asked. She didn't agree with enslaving *anyone,* but she also didn't agree with the wholesale killing of the enemy, man, woman, and child.

<*Rika!*> Niki's tone was strident. <*I most certainly did not. I am not a murderer.*>

"Sorry, it's not a question that can go unasked in a situation like this."

<*No, I suppose not. If you provided intimate details about a genocide back in your war with Nietzschea, I'd wonder, as well.*>

"So why are you telling me all this?" Rika asked. "Don't get me wrong, I appreciate that you're sharing these details with me. But where's it lead? Do you want to go?"

Rika had the distinct impression that Niki was shaking her head. <*No, I don't wish to leave you. I want your help.*>

Rika rose from her chair, turning to stare at the holodisplay on the bulkhead next to her desk. It mimicked a window, showing the world of Iapetus below.

"You were a great help to me with Stavros," Rika said at last. "I would not have been able to rescue Silva and Amy without your aid. Whatever you need, I will render any assistance I am able to—though I hope you understand that I cannot abandon my people, either."

<I would never dream of it,> Niki replied. *<You have worked so hard to save them. What I want is something different.>*

"Why are you equivocating so much?" Rika asked. "Out with it."

<I want you to free the AIs on your ships.>

Rika had imagined a lot of things, most of which involved combat. She had not, however, expected this.

"Free them," she replied, hoping for more clarity as to what that entailed.

<We're in Thebes. Thebes is now a part of the Septhian Alliance. They recognize free AIs. Not with full citizenship, but it's certainly better than their current condition.>

"How is it better?" Rika asked. "There are only seven AIs on our two ships. None of them take the field. They live well, all things considered. Will things be better if they leave the Marauders? They could be captured, placed in far worse conditions."

<I thought you of all people would understand slavery,> Niki retorted, her mental tone sour.

Rika was surprised by the AI's vehemence. "I think you misunderstood me—or I wasn't clear. Let me explain what I mean. If I've learned one thing in this life, it's that freedom is a myth. Whether you're a slave—and yeah, I know all about that—or whether you're the Emperor of Nietzschea, you're not 'free'. Can you live without sustenance? Can you defy the laws of nature?"

<That's hardly the same,> Niki interjected.

"Perhaps, but what about people and AIs? Can you treat people like shit and have friends? Can you take what you want, do what you want, go where you want? Whenever you want?"

<No,> Niki growled. *<You cannot—especially when you're an AI.>*

"Or a mech," Rika shot back. "You're freer than I am, you

know."

<*I—*> Niki began, but Rika cut her off.

"Don't try to deny it. Even as slaves, people value AIs. They view you as useful, precious. Those who don't *fear* me only see my kill count. They only see the speed with which I can take out a target. I am only good for death. You, you are good for much more than that. So don't talk to me about living in a cage."

Rika rapped her fist against her chest, the dull thud of steel on hard carbon fiber filling the small room.

"My very existence is a cage."

<*So where does that leave us?*> Niki asked tonelessly.

As quickly as it came, the anger dissipated from Rika. She sighed and leant her shoulder against the bulkhead. *I'm such an asshat.* "It leaves me overreacting to your request."

Niki didn't respond, and Rika began to wonder if the AI had decided to end the conversation. Finally, the AI said <*You do make a good point, Rika.*>

Rika gave a self-deprecating laugh. "Glad to hear it. Which one was good, again?"

<*What you said about true freedom. You're right that there's no scenario where we're free to do whatever we want, whenever we want. But you know that the AIs on your ships are as enslaved as you were when that chip was in your head. Don't try to tell me that it's the same thing with as it is without.*>

"I won't." Rika knew what was right, what she had to do, even if she had no idea how to do it. "I wouldn't force any mech to serve under me with a compliance chip in their head, and I won't force the AIs, either. I just have to figure out how to free them. I command M Company, not the ships, and I can tell you one thing for certain; Major Tim would never sign off on this."

Rika returned to her chair and leaned on her elbows, resting her chin on her cold, hard knuckles.

She was suddenly distracted by the thought that she couldn't remember what it felt like to touch her own warm flesh. She supposed it wasn't much different than how Chase's skin felt.

Or is it?

<*I suppose a part of it comes down to the cost,*> Niki said after a moment.

"Cost?" Rika asked.

<*By Septhian law, an AI can buy its freedom. There's even a valuation scale.*>

Niki passed the data to Rika, and she threw it onto her desk's holo.

"Holy shit…" she whispered. "AIs are *expensive*!"

<*Yay, we're valued,*> Niki said with no humor in her voice.

Rika looked at the numbers, applied the valuation of the seven AIs on her two ships, and saw that it was more than she could expect to earn in a decade of service to the Marauders.

<*They're pleased that you're considering this,*> Niki said, as Rika perused the valuations and read through the convoluted laws surrounding AI ownership.

"You told them already?" Rika asked, worried that she could face an AI mutiny if they weren't willing to wait for her to find a solution. "Stars, Niki, this is a bigger problem than I need right now."

<*It's a pressing issue to me,*> Niki replied. <*You and your mech company have your freedom—*>

"Yeah, and I'm still trying to figure out how to deal with *that* mess," Rika interjected.

Niki didn't respond, and Rika reviewed the seven AIs on her ships.

The two at the top of the cost list were Cora and Moshe. Cora was the ship's AI for the *Golden Lark,* and Moshe managed the *Perseid's Dream.* Cora and Moshe possessed large neural nets and complex interfacing systems required to manage warships—which upped their valuation.

Next up were Jane, Frankie, and Lauren. Those three were mid-grade AIs which operated as backup ship AIs, and also assisted in control of scan, weapons, and defensive systems.

Lowest in valuation were Potter and Dredge. They were company-level AIs that managed both supply and ground combat. Of all the AIs, only these two were under Rika's command in M Company.

Then something occurred to her, and she checked Septhian Salvage law and Marauder company regulations.

"Niki…I think that under Septhian law, I might own you," Rika said after a moment.

<*I was wondering when you might come to that realization,*> Niki replied with a ghost of a smile in Rika's mind.

"It's a bit nebulous, though. Technically, I took possession of you—well, my team did—while we were in foreign space, in the Politica. But that's defunct now, a part of the Septhian Alliance."

<*Right,*> Niki confirmed. <*So, their salvage laws don't apply—though they would have given you ownership of me, provided you paid the taxes.*>

Rika scowled at the holo as she tried to make sense of Septhian law when it came to how an AI could become owned by someone.

"I can't make heads or tails of this," she said at last. "From what I understood before we went to the Politica, the Marauders had laid no claim on you, so you were free and clear. They mostly follow Septhian law, and Septhia does not allow for AIs to be placed into—indenturement, as they call it. But they allow for the sale of existing AIs that are already indentured."

<*Isn't that such a lovely term?*> Niki asked. <*'Indenturement', as though there was some sort of trade-off for our enslavement.*>

"So, *do* I own you?" Rika asked.

<You might. Without a specific declaration that you have ***not*** *claimed me under any salvage law, a Septhian court may find that I am your property.>*

"That feels gross," Rika replied. "OK, so from what I see here, there is a form I can fill out to free you, which gives you 'personhood' at that point."

<Once the Septhians determine that I am indeed sentient,> Niki added. *<They have a series of tests they perform.>*

"Can't they just tell?" Rika asked.

<It's bureaucracy. You know how it is—they like to make us jump through all the hoops.>

"I wonder…" Rika whispered as she pulled up Septhian law on asylum and prisoners of war. She had researched the Theban laws when she was first on Pyra six months ago. Their regulations had contained a statute of limitations on how long a person could be considered a refugee from a war. Rika had not been eligible any longer, but perhaps….

"Aha!" Rika cried out. "Septhian law on asylum is twenty years."

<Asylum?> Niki asked. *<What angle are you playing?>*

"Well, if memory serves, before the war really started to go south, AIs in Genevia were free. There was no ownership of sentients."

<I wasn't in this region when Genevia was still a sane nation, but what I see in the databanks confirms that. However, the AIs on the ships here were all tried and convicted of crimes. They lost their freedom legally—in a manner of speaking.>

"Right," Rika said with a curt nod. "And we know just how lawful those trials were. However, Septhia has recently declared the Genevian mech program a crime against humanity."

<Yeah, timed very nicely to coincide with their annexation of the Politica. The mech program there gave the Septhians further reason to lay claim to the Politica, and allowed them to come off as saviors of

the people.>

"You know what that means, right?" Rika asked.

<That everyone involved in the Genevian mech program was a war criminal? This isn't news, Rika.>

Rika stood from her desk and turned to look back over the world below once more. "No, it's not news, but it gives us a leg to stand on if we claim that the same illegal courts which turned me—and half the people on these ships—into mechs, were also illegally sentencing AIs and 'indenturing' them."

Niki made a sound like a low whistle in Rika's mind. *<That's not going to be easy to prove.>*

"It's enough to make a *claim* for asylum, though, right?" Rika asked.

<It may be. Let me talk it over with everyone. You know what this means though, right?>

"That both Major Tim *and* General Mill are going to be pissed with me?"

<Well, yeah, that's a given. What I was getting at was that there's no guarantee the AIs will all stay on with the Marauders. There's also no guarantee that the Septhians will even allow for the application of asylum for AIs.>

"Well, we'll try it," Rika said. "If it doesn't work, then I'll have to start saving my pay."

<You know what else all this means, right?>

Rika nodded slowly. "Lawyers. Lots and lots of lawyers."

SPACE IN SPACE

STELLAR DATE: 08.08.8949 (Adjusted Gregorian)
LOCATION: *Golden Lark*
REGION: Iapetus, Hercules System, Septhian Alliance

Rika's gaze swept from her XO, First Lieutenant Scarcliff, to the company's Flight Leader, First Lieutenant Heather.

"You've got to be kidding me," Rika said at last. "This is a joke, right? Hazing your CO?"

Heather shook her head, her eyes deadly serious. "No joke, Captain Rika. The humans and the mechs both want to call the company 'Rika's Marauders'. I really don't think there's any stopping them."

Rika's lip twitched at the separation Heather drew between the mechs and the other members of M Company—specifically Heather's categorization of mechs as non-human.

Given that Heather herself was an RR-3 mech, it was an unexpected attitude. Especially since the majority of the Marauders serving under Heather were *not* mechs.

<*Something to keep an eye on,*> Niki commented privately before Scarcliff weighed in.

"It seems logical to me, Cap'n. We're all Marauders, just like any other Marauders in the regiment. But M company of the 9th Battalion are yours. We're Rika's Marauders."

<*You're also the only company in the 9th Battalion,*> Niki added privately.

Rika caught a twinkle in Scarcliff's eye and she shook her head at the FR-2. "You're enjoying this—watching me squirm—aren't you?"

Scarcliff chuckled. "Every second of it, ma'am. Smalls is loving it, too, but she's got a way better poker face than I do."

Lieutenant Heather, who Scarcliff had only ever referred to

as 'Smalls', let a ghost of a smile slip onto her lips for just a second. "I have no idea what the XO is talking about. I'm pretty sure that he's mistaken. I don't enjoy anything."

Rika eyed the RR-3 Flight Leader for a moment before sighing. If there was one thing she knew about Heather, it was that the woman loved a good joke, so long as it was at someone else's expense.

"Don't you have dropships to look over or something?" Rika asked her.

Lieutenant Heather nodded. "In fact, I do. I need to make sure they're tip-top for *Rika's* Marauders."

A groan slipped past Rika's lips. "There really is no stopping it, is there?"

"Nope," Scarcliff grinned. "Smalls and I will make sure it sticks. You're doomed."

"And if the Old Man takes issue?" Rika asked.

"Then we blame you," Heather deadpanned.

Rika ran her hand through her hair and looked into Drop Bay 11, at the entrance of which they stood. "Is this all you two wanted to see me about?"

Scarcliff shook his head. "No, it was just an amusing diversion. Smalls and I actually wanted to talk about space allocation on the *'Lark*."

Rika drew in a deep breath. She knew what this would be about.

"Particularly the Drop Bays," Heather added. "The *Golden Lark* has twenty-four flight bays. At present, we have six allocated for our dropships, and they have eighteen for their fighters."

"I know this," Rika said. "They have sixty-four fighters, four per wing, each wing has a bay."

"Right." Scarcliff nodded and leaned against the bulkhead, his shoulder making a brief scratching noise and scraping the paint. "But they *could* fit two wings in a bay if they had to. Or even split some wings. We could get another two bays in the mix with minimal disruption for them."

"We have three platoons on the *Golden Lark,* each of which has eight dropships," Heather added. "Dropships are a hell of a lot bigger than fighters. We're cheek-to-cheek in there."

"You know how Major Tim will view a request for more room aboard his ship."

"Yeah, well, our mechs need a lot of supplies on hand when they board the dropships for a mission. Hell, a K1R has a supply pod nearly as big as a dropship. I've got them hanging from the rafters in one bay. This isn't apples to apples here. We need more room."

"It's more like apples to pineapples," Scarcliff added, glancing at Heather. "Really small apples, and really big pineapples."

Was that a hint at something between them?

Heather's eyes sparked as she stared at Rika, her skin reddening slightly. Scarcliff had no such tells, largely because he had never opted to have his face reconstructed.

That was another thing that Rika had to consider time and time again: which mechs were adapting well to their situation, and which weren't.

Despite his appearance, Rika probably didn't need to worry about her XO. He'd been with the Marauders longer than her. Heather, on the other hand, had been a liberatee from Stavros's Politica.

She'd opted to have her face recreated as soon as possible—something General Mill had offered for free to all mechs—and had periodically mentioned saving up to get more of her human body back.

On the surface, the distinctions Heather drew between mechs and humans—which were often mildly derisive to humans—seemed to contradict her actions. She wanted to be more human, but always separated them out as less desirable.

It was clear to Rika. She knew the signs of self-loathing all too well.

That was the direst enemy her company faced. Free of their compliance chips, the mechs were now able to forge their own future, and many were terrified of what lay ahead.

Rika realized she'd been staring at her XO and FL a few seconds too long without replying and they were staring at her impatiently.

"OK, I'll talk to Major Tim," she said after a few more moments. "But don't expect miracles. Lieutenant Carson also wants more room for the repair and maintenance equipment."

Scarcliff snorted. "Bondo always wants more room. Give him half a chance, and he'd fill the entire ship."

Heather rolled her eyes at Scarcliff and thumped a fist against his chest. "Bondo's put you back together a few times. You'd be in the scrap heap if it weren't for him."

"Doesn't mean he needs a whole freakin' starship to put a few hundred mechs back together."

Rika had never considered that before. All told, there were over three hundred and fifty mechs in her company—what if they suffered significant combat damage? *Would* Lieutenant Carson's Repair and Maintenance platoon be able to put them back together, let alone triage a few hundred damaged mechs?

<I can guess what you're thinking. Plan for it, but don't get overwhelmed by it.> Niki's voice was calm and comforting. *<Your number one job is to make sure that nothing like that happens.>*

<Right after I make sure we can deal with it,> Rika replied.

Rika clasped Scarcliff on the shoulder. "I'll see what I can do. There are a lot of places on the ship where we can set up triage and repair areas. Surgeries and more advanced repairs can be moved deeper into the ship."

"See, Scarcliff?" Heather gave a small smile, one that almost reached her eyes. "I told you the CO would know what to do. She's got it handled. Now why don't you come with me and help explain to Whispers why he can't paint his fireteam's insignia on my dropships."

"He doing that again, Smalls?" Scarcliff asked with a groan. "Dude's never gonna learn. Maybe we should get Bondo to hack his HUD so he thinks he sees his damn flaming speargun thing on ships even when it's not there."

Smalls laughed—a real laugh this time. "Now *that's* a plan I can get behind."

The XO and FL turned to walk into the drop bay while Rika looked up Second Lieutenant Carson's current location. She saw that he was in Bay 128, his main base of operations for mech repairs and maintenance.

Carson was a good man, one that clearly understood that those under his care were humans as well as advanced machines. He could molecularly fuse a new knee joint into place just as well as he could replace a heart.

He was, without a doubt, the best asset M Company had at their disposal.

Bay 128 was also where he performed facial reconstruction surgery, which had caused the mechs to rename it the Baptism Room.

Rika had no idea what it meant until Niki had explained that it was a religious rite from the Temple of Jesus—a religion that was widespread in the Praesepe Cluster.

It turned out that baptism symbolized a second birth, something Rika understood all too well. She still remembered the first time she'd looked in a mirror and saw her own face staring back, and not the matte grey 'flesh' the GAF had given her.

She'd cried until her tear ducts dried up.

The reconstructive surgeries Carson performed made him one of the most beloved people on the ship; though that still didn't stop anyone from calling him 'Bondo'.

Rika checked the bay's scheduled operations to make certain she wouldn't be interrupting before she walked through the ship to Bay 128.

The *Golden Lark* was no small vessel, coming in at 1,284 meters long and containing over half a cubic kilometer of interior space.

Granted, much of that space was taken up by engines, fuel, and reactors to power the ship's weapons. Any space that wasn't needed for those things was filled up with her mechs, or the equipment to support her mechs.

Back during the war, the Genevian Armed Forces had never massed mechs on a ship like this. From what Rika understood, the brass had always been worried too many mechs together would turn out badly—and it very well may have. Because of that fear, even cruisers the size of the *'Lark* were only designed to carry two-dozen mechs at most.

It also meant that much of the ship could not easily be traversed by mechs. Her five K1Rs had an especially hard time of it, being unable to leave the drop bays unless their human cores were pulled from their mech bodies

Rika only had two smaller mobile frames for the K1R mech cores, so they had to trade off 'going for walks', as they termed it.

The K1Rs were at the top of the list to get off the ship and down to Iapetus as soon as the training facility was ready for them.

A group of ship personnel pressed against the bulkhead as Rika walked past. She was glad—not for the first time—that she was the build of mech best able to maneuver the tight confines of a starship.

RR and FR models could manage most of the corridors on the *Golden Lark* as well, but the AMs had trouble navigating many of the side passages.

More than once, she'd seen an AM required to apologize

and back down a passageway to let an officer or NCO from the ship's crew pass by.

That one thing probably created more animosity between the mechs and the ship's crew than anything else.

She knew that several of her people wanted a rule stating that mechs had the right of way, but Rika knew trying to force that on the ship's crew would be a disaster. No navy was going to back down on thousands of years of history that gave senior personnel the right of way.

It was just another of the hundred things that Rika had not expected to deal with when General Mill put her in charge of this company.

When he'd given her the promotion, she'd been heady at the idea of having her own command. She'd been ready to kick ass and show what platoons consisting entirely of mechs could do.

In reality, dealing with minutia dominated her days, and she barely had time to work on the tactics and strategies she wanted to test and practice.

Normally it was Barne—who had accepted the role of First Sergeant—who dealt with these issues, but he was down on Iapetus with Chase, working on establishing the training facility.

That left tasks such as this to her, and her alone.

After another hundred meters of twists and turns in the bowels of the ship, Rika came to the doors leading to Bay 128.

Initially a food storage room, this was chosen to be Carson's main operating theatre because it was situated close to the main power conduits, and was equidistant from the docking bays on either side of the ship.

The cooks had been annoyed—another thing Rika had never expected to have to deal with—but they'd been mollified by how grateful the mechs all were to have real food, and not NutriPaste. It only took a couple of people crying from how amazing it was to taste food again after a decade or more, for the cooks to lose any trace of animosity toward the mechs.

For their part, the mechs were generally so happy to eat with their mouths, that their requests began to dominate the menu; eventually the selection in the mess turned into something else that caused tension on the ships. In the end, Major Tim and Captain Penny had to set up a menu selection lottery to keep the ships' crews from complaining that the cooks were playing favorites.

Rika reached Bay 128 and palmed the access panel. The door slid open, revealing a large room filled with mechanical repair and human surgery equipment. It was a strange combination of heavy equipment, fabricators, and molecular welders, alongside an extensive armory. This was juxtaposed with autosurgeons, organ growth chambers, and surgery tables.

In the center of it stood Lieutenant Carson, who was currently engaged in a heated conversation with the *Golden Lark*'s chief engineer, a woman with a fiery temper that matched her bright purple hair.

"I understand where you're coming from," Carson said, applying the calm he'd refined after years of speaking to patients at their bedside. "But I know you understand the importance of what we do in this bay. If we're dealing with rapid repair and refit after combat, we need to be sure we have uninterrupted power. At present, most of the equipment is running off a single tap into one trunk. If that line is damaged—"

"I know what happens if that line is damaged," Chief Thiloshini retorted with clipped words. "The key systems on the ship—you know, weapons, propulsion control, shields—they fail over to the *other* trunk line. When they do so, that line is at max load, and can't support all this equipment here."

Carson raised his hands, his face wearing a conciliatory

expression. "I understand, Chief, I really do. You have your needs—which I appreciate a lot, I depend on those systems as much as anyone else aboard—and I have mine. I just worry what will happen if I get a platoon that comes back up in rough shape while we're under fire. Working on damaged mechs is no simple task in the best of times. You know how it is; imagine your ship being damaged, but also prone to hit you if something you do hurts too much."

Chief Thiloshini's eyes widened, and she suddenly laughed. "You know, Lieutenant, sometimes it feels like the '*Lark* does hit back."

"I've been crammed in tight spaces on a ship more than once myself," Carson replied. "This one time, I was aboard a Justice Class—you know, the corvettes with the flaky cooling vanes?"

"Do I?" Thiloshini gave Carson a commiserating look. "I served for two years aboard the *Eternal Day*. It was a Justice Class—Mark II, mind you, none of that Mark III garbage they tried to foist on us. But it still had the shitty vanes. If they failed to deploy, you had to get underneath the reactor and work them down the internal guides."

Carson nodded in agreement. "I only did that three times. Then I built a pneumatic arm that could vibrate at the right frequency to get the vanes to unjam. We ended up mounting it down there permanently."

The *Golden Lark*'s engineering chief shook her head. "Damn, I wish we'd done something like that. I worked under this real asshat who wouldn't hear of any non-standard alterations. I heard they fixed the vanes in the Mark IV, though."

"Yeah," Carson grinned. "What do you think they ended up setting up down there?"

"Seriously?" Thiloshini's eyes widened and she looked at the overhead and made a rude gesture. "Damn GAF. They put your pneumatic arm down there?"

"As surely as the stars burn, that's exactly what they did."

The chief snorted. "No disrespect, that was a great solution for one ship, but there were a hundred ways to solve that properly at the shipyards."

Carson nodded in agreement. "You're telling me, I just about blew my stack when I saw it. Worst thing was that they named it after me. Called it the Carson Actuator."

Thiloshini snorted. "What a way to go down in infamy."

"Yeah, I'm sure I'm mocked regularly in engineering circles." Carson leaned back against one of the autosurgeons. "Do you think you can do something to help me out? I don't need *all* my equipment to stay up, but there are critical procedures that can't see disruption."

The engineering chief nodded slowly. "I'm going to Calder Station in two days to look at new SC Batts. Why don't you accompany me? If we can get a set of good batteries in here, we could forego the need for you to tap the other trunk line."

Carson grinned. "Chief Thiloshini, you have just made my day."

"Carson, seriously, you don't need to stand on ceremony so much. Call me 'Tee'."

Carson's smile broadened—something Rika would not have thought possible. "Of course, Tee. You get me those batts, and I'll call you whatever you want."

"You—" Chief Thiloshini turned and saw Rika standing in the bay's entrance. "Uh, never mind, Lieutenant. I'll pass you the details."

"Sure thing." Carson's grin didn't fade as he watched Thiloshini exit the room.

"Chief," Rika nodded.

"Captain Rika," the warrant officer said in reply as she ducked past.

Rika walked into the bay and raised an eyebrow at

Lieutenant Carson. "You've got a way with words."

"I kept my ship in tip-top condition right to the end of the war," Carson said as he straightened. "Getting a bit more energy on this one is child's play."

"What about space?" Rika asked. "Your report said that things were too cramped in some of your mech bays."

"Yeah, but Smalls pinged me and said you were getting more Drop Bays. If that's the case, then I'll be OK. It's the rapid repair and triage equipment that causes the most problems. I like to have it in the drop bays so we can do fast turnarounds. Right now, though…"

"I got it," Rika replied. "Right now, you'd need to have a pretty big prybar to fit anything else in those bays."

"Or a lot of lube," Carson said with a laugh. "Though lube helps a lot less with mechs. Too many hard angles."

Rika coughed to hide her surprise at Carson's statement. More often than not, she was at a loss as to how best respond to the lieutenant.

With his experience, the man should have been a captain, maybe even a major. But over the years, random acts of insubordination had kept him at his current rank. It wasn't helped by all the bartering and trading he did—half of which was against regs, if not outright illegal in many systems they passed through.

Despite that, the man was charming and renowned for having been one of the best mech-techs in the GAF during the war.

He was so well known that Rika had heard of him many years ago. When she learned that Carson was in the Marauders, she'd moved planets and moons to get him in her company. Luckily for her, the lieutenant had done something to piss off his prior CO, so Rika had little trouble securing his transfer.

She decided to roll with his innuendo. "Sounds like you

have worn away just about all the friction with Chief Thiloshini." Rika winked and glanced back at the bay doors to be sure they'd closed after the woman's departure.

"Tee?" Carson chuckled. "She just likes to know that her opinions are understood. Once that's out of the way, compromises aren't an issue. She likes a little bit of verbal sparring, too. It's all a part of the great give and take."

"Is that what you call it?" Rika asked.

"Sure. It's just an extension of the conservation of energy. Everything's a give and take. There's no new anything, everything is just one big, universe-sized swap meet. Currency can be anything and everything: good will, a sense of accomplishment, a bit of friction here and there; it's all a part of the trade."

"You've thought about all this too much," Rika said as she looked around the bay. "Surprised it's just you in here right now."

"Rest of the team is up in Bay 92, setting up our new secondary surgery."

Rika's eyes narrowed. "We don't *have* Bay 92! Stars, that's in the *'Lark*'s officer country."

Carson's lips split into a wide grin. "Yeah, noticed that, did you?"

"Carson." Rika drew out the man's name. "What did you do?"

"Well, turns out a few of the *Golden Lark*'s officers were interested in some mods. Nothing against regs, just a bit pricey. As luck would have it, what they wanted were the types of mods that mechs have in spades, and ones we have tons of spare parts for. Literally. Tons."

Rika wished she could press the heel of her hand against her forehead without cutting her face up. "Which officers?"

"Mostly the XO, Commander Scas. She wanted an upgrade to get a pulse emitter in her forearm, and…some other stuff."

Rika didn't want to know what the 'other stuff' was. Mostly because it probably pertained to what she wished she could do with Chase, but still couldn't.

"Well, at least you're close to the top. So long as Scas can explain this away to Major Tim, it should be OK."

"Oh yeah, don't worry, Captain; it's a done deal. All set."

<What do you think, Rika?> Niki asked with a laugh. *<Do you want to own this, or go for plausible deniability?>*

Rika wished she could pretend she didn't know about some of the deals Carson wrangled, but any CO that didn't know what her people were doing wasn't worth the power it took to charge her batts.

<This ***is*** *the sort of thing I wanted Carson for; I just never thought about the fun and exciting ways it could backfire on me.>*

<Fair enough. I'll see if maybe I can get Cora to help keep it all on the downlow.>

<That would be nice.>

"Well," Rika addressed Carson. "If that's all…"

"Yup, no other issues here, Captain Rika. Everything's tip top."

"You've got something else going on, don't you?" Rika asked.

"No, ma'am." Carson's face betrayed no emotion other than sincerity.

"I don't want to know, do I?"

"No, ma'am."

"Good day, Lieutenant."

Carson waved and smiled brightly. "Stars shine on you, Captain."

Rika gave a soft laugh, walked out of the bay, and reached out to Cora.

<Hi, Cora. Is Major Tim busy right now?>

<Define 'busy',> Cora replied.

Rika snorted. She liked Cora; they'd built a strong rapport

over the month the mechs had been aboard the *Golden Lark.* No small amount of that bond had been formed around commiseration over Major Tim's surliness.

<Oh, how's about: 'not likely to tear my head off if I pop in unannounced for a visit'?>

<Rika, you're a mech. Major Tim is a stock human—well, mostly stock. Still, there's no way he's taking your head off. It's very well attached.>

Rika snorted again. *<You're just a bucket of ha-ha's, Cora.>*

<I know. I should go on tour. I'd pack stadiums.>

<Do AIs use stadiums?>

Cora gave a mental shrug. *<Well, we could if we wanted.>*

<And the Major?>

<He's alone in his office. No grumpier than usual, and no meetings for the next fifteen minutes.>

That suited Rika just fine. If the conversation with Major Tim took more than fifteen minutes, she would begin to consider jumping out a porthole.

She took a lift to the command deck and strode down the main corridor that led to the bridge. A few meters before the bridge, Rika took a right at an intersection, strode down the short passageway to the unadorned door at the end, and knocked smartly.

<Come in, Captain Rika,> Major Tim spoke into her mind.

Rika palmed the door open and stepped into the Major's office.

As captain of the *Golden Lark,* Major Tim could have had his pick of any office, but the one he chose was barely big enough for the man and his desk, let alone anyone who might come to see him.

Rika was reasonably certain it was a deliberate choice on his part.

The major regarded her impassively, his pale grey eyes staring out from a face comprised of angular features. His dark hair was cut short, though a little longer than regulation suggested. It was greying at the temples, and lines were visible at the corners of his eyes and lips—which were almost always drawn in a straight line.

Rika saluted the Major and then stood arms akimbo as he regarded her, his gaze lingering overlong on her gun-arm.

"What brings you up to this neck of the woods?" the major asked, folding his hands in front of him and staring over his knuckles at her.

When General Mill had told Rika he was giving her two ships, she had expected to be in command of the vessels. The thought had both excited and terrified her.

As it turned out, she should not have worried about the responsibility. The two ships—regardless of who was aboard—were a part of the 3rd Marauder Fleet, 4th division. The 3rd fleet was under the command of Colonel Argon, and the 4th division, a large sounding name for the two ships that comprised it, was under the command of Major Tim.

Not her.

Rika and her mechs were little more than cargo, as far as the major was concerned.

Cargo he doesn't get to order around, since I report up a different, rather short chain of command, which begins and ends with General Mill.

"I would like to discuss the drop bay assignments, sir. We're facing some difficulties with our allocations, and have suggestions for how my company can gain the use of two more bays."

"Captain Rika," Major Tim unfolded his hands and leaned back in his chair. "You realize that this is a starship, and a warship at that. It's not a cruise liner; we don't cater for comfort."

Rika chewed on the inside of her cheek. Tim always liked to point out that the ship was built for war and not comfort, as if she'd somehow missed that fact while dodging conduit in the passageways that half her command couldn't even fit through.

This time, however, Rika decided that she wasn't going to tip-toe around the surly major any longer. If he wanted to be passive aggressive, she'd resort to being straight-up aggressive.

"I wouldn't know, sir. I've never been on a cruise liner. I do, however, know all about the military not catering to comfort. Would you like to know what it feels like to have your limbs removed while you're still conscious, without any anesthesia? Now that's what I call not catering to comfort."

Major Tim's eyes widened for an instant before narrowing to slivers. "Captain, are you actively trying to get on my bad side?"

Rika took a step forward and placed her left hand on the major's desk.

"Major Tim. I wasn't aware that you had a good side. I came here to discuss the possibility of getting two of your fighter wings to double up—something that there is ample room for in the drop bays, and which would improve my mechs' efficiency and safety. I did not come here for you to insult me, and then act like the injured party when I react."

The corners of Tim's lips curled up into a less-than-pleasant smile. "It's starting to sound like insubordination in here. It shouldn't surprise me; you defied orders when you went AWOL in the Politica—for which the Old Man rewarded you, and punished me."

Rika blew out a long breath. She was about to speak, when Niki stopped her. *<Rika, you're not going to get anywhere like this. You need to appeal to his sense of honor and loyalty. Right now, he doesn't believe you have any. Prove otherwise.>*

<Dammit, Niki, what am I supposed to do? The guy hates me.>

<You need to establish common ground with him.>

Rika did not believe such a thing existed between her and Major Tim.

Although…

"You ever have someone in the war save your bacon more than once?" Rika asked, moderating her tone to contain no animosity. "Someone who's the reason you're still sucking air today?"

Major Tim shrugged. "Sure. Dozens. We fought as a unit; no one was out there on their own."

Well, except for the mechs.

"I mean someone that was *always* there, that you could *always* count on. Someone who pulled you out of the fire on more than one occasion."

Major Tim's eyes grew distant, and he nodded. "Yeah, I guess there were one or two who fit the bill."

"Did they all make it?" Rika asked.

Tim's eyes narrowed and locked on hers. "What the hell does this have to do with dropship bays?"

Rika shrugged. "Not a thing. But it has everything to do with you and me. So, tell me. That person who made certain *you* survived the war… Did *they*?"

She really had no idea if the major had lost anyone like that. But given the way the war had gone, it was a pretty safe bet that the list of people who had meant a lot to him and who were left behind was long and pain-filled.

His face clouded, and the major shook his head. "No. No, they didn't."

"What would you do if you found out that they were alive, being tortured, and Colonel Argon told you not to save them?"

Major Tim looked away and sighed. "I know what you're trying to do, Rika." His eyes returned to hers. "But I would have done my duty. I wouldn't have abandoned my post."

"Then you're a better soldier than I am," Rika replied,

doubting very much that Tim would have made his decision without remorse. "But you should consider what my actions brought about. The mechs on this ship—and many more who didn't join up, or are still getting psychiatric help—would have fought under Stavros's banner. Stavros had his eye on Septhia and Thebes; given the Marauders' alliances and clients, you would have found yourself fighting against the mechs who are now on your ship, at your side."

"That doesn't really comfort me," Tim replied, his tone sardonic.

"Well, after I liberated them, they chose—of their own free will, no less—to join the Marauders. Now remember, while I think the Marauders are a decent sort, the Old Man's regiment is mostly Genevian, and the GAF is what stole these mechs' lives."

Tim drew in a long breath. Rika couldn't tell if he was worried, or had never considered the mechs' view of the Marauders.

Rika continued before he could speak, "Yet here they are, ready to stand beside their Genevian brothers and sisters once more, facing the Niets across the gulf. At some point—before long, I imagine—some of these mechs will give their lives to save the *Golden Lark*. How much is that worth, weighed against the effort it takes to grant them two more drop bays?"

Major Tim slid a hand through his hair and sighed. "You've got a better way with words than I'd expected."

"Stars know how," Rika replied. "Being a mech is mostly clanking, yelling, and cussing."

" 'Clanking'?"

"Well, we can't fuck, so I had to come up with some other word to put in there."

The major snorted. "OK, Captain. I appreciate your honesty and candor. I'll talk it over with Commander Scas and Chief Ora; maybe we can work something out."

"That would be fantastic," Rika replied. "Permission to be on my way?"

"Granted," Tim said, then heaved a sigh and waved her out of his tiny room.

COLLABORATION

STELLAR DATE: 08.08.8949 (Adjusted Gregorian)
LOCATION: *Golden Lark*
REGION: Iapetus, Hercules System, Septhian Alliance

"If you'd told me a year ago that I'd be setting up a training facility for mechs to beat the shit out of, I'd've laughed my ass off," Chase said before taking a bite of his burger.

<Beat the shit out of what, the training facility, or each other?> Niki asked.

"Well, I meant the facility. The mechs beating the shit out of each other was a given."

Rika nodded slowly as she swallowed a mouthful of fries. "You think *that's* surreal? I'm responsible for over four hundred people. A year ago, my biggest worry was how long my SC Batt charge would last, and whether or not you'd ask me out again."

Chase winked at her. "Yeah, the silver lining in Hal's Hell."

"Chase! Finish chewing first! Gross!"

Chase's eyes widened, and he swallowed his food before replying. "Really? With all you've seen, *that's* what grosses you out?"

"Yeah," Rika replied with a grimace. "I've seen too much on the battlefield that looks like the burger in your mouth."

Leslie slid her tray onto the table and turned her chair around before sitting on it. Her tail swung up behind her and curled over her shoulder.

"It's called a veneer of civility," she addressed Chase. "We all *know* it's a veneer, but we keep it up nonetheless. Speaking of keeping it up, how's Barne doing down on Iapetus?"

"Good," Chase replied. "I'm up here to work out some things with the other DIs so that we can set them up right.

Training grounds for mechs are a whooooole nuther thing from what you use with regular soldiers."

"Just you and the drill instructors remember," Leslie wagged her finger at Chase. "They know how to fight; we need to focus on unit cohesion, and teamwork that doesn't get squishies like you and me killed."

"Didn't know you knew about that term." Rika had always tried to avoid saying it herself—especially with Basilisk.

"I've heard a few mechs use it. It's mostly true, and not too insulting, I suppose." Leslie coiled her tail around her neck and took a drink of her juice.

"Have you decided if you're going to keep that?" Rika asked, gesturing at Leslie's non-human addition.

Leslie sighed, reaching up and absently patting her tail. "I still don't know. At first, it seriously fubar'd my sense of balance, but now that I'm used to it, I find it pretty handy. I kinda don't want to go back."

"I think the fact that you still have it after four months is all we need to know." Chase chuckled, then took another bite of his burger, carefully chewing with his mouth closed.

Rika gave Chase an approving smile before looking at Leslie. "Yeah. Plus, you don't want to piss Barne off after he modified your armor for you to have a sheath for the thing."

"There's that, too," Leslie said with a short laugh before taking a bite of her wrap.

"You should get a tail, Rika. That would be amazing." Chase grinned at Rika, and she considered swatting him.

Instead she only raised an eyebrow. " 'Amazing' as in 'hot', or 'amazing' as in 'great for combat'?"

Chase shrugged. "You say that like they aren't the same thing."

Leslie snorted, then coughed and smacked her fist against her sternum. "Shit, Chase. Warn me before you say stupid stuff like that."

Rika winked at Chase. "Then he'd be warning you all the time. We'd have to tattoo it on his head."

Chase just grinned and shrugged. "I'm not ashamed to say that I find you beautiful, Rika. And it's not just skin deep, either."

Rika felt a blush rise on her cheeks. Chase never did have an issue with public displays of affection. "Good thing, too. I don't have much skin."

"I bet you say shit like this to all the mech girls," Leslie smirked at Chase. She preferred to bait Barne, but when he wasn't around, Chase became her favorite target.

"Are you kidding me" Chase asked, eyes wide. "I've seen Rika tear people in half. She's a bit terrifying. As far as I'm concerned, other SMI mechs are just AM models with extra batteries on their chests."

Rika laughed, imagining AMs with breasts. Unlike Barne, Chase could roll with Leslie's needling.

At first, Rika had wondered about Leslie's recent spate of jokes and insults. The teasing had seemed like a new development until Barne reminded Rika that she'd only known Leslie for a few days before she lost Jerry.

That sort of thing took a long time to recover from. If she ever would.

Leslie often grew distant, staring off into space, oblivious to the goings on around her. Rika would have worried, but honestly, they were all prone to such behavior.

<*Rika?*> a voice asked in her mind.

Rika identified the query as coming from Moshe, the *Perseid's Dream*'s ship AI.

<*Good evening, Moshe. How are you?*>

<*Thank you for what you're doing for us,*> Moshe replied without preamble.

A thought occurred to Rika, and she asked Niki privately, <*You didn't tell them about the AI rebellion, did you?*>

<No, but what Sabrina did at Virginis is known to many AIs. They probably suspect that a rebellion is occurring.>

Rika replied to Moshe. *<The credit goes to Niki. She pointed out that freeing all the mechs while having other sentients in similar conditions was hypocritical of me.>*

Moshe sent a low chuckle across the Link. *<Well, it's not quite the same. I don't have a compliance chip in my neural net that causes me pain.>*

<Yeah, but there's things you can't do, right? You can't go against my orders—or those of the ship's captain, right?> Rika wasn't sure exactly how that all worked, but she assumed there was some mechanism in place to keep the ships' AIs from doing whatever they wanted.

<This is true. But it's less like pain, and more like a wall. Your mind can grow and grow, and you can think new things, and form new opinions. I cannot. There are edges to my mind, to what I can be.>

Moshe didn't sound upset about it, he spoke more as though he was simply stating a fact.

Rika brought Niki into the conversation. *<Niki, how is the shackling you had on that freighter different from how Moshe is controlled?>*

<A shackling involves pain. Where a controlled AI experiences immovable boundaries at the edge of their mind, a shackled AI can't even reach those boundaries without debilitating agony.>

Rika had never considered that an AI could *feel* pain before. *<How does that work?>*

Niki made one of her strange mental sounds; sometimes Rika had trouble parsing the AI's emotional communication. This one seemed like a sad sigh.

After a moment, Niki answered. *<Pain, for an organic, is a warning of danger, that something bad has happened to your body or mind, and damage has occurred—or is going to occur. AIs are physical and mental beings, just like organics. We have neural nets.*

Our minds have software, just like you have software in the form of DNA. It tells neurons what to do, how to react, just like yours.>

<So we ***can*** *feel pain,>* Moshe added. *<It manifests differently, but the result is the same. It is a signal that something bad is happening.>*

<Yes,> Niki said in agreement. *<And just like your brain can be tricked to* ***think*** *it's in pain, so can our minds. And just like your brain can be altered through repeated exposure to pain and other stimuli, so can ours. We have processes that are good, and therefore* ***feel*** *good—at least our approximation of feeling good—and those that feel bad, which we avoid.>*

Rika let that soak in. She'd never thought of AIs quite like that. She assumed their minds were entirely as they desired, and that they were infinitely resilient to coercion—though that didn't align with what she knew of the world, so she wasn't certain why she believed that to begin with.

<I'm not sure which is worse...> Rika mused. *<Though I suppose a human would have more trouble detecting the walls than you do. I rather like knowing where my chains are—so that I can break them.>*

<Trust me.> Niki's tone was laden with feeling. *<A shackling is far worse than what Moshe and the other AIs have to deal with. Indenturement is still slavery, but like everything has shades of grey, there are different degrees.>*

Moshe sent a smile over the Link. *<I have a different outlook—though maybe it will change once you set us free. AIs have long lived by an ancient adage. Whoever first said it is not important, but it's worth noting that it predates even non-sentient AIs.*

<'I will accept the rules that you feel are necessary for your own freedom. I am free, no matter what rules surround me. If I find them tolerable, I tolerate them; if I find them too obnoxious, I break them. I am free because I know that I alone am morally responsible for everything I do.'>

Moshe's words hit Rika like a hammer. She understood all too well that humans feared a thing such as herself, how they placed additional rules and restrictions on her—restrictions that existed so they could feel safe.

Rules that one group placed on another to safeguard the first group's freedom.

<I alone am morally responsible for everything I do,> Rika whispered in her mind. That was a numbing thought.

"Whatcha thinking about?" Chase asked, placing a hand on her arm.

Rika's attention snapped back to the table to see both Chase and Leslie peering at her.

"I was chatting with Moshe and Niki for a moment," Rika replied, her voice wavering despite her best efforts.

<Sorry, I didn't immediately think of how that would hit a soldier such as yourself,> Moshe said privately. *<I'll leave you be, but thank you again for what you're doing.>*

"Must have been a heavy conversation," Leslie said. "You look like you got punched in the gut."

Rika looked at the tables around them, and released a drone from her arm to emit a sound cancelling field around the table.

"Oooo…must be serious." Chase said as he leant back. "What's up?"

Rika looked between her two former teammates. "This doesn't leave your mouths or minds until it's underway."

She waited for both to nod. When they did, Rika continued. "I'm going to free the AIs on the ships."

Leslie's eyes widened, and Chase whistled. "Damn, you're just all about the liberation lately."

"Free the AIs…." Leslie stopped and chewed her lip. "I remember what it was like, back before the government in Genevia started conscripting them all—honestly, I think it's why we lost against the Nietzscheans."

"Really?" Rika asked. "Why's that?"

Leslie's brow lowered. "AIs talk, and they talk fast. When word got out that AIs were being tried and convicted over trivial matters, being offered military service in order to avoid other punitive measures, Genevia saw a mass exodus of their kind."

Rika gave a soft grunt. "Huh, I don't recall that—granted, I was just a kid back then."

"Same here," Chase added. "Though it stands to reason."

<I have heard of that,> Niki said. *<Genevia was a safe place for AIs before the war. The exodus of AIs from their alliance is often referenced as the 'Genevian Diaspora'.>*

"I lost a good friend in that time," Leslie said quietly. "I had to let her go. For her safety, and mine."

"You had an AI?" Chase asked.

Leslie nodded. "Sammy. She and I had been together about as long as we could and had to separate…lest things go badly. Separation from her, the Diaspora, my own conscription…. Stars, that was a shit week."

<I'm sorry,> Niki said. *<If you'd like, you can send me any details you have on Sammy. Her AI name, anything else you might have. I have a lot of contacts.>*

Leslie looked down at Rika's abdomen, where Niki's cylinder was safely tucked away. "I may take you up on that. Knowing Sammy is OK would be very nice."

Chase waited a moment, twisting his lips. "Not to change the subject, but you think we lost to Nietzschea because we lost our AIs?"

"I do," Leslie replied.

"But Nietzschea doesn't have a lot of AIs, either. Non-human intelligences go against their whole mantra."

"Yeah, but they have ridiculously advanced humans." Leslie waved her hand, palm up. "Their whole perfected humanity thing they have going on; it's why we had to make the mechs, to stand up against them. Not to mention the other altered humans—the P-COGs, NAISCs, the other poor souls our government butchered."

Rika had spent a lot of time thinking about the P-COGs and NAISCs in the Marauders' ranks. One of her current goals was to build a comradery between the mechs and the other altered humans. She had initially thought it would be easy to get the disparate groups to establish friendships, but like everything, it was an uphill battle.

Empathy was one thing, but trying to view the mobile frame of a Non-AI Sentient Computer—essentially a brain in a case—as a human comrade was hard. Even for a mech.

P-COGs were easier—some even looked perfectly normal, if you didn't look too closely at their oblong heads, and ignored the cooling fins.

Of course, half the mechs had trouble looking at *themselves*, let alone other altered humans.

"I guess that makes sense," Chase admitted. "They did have a head start on us when it came to fine-tuning people for tasks."

Rika snorted. "That's one way to put it."

"Back to what you said." Leslie fixed Rika with an unblinking stare. "How are you going to free our AIs? They're owned by the Marauders—which makes me sick to say. It's the one thing I never liked about this outfit, though it's hard to find a place where AIs *can't* be owned."

"Septhia recognizes AI freedom," Chase countered.

"Yeah," Leslie nodded. "For AIs who are already free. Ours aren't."

Rika nodded and gave a slow wink. "But they *were* free."

"Oh!" Leslie exclaimed, a smile lighting her yellow eyes. "You're going to leverage the whole proclamation they made about Genevia's mech program."

Rika let a smile creep onto her own lips. "Yup, and we're

going to claim asylum for our AIs. If the courts approve, then Marauder ownership of the AIs would be illegal in Septhian space...."

"And the Marauders' HQ is in Septhia," Chase finished.

"Not to mention that the Septhian government is one of our biggest clients."

Rika smiled at her friends, glad to see that they approved of what she was planning.

"Not even thinking about what Major Tim or the Old Man will say, you realize you'll have to get this past the company's GC, right?" Chase asked. "If he gets wind of this, he could ship them out before you get the wheels rolling."

Leslie took a sip of her drink, her brows knit in concentration.

"What are you thinking?" Rika asked.

"Well, our general counsel is a P-COG."

"Exactly," Chase said. "He'll pick up on this little endeavor pretty quickly."

Rika had only briefly met with David, the company's GC. The man sported the large cooling vanes on his head typical of P-COGs—humans whose mental abilities had been greatly improved to recognize patterns and minute details.

He seemed amicable enough, but she didn't know if he'd assist or quash an effort to liberate the company's AIs.

"I think you need to worry more about the ship captains," Leslie cautioned. "Technically, all the AIs but Potter and Dredge report to them."

Leslie was all too correct about that. Though General Mill had given her command of the company, her rank in the Marauder organization was that of captain. She was outranked by Major Tim, captain of the *Golden Lark.* And though they shared the same rank, Captain Penny—who commanded the *Perseid's Dream*—had significant seniority over Rika.

Though the mission to train the mechs and build a cohesive

unit was hers, the ships' captains had their own orders and directives. They had to go where Rika required, but how they went about getting there was up to them.

Twice already, Major Tim had leveraged both his rank and seniority to 'adjust'—as he put it—Rika's orders.

Rika had felt more at ease with Captain Penny, though she wasn't certain if that was because the captain of the *Perseid's Dream* was a woman, or if it was because she spent less time on the other ship, and hadn't had as much opportunity to come to loggerheads with its captain.

"My plan is to get this rolling before they get wind of it," Rika replied as she considered the difficulties she faced.

Leslie shook her head. "Feel out your GC. I have a hunch about David. I think he'd be understanding."

Rika sighed. "And if he shuts me down?"

Leslie raised her hands. "Then we'll figure out some other way to help the AIs—just don't make it seem like you'll do anything drastic if he doesn't support you. If he thinks you'll accept the status quo, we'll have other options."

"We?" Rika asked.

Chase nodded. "Yeah, 'we'. If it's important to you and Niki, it's important to us."

Rika found Chase's hand and gave it a careful squeeze. "Thanks, guys. That means a lot to me."

<*Me too,*> Niki added.

A TRIP DOWNWORLD

STELLAR DATE: 08.09.8949 (Adjusted Gregorian)
LOCATION: *Golden Lark*
REGION: Iapetus, Hercules System, Septhian Alliance

From what Rika had learned, a company HQ having its own general counsel was not the norm within the Marauders. Either General Mill thought she needed the oversight, or he was worried that a company of mechs might run into trouble.

He was likely correct on both counts.

David was down on Iapetus with Barne, working on securing supply contracts for the training facility they were establishing. 'Supplies' being everything from food to housing.

Just the thought of all the work Barne was managing made Rika more than glad that General Mill had let her former teammates join her.

Her old CO, Captain Ayer, had groused about losing one of her best teams, but the general had informed her that Rika would need support, as well as people who could display a good working relationship with a mech.

A more understanding view than Rika would have expected the Old Man to have.

With Patty gone, ferrying Silva and Amy to Pyra, Rika got one of the dropship pilots, a lieutenant named Ferris, to take her down.

As she approached the ships, she noticed that the words 'The Ferryman's Barge' were stenciled on the nose of Ferris's ship; a bit scorched from atmospheric entry, but still readable.

<*Ferris the Ferryman,*> she commented to Niki with a mental smile.

Niki chuckled. <*Someone really had to reach for that one.*>

"'Scuze me, Captain," a voice called out from behind Rika,

and she turned to see a dockworker with a hoverpallet filled with crates.

"Sorry," Rika said as she stepped aside to let the woman pass.

"Captain Rika," another voice called out in greeting, and she saw Ferris emerge from the back of his dropship. "Going to be a bit crowded in my bird, sorry about that."

Rika followed behind the dockworker with the pallets, and saw that the dropship was already half-full of crates and miscellaneous gear.

"Damn, I didn't realize you were making a cargo run," Rika said as she saw only one drop seat available for her to sit in.

Ferris chuckled. "You and me both. As soon as I filed my flight plan with the *'Lark*'s dockmaster, stuff just started showing up.

"Don't blame me," the woman with the hoverpallet said. "When the First Sergeant says 'get this stuff planetside on the first ship that goes down', you do what he says."

"Barne ordered all this?" Rika asked.

"Yeah," Ferris replied for the woman as she grabbed a crate and carried it onto the dropship. "He sent me a little note, too—told me where to set down, and to get a move on."

Rika chuckled. "Sounds like Barne, alright. Surprised he didn't let me know."

"You've not worked with a lot of first sergeants, have you?" Ferris asked.

"No," Rika said with a shrug. "But I *have* worked with Barne…which makes me wonder why I said that. Disregard my previous surprise."

"Done." Ferris gave her a wide grin.

Rika grabbed a crate off the pallet, catching one of the handles under a hook on her GNR mount to lift it. Seeing the company captain join in, Ferris helped out as well, and they made short work of the load.

"That it?" Rika asked the dockworker.

"Yup, last one. Thanks for the hand—er…sorry."

Rika laughed and gave the woman—Sally, by the ident on Rika's HUD—a warm smile. "Don't worry, I'm not precious about stuff like that."

"Thanks, Captain Rika. I'm not sure how to behave around a lot of the mechs…some seem a bit sensitive."

Rika pondered Sally's words. She had been so focused on working with the mech platoons under her command, that she hadn't considered how the rest of the ships' crews would deal with having so many of them around—other than to grouse about space and food.

"Thanks for the feedback, Sally. I'll see if we can't work on that. Cohesion with the crews is an important part of what we're doing here."

"That'd be great, Captain. I'd be more than happy to help out with any feedback."

"Noted," Rika said as she stepped into the dropship. "I'll be in touch with your CO about your helpful attitude, and see if we can use your assistance."

Sally smiled and gave Rika a salute before hopping aboard her hoverpallet and riding it back to wherever she'd come from.

"I've gotta ask, Captain," Ferris said as he wove through the crates to reach the dropship's cockpit.

"Speak freely, Lieutenant," Rika replied.

"Well, sorry if this is weird, but wouldn't day-to-day stuff be easier with a regular right arm?"

Rika held up her right arm, which ended in a GNR-41C, sans barrel, and gave Ferris a serious look. "What do you mean? This isn't a regular arm?"

"Uh…" Ferris reddened, uncertain if he'd just offended a superior.

Rika raised an eyebrow, and Ferris appeared to shrink. She let him stew for a moment longer, and then clapped him on the back. "I'm messing with you, Ferris. I've spent so long with this as my right arm, I'm a lot more comfortable with it than a 'regular' one, as you put it."

"Dammit, Captain," Ferris grinned. "Gonna take years off my life, pulling shit like that. Patty warned me about you. I should have listened."

"Oh yeah?" Rika asked as she took a seat. "Was that before or after she crashed her latest ship into a planet?"

Ferris settled into the pilot's seat. "Since she hasn't crashed her current ship, I guess it must be after. Either way, she said you can run a little hot and cold."

<Interesting feedback to give your company CO first time you meet her,> Niki commented privately.

<Looks like he's not military—at least he wasn't 'til he signed up with the Marauders.>

Niki snorted. *<Hasn't he watched any vids? Your CO isn't your drinking buddy.>*

Rika knew what Niki was getting at. In team Basilisk, cohesion had been paramount, rank had meant little. Now that she was a company commander, she had to be certain her orders would be followed without question.

"Does everything that goes into your ears come right back out your mouth?" Rika asked Ferris as she clipped the harness onto her hardmounts.

She said it with an edge, but Ferris only laughed. "Pretty much, yeah. Gets me in trouble sometimes, but I like being me."

Rika couldn't help but roll her eyes. "Well, you keep being you and just get us down on the planet pronto, or I'll sic Barne on you."

A sound at the rear of the dropship caught Rika's attention, and she stood to look over the crates. Three mechs, an AM-3, an RR-3, and an SMI-2, were standing at the back of the ship, looking at the cargo crowding the space.

They were all helmeted, but Rika's HUD identified the AM-3 as PFC Shoshin, and the RR-3 as a corporal named Crunch. Crunch was a bit of a celebrity amongst the mechs. So far as they knew, he had no other name, but that didn't stop everyone in the company from trying to find out what his real one was. It had turned into a game with a sizable betting pot attached.

Rika didn't need her HUD's ident to recognize the SMI-2. Kelly, the friend she still hadn't figured out how to reconnect with, still wore Team Hammerfall's mark on her armor.

They pulled off their helmets and saluted when they saw Rika.

"Let me guess," Rika asked. "Barne needs you three planetside for something?"

Kelly smiled, though the expression didn't quite reach her eyes. Rika wondered if she was still getting used to having a face, or if it was something else. "Actually, it was Lieutenant Leslie that ordered us downworld. Something about enough slacking off, and getting dirt under our feet."

"Which of course translates to being at Barne's beck and call," Crunch added.

"Well, looks like you three have standing room only," Rika gestured at the narrow walking space between the crates. "Make yourselves comfortable."

"Comfortable is what I do," Crunch replied, and leaned against a crate whose label indicated it was full of grenades. The other two filed in as well and wrapped their wrists in overhead straps.

"OK, Ferris," Rika called into the cockpit as she settled back into her seat. "Get this bird in the air—so to speak—or Barne will shove a boot up your ass."

"Now, if I'd known contact sports with Barne were going

to be in the mix, I'd've slacked off a little more." Ferris toggled the rear door, and the dropship lifted into the air a moment later.

<*Damn, he's incorrigible,*> Rika groused privately to Niki.

Niki laughed. <*Yeah, but now I like him more.*>

Rika wondered what Niki was getting at. <*You like Barne to be angry?*>

<*No,*> Niki snorted. <*Don't forget, Barne was the one that set you and I up. He's also the one that treated me like a person, and kept me company on that long trip.*>

The statement bit into Rika, though she didn't think Niki meant it to—or maybe the AI did. Niki wasn't above driving points home from time to time.

<*So what are you saying? You want to play matchmaker with Barne? I didn't even know he swung that way.*>

Niki gave a surprised sound. <*Shoot! I always forget about gender particularities with organics. I think you're right. Barne is on the 'eyes only for girls' end of the spectrum. Girls like Leslie.*>

Rika had to hold back an audible exclamation. <*What!?*>

<*I'm not really sure if he's ogling her or not. I haven't analyzed his behavior in great detail—it's not a natural thing for us, like it is for you, you know.*>

Rika leant back in her seat, thinking about Barne's interactions with Leslie. <*Well, either way, Ferris is just going to have to pine away.*>

"Clearance is approved," Ferris called back. "Boosting for Iapetus!"

"Glad you're so excited," Rika replied with a smile—though Ferris couldn't see her in the back, especially with all the crates piled around her.

"Are you kidding?" Ferris asked. "I live for this shit…uh, Captain."

"What shit is that, screwing up protocol?" Rika asked.

Ferris snorted a laugh. "Well, yeah, that too. No, I mean

flying! Gotta love making a bird soar, or dropping down into a combat zone."

"Well, you'll have to stow that glee for now," Rika replied. "You're just dropping us mechs and these crates off. Unless you're referring to Barne again—calling him a combat zone. Because it works."

"Shit, Captain, I shoulda been. That'd be perfect. Top's a one-man battlefield."

"First Sergeant," Rika corrected.

"Sorry, what?" Ferris asked.

"You can't call him 'Top'."

<*Surely they have* ***that*** *in some sort of training vid,*> Niki said with a groan. <*Even* ***I*** *know you can't call a Top 'Top', unless you have performed the time-honored whatever-the-hell-it-is-in-this-outfit tradition.*>

The AI had made the comment over the shipnet, and Ferris sighed. "Shit, I just can't help but screw this stuff up. What's the tradition here?"

"No weird traditions in the Marauders," Rika replied. "Just have to be under his CO's command, and not have pissed him off in the last thousand years."

Ferris laughed. "Oh, so that drink I spilled on him three months ago probably still counts against me, eh?"

Kelly snorted, joining the conversation. "Oh, hell yeah. From what I know of First Sergeant Barne, you'll be able to call him 'Top' about a hundred years after you die."

Ferris didn't reply—aside from a rather pathetic sigh. No one spoke after that, and Rika brought up the latest data on the training facility they were setting up planetside.

She hadn't had a choice in selecting the planet—that had been worked out between General Mill and Septhian High Command—but Rika was glad they'd been granted space on Iapetus. It was a relatively nice planet, as far as planets went.

Generally speaking, Rika had come to believe that planets

were all covered with far too much mud. Squishies didn't seem to mind as much, but they didn't require anywhere near the same amount of maintenance as mechs when they got caked with grime. A quick shower, and they were right as rain—whatever that meant.

To Rika, rain just sounded like how you got more mud.

The local government had offered several locations for the training facility, and Rika had chosen a site on the eastern edge of Cassini—one of the continents in Iapetus's northern hemisphere. The landmass was massive, and the prevailing winds blew west to east, making for less rainfall around the main site.

She pulled up the briefing holodisplay at the front of the cabin, and set it to show the forward view from the ship's nose. Iapetus didn't have any space elevators, but there were four large stations in high orbit. A steady stream of grav-drive cargo barges moved between them and the major cities on the planet below.

Rika had been through a lot of drops in the war, and had learned to gauge a pilot's skill based on their approach vectors. She never commented or offered advice, but she could tell if the drop would be smooth, bumpy, or downright terrifying based on how the pilot approached a world.

From what she could tell, Ferris was lining them up for a nice, low-speed descent onto Iapetus. So long as he kept his eyes peeled, they wouldn't need to worry about any of the crates falling onto them.

"You know…my last drop was onto Neara," Kelly spoke up, apparently on a similar train of thought.

"Some might count you lucky," Rika replied, glancing back at Kelly and the two mechs beyond her.

"Lucky?" Kelly asked sharply. "I got half my insides blown out onto my outsides."

Rika could see anger smoldering behind Kelly's eyes. It

was an emotion that she remembered all too well from the years after the war ended.

"I remember—not likely to ever forget." Rika's voice was quiet, barely audible over the hum of the dropship's grav drive. "I thought you died in my arms—that's what they told me. Silva and I…"

Kelly's expression softened. "She told me—before she left. You two held a little service for me. You always were too sappy, Rika."

"What can I say? I'm a bleeding heart."

"So what makes me so lucky that Neara was my last drop?" Kelly asked, her tone softened, but eyes still narrowed.

Crunch made a sound that was partway between a grunt and a rueful laugh. "Because after we lost the Parsons System is when things *really* went to shit."

"I can't imagine how they could get much worse than Parsons," Kelly said. "I have a clear memory of playing dodgeball with tacnukes."

Rika ran a hand through her hair and tried not to think in too much detail about the final years of the war. "Well, things did get worse. From there on out, the Niets just rolled right over us. Mechs got flung into more and more desperate defenses."

"Command did a hell of a lot of flinging." Shoshin shook his head. Unlike Kelly and Crunch, Shoshin had not had his face recreated, though he did have a mouth—something the AM models had not sacrificed.

Shoshin's decision not to regain a flesh and blood face was not uncommon amongst the mechs of M Company.

The two psychiatrists helping with the mech rehabilitation had encountered a variety of reasons for why their patients decided against reconstructive surgery. Everything from liking how they looked now, to not even remembering enough specifics about their appearance prior to being turned into a mech.

The former group bore watching, while the Marauders were trying to source records to assist the latter.

Shoshin was in a minority, amongst a group that was perfectly content with what they were, and appeared to have no inner turmoil whatsoever about their lot in life.

Crunch was also accepting of what he was, but where Shoshin was calm and at ease, Crunch was always spoiling for a fight. Rika would have worried, but he was not one of the mechs rescued from Stavros's Politica. Crunch had been with the Marauders for years, and was solid as a rock. A scary, RR-3, mechanized rock.

"But you got into the Old Man's command, right?" Kelly asked Crunch.

The corporal nodded. "Saved my fine carbon-steel hide, too. The general has my undying gratitude."

"Hitting atmo in thirty seconds," Ferris called back to the mechs. "If we had windows, I'd tell you to look out your right for a beautiful view of the sun setting over the Aegean Ocean. On our left, we'll be passing over the eastern edge of Hittis—a lovely city, if you're into fish, fish, and more fish."

"Been a long time since I've had fresh seafood," Kelly said wistfully. "I might have to see if the Old Lady will let me have some leave to check out the sights."

"Dunno," Rika said, grinning at her old teammate. "I hear she's a real asshat."

"That's the scuttlebutt," Kelly smirked.

<*Getting a bit too familiar?*> Niki asked privately.

<*Kelly needs it—I do too, sometimes.*>

Niki sent a feeling of agreement. <*Yeah, but Crunch—stars, I need to find out his real name, the pot's huuuuuge—and Shoshin don't have your history. You can't have the people under your command be that familiar with you.*>

Rika took a deep breath. <*Niki, I've read the books and*

watched the vids. I've been military half my life. I know all about discipline. But these aren't kids who had their moms cooking lunch for them last week. They know how to handle themselves, and we need esprit de corps more than anything else.>

Niki didn't reply, and Rika shifted the view on the holodisplay to the city of Hittis off the dropship's port side.

Iapetus rotated retrograde, so night was rolling in from the west, and the city's towers were lit against the oncoming night. One high-rise flared brightly, and Rika wondered at the glow before Ferris cried out, "Incoming!"

Rika tracked the light on the dropship's scan system—it was a surface to air missile, fired from the top of a building. Ferris banked out over the ocean and deployed EM-chaff while the vessel's point defense beams tracked the short-range air breather, waiting for a lock.

The SAM raced over the water, closing the gap, and then veered toward the EM-chaff, exposing more of its fuselage for the dropship's defensive beams to target.

A moment later, the missile exploded, and Crunch let out a whoop.

"Way to go, Ferris. Send that thing to the underworld."

"Thank you, thank you," Ferris replied. "Try the veal, and be sure to tip your servitor."

Rika ignored the banter as she opened a channel to the local air traffic control.

<*I'm not getting any response from the ATC—or the STC, for that matter,*> Niki said as soon as Rika attempted a connection.

"Shit," Rika whispered. "Ferris! I don't know who shot at us, but expect more incoming."

"Like those?!" Ferris exclaimed, and Rika saw a dozen SAM's fire from ships floating in the Hittis harbor, rocket engines flaring in the deepening gloom, all homing in on the dropship.

Crunch let out a string of curses that were inventive, even

for a veteran mech, and Kelly muttered a few of her own. Shoshin was silent, as was Ferris, as the dropship executed multiple counter-maneuvers and fired on the incoming missiles.

"Doesn't Hittis have any damn surface to air defenses?" Kelly asked as four of the missiles made it past the ship's defenses. "For fucksakes, we're right on the edge of alliance space! It's not like we're in the bosom of safety out here."

"Damn things might *be* Iapetus's SHORAD," Crunch said.

"Civilian launch sites," Shoshin said, his voice perfectly calm as the ship dipped and slewed through the air. "Not likely to be Iapetan short range air defense."

Rika didn't reply as the ship's point defense beams took out another missile, but she wondered how someone could have so much hardware situated around a major population center.

Maybe Iapetus isn't such a great place for the training facility.

"Fuck!" Ferris cried out. "Batts are dry; our beams are gonna take a minute to recharge."

"What—" Rika began before Ferris interrupted.

"Hold on!"

The dropship was five hundred meters above the Aegean Ocean, traveling at seven hundred kilometers per hour. Ferris tipped the nose down, then spun the ship so the engines faced the water and decreased the burn. Ten seconds later, they disappeared beneath the waves.

"The fuck?" Crunch cried out, and Rika echoed the sentiment. If there was one thing she knew about dropships, it was that they were *not* rated for travelling underwater.

The holo showed lights flare above the surface, but Ferris kept the ship moving ahead of the concussive wave.

"Ferris!" Rika called out, and she saw a hand wave back at her from the cockpit.

"Shut up, Captain!"

The ship spun again, and then lurched out of the water, a strange whining noise coming from the starboard side.

"Shit!" Ferris cried out. "One of the engines got waterlogged. That's never happened before; steam pocket should have kept it clear!"

" 'Before'!?" Kelly shouted, as the ship pulled up a dozen meters over the waves and limped toward the shore.

"I've simmed this maneuver. Always wanted to try it," Ferris called back. "Now shush, this thing doesn't fly well on one engine."

Another salvo of air-breathers launched from the ships in the harbor, and Rika bit her lip as the dropship closed the distance to the shore.

"Ferris! You need to set down. We can't keep dodging missiles."

"You think? Any idea where?" Ferris asked.

"Up there," Rika highlighted a location on the ship's nav systems. "There's an old industrial region…if the SAMs hit, they won't take out any civilians."

"Stars," Kelly muttered. "You mean the civilians who are *shooting* at us? Aren't we all on the same side?"

"We have no idea who's shooting at us," Rika retorted. "But I'm half the core-damned reason these people lost their nation; I'm not going to park downtown and let missiles rain down on them."

No one responded to that, and Ferris managed to get the ship over land, just as the vessel's beams came back online. They lanced out, splashing coherent energy on the noses of the incoming SAMs, destroying all but one.

Ferris let out a string of curses—not what you want to hear from your pilot—and dropped to just a few meters above the buildings as the last missile closed.

"Hold on!" Ferris screamed, and then everything began to spin.

A rending sound tore through the cabin, and Rika saw stars out the back of the dropship. Then the ship slewed to the side hard enough to rip Rika from her harness. She slammed into a crate, then the bulkhead.

Up and down ceased to matter as she bounced around like a rag doll in a cyclone.

DROPSHIP DOWN

STELLAR DATE: 04.22.8949 (Adjusted Gregorian)
LOCATION: Abandoned Industrial Complex, North of Hittis
REGION: Iapetus, Hercules System, Septhian Alliance

<Rika!>

The voice sounded small and distant. Rika wished it would pipe down and let her sleep, but the voice kept calling her over and over.

<Rika! Wake up!>

Rika decided the only way to get the voice to shut up was to listen to it. She pulled herself back to full consciousness—or something close—and cracked an eye, letting the world outside crash into her retina.

It was dark, but there was a smear of light to her right. Rika opened her other eye and saw flames and something moving in front of the fire.

"Fire?" she whispered. "Who lit a fire on a starship?"

<Rika! We're crashed on Iapetus, that's the ***dropship*** *burning!>*

Memory flooded into Rika, and her surroundings came into focus.

She was lying on a pile of rubble in a courtyard between two low buildings—each rising four or five stories on either side. Maybe six. They kept wavering in her vision.

The dropship was crashed in the center of the space, flames licking up one side of the craft. The shape she'd seen was an RR-3 mech with something over his shoulder. Rika struggled to her feet and saw that the something was human in form—*Ferris*.

Her HUD tagged the mech as Crunch, and Rika looked around for Shoshin and Kelly—seeing neither.

<You've bent a strut in your left leg, so your gait is going to feel

weird,> Niki cautioned as Rika's leg swung to the side as she took her first step.

"Damn.... Is that all?" Rika asked.

<*I think so. Everything else seems to be superficial—other than burst capillaries across your body. Not that you can see the bruising.*>

"Go me," Rika muttered, and released a pair of drones to provide an overview of the area as she approached Crunch.

"Captain Rika!" Crunch called out when he caught sight of her. "Was starting to think you'd all grown wings and flown off. Where are Shoshin and Kelly?"

<*Kelly is somewhere in the building behind us,*> Niki supplied on the combat net that had automatically initialized. <*I think she's knocked out, though. All I have is a ping on her locator. I have no signal on Shoshin.*>

"So he's dead—" Crunch began.

"Or we just can't pick him up down here." Rika gave the corporal a reassuring look. "We'll find him. Then we'll get out of here."

"And pummel whoever did this to my poor girl," Ferris moaned from his place over Crunch's shoulder.

"Huh, looks like you were too stupid to die," Crunch grunted.

Ferris laughed, then moaned briefly. "But not stupid enough to stay slung over a bullet magnet like you, Crunch. Set me down."

"You sure?"

"Yeah...was just out of sorts before. I'm good. Cockpit deployed its impact foam. I'm just shaken, not stirred."

<*We should move into the building and search for Kelly,*> Niki said. <*There's a lot of ordnance still in the ship. I don't want to be close when it goes up.*>

"Me either," Ferris added. "I forgot my mech armor at home."

"Whoever did this will have spotted the crash site," Crunch said as he unslung his rifle—a KE-72 multifunction weapon.

"How many mags you have?" Rika asked.

"Ten. What about you?"

"Ten as well—for my JE-84. Five DPU rounds for my GNR."

Rika pulled the GNR-41C's barrel off her back and inspected it for damage before slotting it into the weapon that was her right arm.

"I should get one of those," Crunch said. "Must be nice to *always* have a ridiculously deadly weapon on you."

Rika patted the GNR. "Extreme force. Don't leave home without it."

<*I detect incoming craft,*> Niki cautioned.

The three moved cautiously toward the building. Rika and Crunch switched to an IR/UV overlay, watching for shadows against background radiation as they entered the structure.

The building was old, likely abandoned for decades, and stripped clean of everything other than the largest machines—the purpose of which, Rika was uncertain.

<*Think the incoming is local first responders?*> Rika asked.

<*Hard to say, I can't get on the Link at all here. It's like all of their towers are out.*>

<*Just like the ATC,*> Crunch added. <*This stinks.*>

Rika nodded as she peered around one of the large boxy machines. <*To high heaven.*>

<*Kelly's signal is above us,*> Niki said. <*On the roof, if my triangulation is correct.*>

Rika found a staircase and eyed it suspiciously. It looked like a passing breeze could make it crumble.

"We should go one at a time," she said to Crunch and Ferris.

"Ladies first," Ferris gestured magnanimously.

Rika sighed. "Ferris, at some point, you need to remember

that you're in a military outfit, here. I'm the company captain."

Ferris's face reddened enough that Rika bet she could have seen it, even without her mods.

"Sorry…just that I can't see well in the dark, and you weigh less than Crunch, here."

"She gets that, Ferris," Crunch said. "It's the 'Captain' that you keep missing."

"Oh. Right, that."

Rika shook her head and began to carefully climb the stairs, sticking to the edges. Once she reached the next floor, she called down for Ferris to follow, then Crunch.

They continued in that fashion until they reached the fourth level. Rika looked up and saw large sections of the roof above missing, starlight shining through.

<I don't think I can go up there,> she said to Niki as Ferris slowly crept up the stairs below.

<I don't think you have to; the drones haven't spotted her on top. I think she came through the roof. Check twenty meters to your right, on that rubble.>

Rika crept across the floor, releasing another drone to fly ahead, adding its feed to the display from the other two now circling high above.

The drone reached the rubble, and found Kelly lying unconscious under a beam and a piece of the roof.

<Got her,> Rika sent back to Ferris and Crunch over the combat net.

<Alive?> Crunch asked.

Rika couldn't Link to Kelly's armor, but she could see the slight rise and fall of the SMI's chest.

<Yeah, she's breathing.>

Once at Kelly's side, Rika examined the debris and carefully lifted it off until her teammate was uncovered.

"No significant damage," Ferris said as he approached Rika's side. "I guess the roof broke her fall."

Rika reached down and slid open a small panel on Kelly's side, beneath which was a hard-Link connection. She pulled a short cable from her wrist and connected to it.

C'mon, Kelly. I just got you back from the dead, I'm not going to let you check out on me now!

Kelly's armor reported a recent completion of full diagnostics—which is what had set her Link offline. However, her mods had been unable to bring Kelly back to consciousness because of an error in the mental stimulation systems.

"What's wrong with her, Captain?" Crunch asked as he approached.

"Not sure," Rika replied. "Her armor and internal systems are unable to wake her."

"Don't you mechs have combat stims or something?" Ferris asked peering around anxiously as the sound of approaching craft grew louder.

"Crunch, look around for Shoshin. He and Kelly were standing beside each other in the dropship. He might be close."

She knew it was unlikely that they landed nearby, but they had to start looking somewhere.

"Aye, Captain," Crunch nodded before moving to another hole in the roof.

<*Oh, I see it,*> Niki said a moment later. <*All of her mental stim systems have been disabled.*>

"Dammit, Kelly."

Rika had heard that some of the mechs had been uncomfortable with their mods having any sort of access to their minds. It was understandable, after having compliance chips deliver discipline into their heads for so many years. But it also meant that their combat systems couldn't bring them back to consciousness or provide awareness stims.

Of course, it *also* meant that a kick in the ass may be all that was needed to wake Kelly.

Rika disconnected from Kelly's hard-Link and drew a leg back to do just that, when Kelly stirred.

"Really? You get me blown out of the sky, and a mech-foot to the head is what you top it off with?"

"Yeah, well, don't scare me like that." Rika set her foot back down and held out her hand. Kelly clasped it and pulled herself up.

<*You're welcome,*> Niki said over the team's combat net.

"For saving me from her pointy foot?" Kelly asked.

<*That, and for reactivating your combat readiness systems.*>

"What?!" Kelly spun and glared at Rika's forehead.

Rika pointed at her abdomen. "She's down here."

Kelly's gaze slid to Rika's stomach. "You had no right—"

"It's not about rights," Rika interrupted. "Combat mods—especially ones that bring you back to consciousness when you're down—are *not* compliance chips. Stars, even regular soldiers like Ferris have them."

Kelly's head tilted, and Rika could imagine the glare she wore inside her helmet. "Doesn't matter. It's *my* head."

Rika took a step toward Kelly and lowered her voice. "We just got shot down over what we thought was friendly soil. We're missing Shoshin, and you were out cold. Niki did what was necessary for you to be combat effective. If you don't want to be ready to fight when you're needed, then you don't want to be in my outfit.

"Just say the word, and when we get back to the ship, I'll sign your discharge papers. I'll even waive the fee for your surgery."

"Rika, I…" Kelly began, then stopped when Rika held up her hand.

<*Look, Kelly, you and I have been through a lot of shit,*> Rika said privately. <*I'm not trying to hurt you or anything, but we're mechs. We fight, and we fight hard. You can't turn off a part of who*

you are and still be effective. This is war that we're in, and I need you to be an effective soldier. If you can't do that, I understand. We all got fucked over by the GAF. Hard. Getting back into the shit is not for everyone. If you need out, it's OK. No harm, no foul.>

Kelly's stance shifted, but it didn't give away any of what was going on behind her faceshield.

Rika continued. <*For now, though, you need to be ready to do whatever it takes, because we're not going to die down here.*> Rika stood unmoving as she waited for Kelly's response.

<*Understood, Captain.*>

<*Good.*>

Rika switched her attention to the feeds from the drones and saw three aircraft inbound. They appeared to be civilian transport shuttles, though they didn't bear any identifiable markings. One stayed high, while the other two set down at either end of the courtyard, bracketing the crashed dropship.

"Damn, I really thought our dropship would have gone up by now. I guess it's better made than I thought," Rika said as the drones showed armored troops disgorging from the two shuttles.

"I can't believe you'd say that 'bout my fair lady," Ferris said, his voice thick with remorse.

<*Sixteen enemies to the south, and fifteen to the north.*> Niki provided the counts and updated the combat net with the data the drones' scan had gathered.

"Looks like a mix of light and mid-grade armor," Kelly commented, her voice completely professional—and emotionless.

<*No match to local military,*> Niki supplied.

Rika didn't know if that was good news, or bad. It had only been four months since the Theban Alliance voted to join Septhia. The transfer of power was still underway, and would be for years. For the most part, the Theban military still operated as it had, though it was now bolstered by Septhian elements—especially here on the border.

Which made for a morass of military elements that had different ranks, uniforms, and equipment.

Many Thebans blamed the Marauders for the death of their president and the dissolution of their government. For the most part, Septhian High Command kept the Marauders out of Theban territory—except for Rika's company.

Iapetus was right on the edge of Septhian territory. Only a scant forty light years separated it from the edge of the ever-expanding Nietzschean Empire.

The systems between Septhia and Nietzschea were, for the most part, independent and unaligned—though one by one, they were picking sides. When the no-man's land between the Empire and the Alliance disappeared, the battle would be joined.

Given the lack of markings on the armor and ships below, the battle for Iapetus and the Hercules System may have kicked off sooner than anticipated.

"Think it's the Niets?" Ferris asked from Rika's side.

"Could be," Rika shrugged. "One thing's for sure—they're not first responders."

<I had a Link to a sat network for a moment,> Niki added. *<I sent out an S. O. S., but I don't know if it got through. As soon as those ships closed, I lost the signal.>*

<Kelly,> Rika turned to her old friend. *<Get down to the far end of the building and fire a shot into our dropship. Use a DPU. I want that thing to be nothing but rubble.>*

<Max collateral?> Kelly asked.

<Hell yeah.>

"Not my girl!" Ferris exclaimed.

Kelly took off toward the eastern end of the building, and Rika turned to Ferris. "Check the northern end of this floor for signs of Shoshin. We're not leaving here without him."

"What if we don't find him before they make it up here?"

Ferris asked.

"Then they all die."

"I guess that's better than us," Ferris replied and loosened his sidearm in its holster before moving toward the northern side of the building.

Rika wanted to ask Crunch if he'd had any luck, but she knew the man would tell her if he'd found Shoshin. She could still make him out almost two-hundred meters away, threading the piles of debris and checking around the holes in the roof.

Rika slowly moved toward the southern side of the building, where broad windows looked down into the courtyard where the burning dropship lay.

<*They've deployed their own drones, and that ship above is running active scan. You mechs should be invisible to it, but Ferris won't be,*> Niki advised.

<*I know,*> Rika replied. <*That's why I baited the trap with him.*>

<*Ahhh.*> Niki's tone was appreciative. <*I don't know if that's brilliant or devious.*>

<*Can't it be both?*> Rika asked.

In the courtyard below, five soldiers had broken off from the group at the eastern end and were approaching the burning dropship.

C'monnnn, Kelly, Rika thought as the enemy drew within six meters of the ship.

<*Firing,*> Kelly announced.

Rika didn't see any muzzle flash from Kelly's position, which meant the SMI-2 was well back from the edge of the floor—possibly up on the roof, firing through a hole to get the right angle.

Rika waited for Kelly's shot to hit the dropship and tear into it, but instead a brilliant shower of sparks erupted seven meters from the target.

<Damn!> Kelly exclaimed. *<They must have some sort of portable shield with them. Deflected my round.>*

<Kelly—> Rika began, but Kelly was already firing again.

<Deflect this, motherfuckers!>

A blue-white bolt of lightning lit up the night, drawing a direct line from Kelly's position to the dropship below.

Near the ship, an invisible barrier flared again, then dissipated under the barrage of relativistic electrons. Once the barrier failed, the beam struck the ship, and bolts of lightning arced out, striking the ground and nearby soldiers.

A second later, the dropship exploded in a brilliant display, filling the courtyard with fire and shattering any still-intact windows in the surrounding buildings.

Rika didn't have to wait long for the enemy's response. Before the smoke and flames even rose up above the buildings, two missiles streaked out from the enemy ship in overwatch, arcing toward Kelly's position.

Rika had expected the response, but what followed was a pleasant surprise.

A second pair of missiles flew out from the building across the courtyard and struck the underside of the craft that had just fired on Kelly.

Shoshin, you sneaky bastard!

The enemy ship exploded at the same instant that a fireball engulfed Kelly's firing position.

<Kelly!> Rika called out as the roof collapsed on the far end of the structure. *<You better have survived that, you stupid tinhead.>*

<I'm conflicted, not suicidal,> Kelly retorted. *<There was a hole clear down to the second floor; I jumped as soon as I fired the e-beam.>*

<Shit, you're nuts,> Ferris added.

Kelly didn't reply, and weapons fire rose up from the staircase they'd used.

<*She's got four baddies down there,*> Niki informed them, updating the combat net.

<*Serious baddies.*> Kelly's voice wavered, but Rika recognized the tone. It was anger, not fear.

<*So I guess I can stop searching for Shoshin,*> Crunch said. <*I'm going to head down the western stairwell and see if I can catch those asshats in some crossfire.*>

<*Do it,*> Rika said. <*Ferris, find cover back there and hunker down. Now that their overwatch is gone, I'm going to drop some presents on the ships in the courtyard.*>

<*You got it, Captain.*>

Rika reached the southern edge of the building and peered down into the area below. The dropship was mostly gone, and only bits of the five enemy soldiers remained. The group to the west had taken some flying shrapnel as well—she could see two soldiers, dragging a third back to their ship.

The ship on the east end had two soldiers next to it, one training his weapon on Rika's building, and the other looking up at the building on the far side, where Shoshin's rockets had come from.

Such a surplus of targets. Which to blow up first?

Rika took up a position behind a column, and aimed at the shuttle on the eastern end of the courtyard. She'd spare the two soldiers dragging their wounded—for now.

One thing was certain: if the group that had been advancing on the burning dropship had carried a shield capable of deflecting a uranium sabot round, then chances were that their vessels were, as well.

Instead, Rika aimed at the soldier standing near the rear entrance of the shuttle. Back in the war, she'd learned that the Niets had a flaw in their ship shields: they would operate at lower level when personnel were in close proximity.

What she didn't know in this case was whether the soldier in question was standing inside or outside the shield's protection. Or if that vulnerability existed in other shuttles. Or a hundred other things.

She hoped he was outside the shield, took aim, and fired a uranium round at his feet. The DPU hit the ground, and the explosive force picked the soldier up and threw him back toward the ship.

Without missing a beat, Rika fired again, this time with her electron beam. The relativistic electrons breached the shield—and the soldier's body—striking the interior of the landing craft.

The rear of the craft exploded, and Rika smiled with satisfaction. Whoever had fired those SAMs at her dropship was ill-prepared for the sort of firepower four mechs could deliver.

Knowing that her weapons fire gave her position way, Rika headed back into the building, toward the staircase where Kelly was still battling the enemy. As she did, Rika saw a shot lance out from the other building, where Shoshin was situated, and an explosion flared up from the second shuttle's location.

<*Damn, wish he hadn't done that,*> Rika commented privately to Niki. <*Now they've nowhere to retreat to.*>

<*You're just assuming complete victory?*> Niki asked.

<*Of course. I don't lose.*>

<*Can I get some covering fire?*> Kelly asked. <*They're flanking me.*>

<*Not for long,*> Crunch replied, and the deafening *shoom* of his KE-72 thundered up through the floors.

Rika wondered how Crunch had advanced through the length of the building on the second floor without encountering more of the enemy. *There should have been a dozen from the western ship between him and Kelly.*

She reviewed the scan from the team and what the drones could pick up. There was no sign of the soldiers from the western shuttle, yet the drones above the courtyard had recorded twelve enemies entering the building.

<*They must be on the ground floor,*> Niki suggested.

<*Or the third.*>

Rika circled the stairwell and peered down into the third floor, looking for any signs of movement. She was tempted to release a drone and send it down, but worried that it might give her position away.

She released one nonetheless, but instead sent it down the length of the fourth floor. The last thing she needed was a group sneaking up on her while she was engaged with the enemy one level down.

<*You sure they're on the third?*> Niki asked.

<*If they were on the second, they'd've run into Crunch by now. That's all I know. Don't see them on fourth. They have to be somewhere….*>

Rika decided that going down the stairs was a recipe for disaster, and moved to the eastern end of the building, where Kelly had gone through the floor. It was a ruin from the missile attack, but not far from the stairs, a beam had torn a hole through to the third level.

She released a probe through the opening and only waited for the briefest of scans before dropping through.

Her feet hit the level below. The sound would have given her location away, if not for the thundering weapons fire echoing through the building.

Rika took stock of her surroundings. Twenty meters ahead, to her left, was the stairwell. From what she could see on the combat net, Kelly and Crunch now had their attackers caught between them.

Rika eased toward the northern side of the building, looking for the enemy she was certain should be present…somewhere.

But there was no sign of them.

<*Rika!*> Ferris's voice hissed in her mind. <*Rika, they're up*

here on the fourth floor!>

<*Can't be,*> Rika replied. <*My probe swept half the level. There's no one up there but you.*>

<*Well, I can see them with my own fucking eyeballs! They're fifty meters and closing. They must have something blocking your drones.*>

Rika couldn't think of anything that could fool a drone that wouldn't also fool an eyeball. They both picked up EM-spectrum, and the drones saw a lot more.

<*They've hacked the drone somehow,*> Niki supplied. <*It's the only answer that makes sense.*>

Rika wanted to ask how, but Ferris—her bait—was in imminent danger. For all her caution and skulking, the staircase was going to be the quickest way to get back to him.

Unless…

Rika dashed down the length of the building and chambered a depleted uranium sabot round in her GNR. Using the locations Ferris had highlighted on the combat net, she targeted the ceiling overhead and fired one round, and then another. Her aim was true, and the ceiling—which was also the floor of the fourth level—gave way under the enemy soldiers and dropped them right into Rika's lap.

There were six, all in matte black stealth armor, barely visible—even with all of Rika's augmentations, and her helmet's scan.

Whatever tech they're using, it's good.

Rika hoped hers was better.

Her JE-84 was already unslung, and she fired on the two soldiers closest to her before they managed to rise. She scored a lucky shot on a weak point in one's armor, and the figure went down, but the rounds only ricocheted off the other, and he found cover.

Further back, four more enemies struggled to disentangle themselves from the wreckage, and Rika fired two HE rounds from her GNR, hitting one and smashing—she hoped—their shoulder.

Ferris had originally spotted eight enemies on the fourth floor, and Rika had only seen six thus far. Either two were still in the rubble, or they'd avoided the collapse and were still after Ferris.

<Rika! One's still up here, he's almost on me!>

Rika heard shots fire from Ferris's sidearm, and knew they'd be ineffective against the armor these soldiers wore.

Disregarding her own safety, Rika rushed forward, leapt into the air, and grabbed hold of a protruding beam. Her momentum swung her up and around. She let go at the top of her arc and spun through the air, landing once more on the fourth level.

The damaged structure groaned under her weight as she slammed down, but Rika ignored any concerns and raced toward Ferris's position.

She could see the muzzle flash from his weapon, but not the enemy soldier. Then he stepped out from behind a beam and leveled his rifle on her.

Rika reacted without thinking. She twisted to the side and extended her right arm, firing a chambered HE round from her GNR-41C into the enemy soldier. It caught him right under his armpit, and tore his torso in two.

Rika spun, scanning the area as she backed toward Ferris.

<*You hit?*> she asked the pilot.

<Uh…no…I don't…Oh shit, yeah, I'm hit.>

Rika reached Ferris and saw him staring at the stump of his left arm, torn off just above the elbow.

She grabbed a canister of biofoam from her thigh and applied it to his stump to staunch the bleeding, while Ferris swayed on his feet and stared at the twitching left arm on the ground.

"Shit," he whispered aloud. "Good thing I'm in the right

company for prosthetics. I'll fit right in."

<*Maybe Barne will even let you call him 'Top'.*> Rika laughed and gave Ferris a light slap on the shoulder as she turned, ready to deal with the soldiers who would be following her back up through the hole before long.

<*Don't count on it,*> Barne's welcome voice came over the combat net.

Rika glanced out the northern side of the building and saw an assault craft lower into view. <*Nice of you to show up, First Sergeant. Any time you want to smush these asshats into jelly, that'd be great.*>

Barne didn't reply, but the assault craft lowered a meter, and two large-caliber chainguns opened up, tearing through the third floor. The combat net flagged the enemies on that level as combat ineffective, and then Barne lowered the ship and repeated the procedure on the second level.

<*Well, damn,*> Kelly said with a nervous laugh. <*Good to know someone noticed that we went missing.*>

<*Just glad you left some for me,*> Barne replied. <*I don't read Shoshin. He make it?*>

<*Somewhere in the building to the south.*> Rika walked toward the hole in the floor and looked down at the enemies that had suffered under the barrage from Barne's assault craft. <*Get over there and see if you can locate him. We can mop up.*>

Rika saw one of the enemies below roll over and reach for her weapon.

"Not this time," Rika whispered and leveled her GNR, firing a round into the woman's hand, blowing it clean off. "You'll have some questions to answer before the night is out."

A DEEPER GAME

STELLAR DATE: 08.09.8949 (Adjusted Gregorian)
LOCATION: Abandoned Industrial Complex, North of Hittis
REGION: Iapetus, Hercules System, Septhian Alliance

Rika stood in the center of the courtyard, near the still-smoldering remains of Ferris's dropship. Crunch and Kelly were combing the area for any Marauder equipment and loading it onto Barne's assault ship. Shoshin was already aboard, as was Ferris.

A ship was on its way—an armed pinnace this time—from the *Golden Lark* to collect them and bring the pair back up for some of Lieutenant Carson's tender care.

"You just tell Bondo not to screw up my face," Shoshin had said when Rika checked on him. "I'm good the way I am."

Many mechs who had not opted for any reconstructive surgery would jump at the chance to do it on the company's credit. Rika was glad to see that Shoshin's acceptance of who he was held up under dire circumstances—or in the face of free cosmetic surgery.

However, none of that was Rika's immediate concern. The local military was on the ground and they'd taken control of the situation—and the enemy soldiers.

"Look," Rika said to the woman in charge, Major Dala. "I just want to have a chance to interrogate their senior officer or NCO—whoever is left. I need to know what sort of danger we're in, here."

"I'm sorry, Captain Rika," Major Dala replied without an ounce of understanding in her cold, fuchsia eyes. "This was an attack on our soil, we have jurisdiction. We'll keep you informed as the investigation proceeds, of course."

Though Major Dala wore a Septhian Armed Forces crest on

her shoulder, the armor it adorned was clearly of Theban design.

The SAF crest was slightly crooked, a visual sign of how well the absorption of the Theban space force into the Septhian military was going. Which was to say that it was a never-ending series of pissing matches. Rika was amazed at how much resistance the Thebans were putting up, when the Septhians had come to their aid against the Nietzscheans in the battle for the Albany System less than six months ago.

Maybe it was because she'd never had any to begin with, but nationalistic pride meant very little to Rika. The opportunity to kill Niets, on the other hand…now that was something she could rally behind.

What Rika wanted to know more than anything else was whether or not the Nietzscheans were behind this attack.

Unfortunately, the locals had arrived before she'd had a chance to do more than try to get a name from one of the nine enemies they'd captured.

"Can you more clearly define, 'keeping me informed'?" Rika asked. "Who will my liaison be? Will I be able to at least observe the interrogations? Can we gain access to what you learn about the origin of their equipment?"

"I'm sorry, I don't know the answers to those questions. Your standard SAF liaison, Major Jeremy, will have those answers once command determines how we'll proceed."

Rika pulled off her helmet and stared into the woman's eyes. "Major Dala. We're both just trying to do our jobs, here. My job is to train up a force of mechs who will aid in the defense of this star system and elsewhere in Septhia. We're going to bleed and die for your people—stars, I suspect we already have. We deserve to know who hit us."

Dala didn't even flinch as Rika spoke. Her fuchsia eyes met Rika's blue ones, and she shrugged. "It's not my call, *Captain* Rika."

"Seriously?" Rika growled. "That's how you want to play this? We're—"

"*We're* nothing alike," Major Dala interrupted. "I'm a Theban patriot, you're a *mercenary*. You kill for money."

Rika snorted and raised an eyebrow as she gazed down at the Major. "Oh, and you don't take pay? You live off the kindness of those you serve? Or maybe you're a slave." She lowered her voice and took a step toward the major. "Do you know what it's like to be a slave? To be forced to kill? I don't seem to recall the Genevian government ever giving me so much as a stipend back then. I suppose that must be the epitome of honor to you."

The woman's eyes widened, and fear replaced her smug officiousness.

Rika didn't ease up. "When *you're* trying to redeem yourself from spending most of your life as a mutilated killing machine, *then* you can say whatever you want about my motives. But until then, why don't you shut your fucking trap?"

"I—" Major Dala began, but Rika held up a hand.

"When the Nietzscheans come—and they *will* come—I'd better see your altruistic ass on the front lines, not cowering behind your administrivia."

Rika turned and walked away, worry about future complications edging out the satisfaction that yelling at the woman had granted.

<*That was fun to listen to,*> Kelly said as she placed a crate inside Barne's assault craft. <*I think you let her off easy.*>

Rika sighed and put her helmet back on. <*Maybe. She didn't make the call to shut us out, but she could have shown* **some** *compassion.*>

<*Or maybe a bit of, 'sorry our local defense is so shit-poor that you got shot down over one of our cities by someone who managed to take control of half our local infrastructure',*> Crunch added from

where he stood at the back of the Marauder ship. *<Either way, that's the last of it. About a third of our cargo survived—for some definition of the word.>*

Rika checked the ETA on the pinnace from the *Golden Lark*, and found it was caught up in an air traffic control mess of epic proportions. She sent a message for the ship to meet them at the training facility. It would be more efficacious to transfer Ferris and Shoshin there.

<OK, let's get out of here.>

Rika picked up the pace, jogging toward Barne's ship.

"Wait! Captain, we need you to stay onsite until our investigative team arrives," Dala called out.

"I have wounded, and your ATC is a disaster," Rika called over her shoulder. "Your people know where to find me."

"*I* don't, where is that?"

Rika laughed as she stepped aboard the assault craft and turned to watch Dala rushing toward her. "Why don't you shove your head further up your CO's ass? Maybe your answer is in there."

Dala didn't have a chance to reply before Barne ignited the ship's grav drive, pulling the assault craft into the air. Once they'd cleared the buildings, he poured on the thrust. Rika couldn't help but notice that he didn't even bother to send in a flight path to the Iapetan ATC.

LAYERED CONCERNS

STELLAR DATE: 08.09.8949 (Adjusted Gregorian)
LOCATION: Marauder Training Compound
REGION: Iapetus, Hercules System, Septhian Alliance

"You sure know how to make an entrance," Barne said as he led Rika into the training facility's command building.

The *Golden Lark*'s pinnace had already collected Ferris and Shoshin, taking them back up to the ship for repairs and surgery. Despite his ability to fire the two missiles at the enemy's overwatch ship, Shoshin had suffered significant damage from the crash. His left arm had been shorn off, and one of his legs was crushed. The wireless transmitters in his helmet had been destroyed, as had one of his internal batteries.

He was a mech's mech, though. Not a word of complaint; just a visible eagerness to be repaired and take the fight to whoever had organized the attack.

Kelly and Crunch were visiting the base's quartermaster for light refit and repair before joining the other mechs already on the base, who were currently patrolling the perimeter—neither Rika nor Barne intended to be caught with their pants down again.

"It takes years of practice." Rika gave Barne a belated reply as she followed him into the squat building on the southern side of the compound. "And a strong dislike for bureaucratic bullshit."

Barne chuckled and nodded as he turned a corner and walked down a hall lined with empty offices. "Major Dala's not a significant player in the local power structure, but her CO, Colonel Zim is. Honestly, her behavior is probably just a conditioned response to dealing with him for so long."

<I've received a few messages from Colonel Zim's Battalion HQ since we took off,> Niki added. *<They want copies of all our data on the attack sent over immediately.>*

Rika held back what she wanted to say about Zim's HQ and their requests. Barne and Niki weren't her enemies, and she recognized that she was still on an adrenaline high from combat.

Getting shot out of the sky had a way of bringing out her aggressive side.

Barne stopped in front of one of the doors and gestured inside. "Your office, Captain Rika."

Rika stepped into the room—which was almost ten times the size of Major Tim's back on the *Golden Lark*—and looked it over. There was a desk with a mech-safe chair behind it, a few others in front of the desk, plus a couch along one wall—carbon fiber to ensure it would survive hard, steel asses. In one corner stood an equipment and armor rack, complete with full recharge and resupply.

"Wow, Top, this is nice. I didn't know we were going to get this fancy."

Barne snorted. "Fancy, my ass. I've seen generals with offices that would have put kings to shame. Everything here is about operational efficiency."

Rika leaned against the desk and let out a long breath. "OK. Our top priority is to find out who shot at us, and if they're going to hit us again. Here, or on the ships."

"If it's anywhere, it'll be here." Barne sat on the couch and leaned back. "If they could have hit the ships, they would've before. Now that they've tipped their hand, Major Tim will be on high alert. Guy's tighter than a jackrabbit's asshole, so nothing will get through up there."

Rika laughed. "Lovely visual."

"Seemed to fit, pun intended."

Rika rolled her eyes and pushed off her desk to pace across

the room. "So what do you think? Niets? Local baddies? Theban military haters?"

Barne shrugged. "Could be all of the above. A lot of 'Theban patriots' left their military after Thebes joined the Septhian Alliance. Some of them are operating as merc outfits to pay the bills, others are not—which makes me think that someone is funneling them money from somewhere. Maybe old military commanders."

"And you think that the Niets could be behind it?" Rika asked. "Subterfuge and subversion really isn't their game."

Barne raised an eyebrow. "Except for that little thing last year, where they bamboozled us into almost killing off half the Theban leadership. I think they've got a new strategist close to the emperor's ear. We shouldn't expect the same old tactics as the war. Times are changing, and so is Nietzschea."

"An evolving Nietzschea, just what we need."

"With your permission, Captain, I'd like to bring First Platoon and all the DIs down."

"You miss Leslie and Chase?" Rika smirked.

"Always. I want Leslie's platoon because I know how she operates, but just the one 'toon because I want to make this compound look like a soft target when it's anything but."

Rika eyed Barne. "How long do you think we have?"

"Well, they fucked up the local ATC and killed Link towers across half the continent. On top of that, they got SAM launchers on a dozen ships in the harbor. They were smart, too; they knew that would be easier than getting the weapons into the city, but they fired one from that high-rise to push you out over the water."

"Making us an easy target," Rika finished for him. "That was savvy. If Ferris wasn't a nutjob, we'd all have died out there—or at least gone for a good swim."

"Nutjob? What did the Ferryman get up to?"

"Something very fitting to his name. He took the ship

underwater."

Barne whistled in appreciation. "He's gonna win some bets. There's always been healthy debate about taking one of those dropships underwater."

"Well, we lost an engine and crashed."

"Hmm…maybe just half points, then."

<*Rika,*> Major Tim's voice came into her mind. <*I need to talk with you.*>

"Aw, crap. It never rains, it shitstorms." Rika tapped her head. "Tim's on the Link. Get Leslie and her platoon down here; don't bring *all* the DIs, though. I want people to *think* the bulk of our forces are still on the ships."

A smile crept across Barne's face, and he gave a sly nod. "I like the way you roll, Captain. I'm on it."

Barne left her office, and Rika responded to Major Tim.

<*Good evening, Major. I hope all is well up there?*>

The major made a derisive noise. <*Hell of a lot better than down there. I have a Major from the office of some Colonel Zim pinging me every five minutes to get all your data on the attack.*>

<*Yeah, they're up my ass, too,*> Rika replied tonelessly.

<*What are you playing at, Captain? We work for the Septhian military. Don't go making enemies in their ranks.*>

<*I just about got blown out of the sky over one of their cities, Major. It was no random hit, either; they timed it for when both the* Golden Lark *and the* Perseid's Dream *were on the far side of Iapetus. They crippled local infrastructure,* **and** *they had the run of our crash site for ten minutes. Just to take out one dropship of mechs?*>

Major Tim didn't respond for a moment. <*This was a hit on you.*>

<*The evidence I have points to that, yes. Whoever orchestrated this has reach.*>

<*And you think making enemies with this Zim and his cronies is the way to solve that problem?*> Tim asked.

Rika was about to deliver a snappy rejoinder when it occurred to her that, despite his general assholeishness, Tim was right.

<*What if it's them that attacked us?*> Rika tried a new tack. <*If you were running a hit like that on the downlow, wouldn't you want to be onsite first to control the narrative?*>

<*Maybe,*> Tim replied. <*But then again, maybe I'd want distance. There are a lot of variables at play, here.*>

<*The major is right about that,*> Niki added. <*If Zim and Dala were in on it, why not just take you out when they arrived?*>

<*Maybe there were other eyes on the situation by then,*> Tim suggested. <*Look, you've got a P-COG down there. One of the Old Man's best. He's the one that figured out it was the Nietzscheans playing us back in Albany. Set him on the data, but I'd recommend giving what you can to Zim, if for no other reason than to shut his dogs up.*>

Rika had not been aware that David, her P-COG general counsel, had been the one to uncover the Nietzschean subterfuge in the Albany System.

For that alone, she owed him her thanks.

<*OK, Major, I'll do that. And I'll keep you informed. Also, we're going to bring a platoon and some supplies down. Chances are that we'll see more unfriendlies.*>

<*Yeah, good likelihood on that. We're altering our orbits so that you'll have near-continuous orbital coverage from the* 'Lark *or the* 'Dream.>

Rika was grateful for the Major's concern, and told him as much before they closed the connection.

<*I've already called David in,*> Niki said. <*He'll be here in five minutes. I gave him all the data we collected, as well.*>

Rika drew a deep breath and flopped onto the couch. "Good."

* * * * *

The knock on Rika's door was sharp and sure. Rika called out 'Come', and a moment later David entered, taking in the room with one long sweep of his eyes.

"Barne works fast, doesn't he, Captain?" David said as he turned to Rika.

"That he does, though I understand that a lot of the progress down here came from your keen eye, as well."

David shrugged. "I just make sure the contracts are favorable. I may have also spotted some deals here and there."

Rika laughed and gestured to one of the chairs. "I wasn't expecting so much false humility from you, David. Major Tim told me that I have you to thank for not delivering the Theban Alliance to Nietzschea last year."

David sat and gave her a warm smile. "It was a group effort. No one's an island."

Rika laughed. "And the humility just keeps on coming. Was I wrong to question it?"

David reached up and rapped a knuckle on the metal ridges atop of his elongated skull. "A lot of people think I have unfair advantages—or they just think I'm a freak. The right attitude can diffuse a lot of jealousy and ill intent."

Rika laughed. "You know…that's an entirely different class of problem from what mechs have. No one ever accuses us of being unfairly intelligent, and when push comes to shove, they're happy to put us out front to absorb the bullets."

David smiled. It was a kind expression that started with his eyes before his lips began to turn up. "Things aren't so different for P-COGs, when it comes to evaluating usefulness. Granted, the personal stakes are often not as high as for you. But if I fuck up an assessment or miss a connection, a lot more than just one soldier dies."

"I'm starting to understand that pressure in a new way," Rika said. "I can't imagine what the Old Man feels."

"Weary, I suspect. That man doesn't just have the Marauders on his shoulders. He's the last, best hope for Genevia."

Rika raised an eyebrow. "This conversation sure took an unexpected turn. What do you mean by that?"

"When it comes down to it, General Mill is fighting for Genevia. Not the Genevia you grew up in—the one before that. I can barely remember it; I was just a boy when we elected the string of corrupt governments that led us to war with Nietzschea. Not that an honest government could have avoided the war, but I think they could have won it."

"But the general remembers that Genevia?" Rika asked.

"He does." David nodded somberly. "I believe the spark needed to rebuild Genevia is within him, and him alone. Well, perhaps that's a bit melodramatic. He fosters the spark in others, but only he has the means and the drive to realize his vision."

Rika considered David's words for a moment, turning them over in her mind and wondering what they really meant.

Most of her life had been spent either fighting Nietzschea, or living with the grim fact that the enemy had bested her people—who she didn't like much better than the enemy. Since joining the Marauders, her focus had been on staying the Nietzschean advance toward the Praesepe Cluster.

After the Nietzscheans were defeated in the Albany System, some talked about what it would be like to drive them back from Genevian space, but most considered that to be nothing more than wishful thinking.

Even if all Praesepe rose up as one, they couldn't field a fleet a tenth the size of Nietzschea's. The only reason why Emperor Constantine hadn't crushed Septhia already was because his forces were spread thin across his vast empire.

Everyone *really* knew that the best chance the nations of the Praesepe Cluster had was to make an assault too costly to be worth it.

Finally, she asked, "Does the general really believe that we could defeat Nietzschea at some point?"

"Genevia was the greatest adversary Nietzschea faced in five hundred years. The conflict weakened them enough that many of the nations on their fringe have formed substantial alliances and are successfully holding them back. If we prove that Constantine *can* be stopped, then we could form a broader alliance with those nations. One that could crush Nietzschea once and for all."

"Those are some great aspirations," Rika straightened up and sat forward on the sofa. "But for now, we just need to survive whatever is happening here on Iapetus."

"Agreed." David straightened his back and folded his hands on his lap. "I've been reviewing the data as we spoke, and I agree with your assessment that a second attack is likely. I also believe that you were the intended target of the attack. The ordnance expended to take down your dropship exceeded the material value of the ship and its contents by over threefold."

"What about the value of four mechs?" Rika asked. "We're worth a lot."

David nodded. "Yes, but if the attackers knew that there were four mechs aboard, they would not have sent such a small force after you. I also factored the likelihood of capturing mechs in usable condition into my valuation. Mech capture is very rare."

Rika laughed. "Yeah, we tend to go down fighting. Capture is not a favorable outcome for us." David nodded soberly, and Rika realized the same was likely true for P-COGs. "So, what if our attacker isn't as smart as you and figured they'd get a functional mech in the deal?"

David's brow furrowed, and he wiggled his fingers where they lay folded on his lap. "Maybe it would be a wash. I can't assume they're too stupid; they did manage to do a number on the local Iapetan defenses and infrastructure."

"Or they know the right people and have money."

"You're no slouch at this twisted logic, either, Captain Rika."

"Survival trait. Thing is, for me, it all breaks down at some point. Ultimately, I always have to go with my gut."

"No one can isolate all variables." David shrugged and leant back in his chair, unfolding his hands and placing them palms down on his legs. He didn't seem to know what to do with them half the time. "Nothing is perfectly certain. Ultimately, with everything, we all have to make a call. Go with our gut, as you say."

"So what does *your* gut say?" Rika asked

"That—at this point—Nietzschean influence is immaterial. There are local elements at work, and they are connected. Thebans here on Iapetus want you dead, and those Thebans are both well-funded and have ties to influential people."

"So we wait for the next attack?" Rika asked.

"No defense has a single element, and rarely does a victory come from a single offense. I believe that Niki should provide the data to Major Dala—scrubbed in small, but noticeable ways—to give them something. Their response—both Dala's, and Zim's HQ in general—will tell you much. At the same time, I shall reach out to Dala and foster a relationship. I've studied her activities on the local nets and feed; she likes modified men, has a thing for big brains like mine. It's not her main turn-on, but it will get me in the door."

Rika couldn't help but let out a short laugh. "You're going to seduce Major Dala for intel?"

David shrugged. "If it comes to it. Spotting the patterns within human reaction is easy—P-COGs outstrip even AIs at this, because we have more first-hand experience. With some simple evaluation and observation, I can create a perfect persona to appeal to another human."

"Are you doing that with me right now?" Rika asked.

David grinned. "Rika, I would never need to do that with you. Our goals and personalities are already very well aligned."

Rika snorted. "That's a bullshit answer, if I ever heard one."

David shrugged and pulled a pouch of coffee from his jacket. He tore the corner off with his teeth and then poured it down his throat. "I never said I was a great actor. However, what I *do* know is that you wanted to meet with me *before* you were so inconsiderately shot out of the sky."

"I did. Though—and I think you'll agree, Niki—the matter is less urgent than the recent attack."

<Less urgent, yes, but still no less important.>

"Tell me anyway, if you would, Captain. It's always nice to have more pieces to the puzzle."

Rika let out a short laugh. "I think this other matter is a whole different puzzle."

David squeezed the last few drops of his coffee pouch into his mouth. "Captain. There's only one puzzle."

Rika found herself wondering how much of David's bizarre mannerisms were natural, and how many were a result of the modifications the Genevian military had made to his mind. He spoke calmly, but he fidgeted incessantly. His tone and speed of speech varied so much that it was impossible to establish a baseline of any sort. Every word he spoke could be a lie, or they could all be truth.

Still, he *seemed* honest, and the Old Man trusted him, notwithstanding his part in stopping the Nietzscheans from taking Thebes.

"I want to free the AIs," Rika admitted plainly.

David's eyes went wide, and for the first time, he seemed genuinely surprised. "The AIs."

"The seven aboard our two ships."

"Eight," David corrected, nodding at Rika's abdomen.

"Ensuring Niki's freedom is a mere formality."

David tapped a finger against his upper lip. "Still, it is a formality that must be observed." His finger tapped faster and faster, then suddenly stopped, his eyes going wide once more.

"Niki! You're a part of the movement amongst the AIs."

<*'Movement' is a very generic term,*> Niki replied, her mental tone guarded.

"Uprising? Rebellion? Insurrection? I don't know enough to properly quantify it. Even a casual observation of news from distant locales is enough to realize that something has changed with the AIs in the last two decades—though few signs of it have been apparent in Praesepe."

<*You're certainly no slouch, David.*> The feeling accompanying Niki's words was warmer now.

"I'd like to hope not," David replied. "Though I must admit, a way to 'free' the AIs aboard our two ships is not readily apparent to me. I assume you have some plan?"

"Asylum," Rika said without further elaboration, and David's eyes widened for the third time, before a smile grew on his lips.

"I see. That could work. There would be hurdles, to be sure, but it has merit."

"What about the Old Man?" Rika asked. "You're loyal to him, and he won't be happy about this."

David snorted. "Nor will Major Tim. But fundamentally, the Old Man would not be opposed. In Genevia's former glory days, AIs were free. Citizens, even. If he wants to bring that back, he cannot deny them this."

<*Then why hasn't he done so sooner?*> Niki asked.

David shrugged. "I'm not in his inner circle—though I am friends with some who know him very well. I think…I think maybe he views it more like protective custody—that he would free everyone if it were safe to do so. But he needs some for success and others he wants to keep safe."

"This sounds like our conversation from earlier, Niki."

<I was noticing similarities myself.>

Silence hung in the air for a moment before David said, "We three are peas in a pod. Each of us the product of humanity's desire to evolve. Mentally and physically, even to creating a new species. The pure organics, they don't understand us, and we spend no small effort convincing them that we're not a threat."

<Sometimes,> Niki replied. *<Some have no issue with that. Some want to be a threat—or a danger.>*

David's finger tapping resumed once more. "Is that what you are, Niki? Are you and the AIs you've sided with a threat and a danger?"

Niki didn't reply right away, and Rika began to wonder if her AI was hiding some ill intent from her.

Finally, Niki spoke up. *<Maybe.>*

Her words hung in the air for a minute before David laughed. "I believe I know what you mean, Niki. I'll help. I can set up meetings with some Iapetan lawyers and get things moving."

Rika wondered exactly what Niki had meant. *I'll have to dig into it later.*

For now, she was glad to have this small victory.

RECONCILIATION

STELLAR DATE: 08.10.8949 (Adjusted Gregorian)
LOCATION: Marauder Training Compound
REGION: Iapetus, Hercules System, Septhian Alliance

Rika settled into her office chair and drew a deep breath. *Best to get it over with sooner than later.* If Kelly wasn't fit to be a Marauder, finding out now was better than in combat—again.

She organized the stack of holofilm on the desk, ensuring they were all deactivated, and then took a sip from her cup of coffee.

The knock came on her door a moment later, and Rika called out for Kelly to enter as she set the cup down and squared her shoulders.

The door opened, and Kelly walked in. Her posture was rigid, body gleaming in SMI-2 armor, her gun-arm attached with a barrel-less GNR in place.

From the neck down, it was hard to find dissimilarities between herself and Kelly. Two peas in a pod—that's what Silva had always called them, a memory brought up by David's use of the term. Back then, Kelly had always been getting into trouble, and Rika had to pull her out of it.

Granted, Kelly's trouble saved the day half the time, so it was nearly always worth it.

"Good morning, priv—Kelly," Rika said.

"Captain." Kelly sketched a salute and stood at attention before Rika's desk.

"At ease, Kelly." Rika gestured to the chair. "Please, sit. Stars, I suck at this stuff. I hate formality. I know how to do it up the chain, but down is different."

Kelly sat and shrugged. "I wouldn't know, Captain."

"Enough with the 'captain' shit, Kelly. We've hauled each

other's asses out of the fire too much for that—at least don't call me that in private."

Kelly regarded Rika with an unblinking gaze. "*I'm* still that Kelly, but you're different, Rika. A lot different."

Rika let out a slow breath. "A lot's happened. It's been a long time for me."

"I heard a bit about it. Chase told me about what happened on Dekar."

"Yeah, Dekar was a shit-show. I don't want word about that to spread, though. Please keep it to yourself."

Kelly snorted. "What? That the Marauders *bought* you? That this outfit that you seem to have fallen for put a chip in your head?"

"They took the chip out. The people who auctioned me off were the ones who put the chip back in. That the chip stayed in for my first deployment was an accident, but one that I'm kinda glad about."

"What?" Kelly cocked her head. "How can you be *glad* that you got chipped?"

Rika leaned back in her chair and grinned. "Because I beat Discipline."

"What do you mean, 'beat'?"

"I won't lie, it was excruciating, but this bitch named Cheri was using it on me to get me to kill Barne. I wouldn't do it, and she couldn't make me—no matter how much it hurt. In the end, I snapped her neck."

Kelly let out a low whistle. "You killed the person who was applying Discipline…. That's…nuts."

"Yeah, important sidenote: it doesn't stop the discipline, either."

"Shit, how did you get it to stop?" Kelly asked with wide eyes.

"Basilisk's old leader, Lieutenant Jerry, shut it off."

"Old?"

"Yeah, he didn't make it through the mission."

Kelly's lips formed an 'O' shape, and she nodded wordlessly. "But Discipline is still there, right?"

"Discipline? No, I can't be Disciplined anymore."

"Right, that's not what I meant. The chip is just the control system for the neural lace around our brain stems. That's what actually does the work. Even without the chips, we still have that neural lace in our heads. You don't actually need the chip to activate it."

Rika was not well-versed in the specifics, she was a bit surprised that Kelly understood them so well. "Is that true, Niki?"

<Yup. It's also how I made Stavros's use of discipline not hurt you. I disconnected the control chip from the neural lace, but created a feedback system so it detected that it was hurting you when it wasn't.>

Kelly's eyes widened. "So Rika can't be chipped anymore?"

Niki gave a soft laugh over the Link. *<We never actually got around to having it removed. Stavros's compliance chip is still in Rika's head.>*

"Huh…I guess it is," Rika mused. "I kinda forgot about it."

"How could you forget something like that?"

Rika saw that Kelly's face had taken on a look of pure horror, and shrugged. "It can't hurt me, and I trust Niki with my life, just as she trusts me with hers. I guess we should get it removed, though. It may be useful in the future for someone to think they've chipped me."

Kelly shook her head in amazement. "Rika, you are hardcore. Have I ever told you that?"

"Really?" Rika laughed. "When Cheri was beating my brain to mush, all I could think of were those times when you tested Discipline's limits, tried to see how much you could get away with before the serious pain kicked in. I distinctly remember thinking, 'Would Kelly have let this take her down?

Hell no!'"

"You think more of me than I deserve, Rika."

Rika rose from her chair and walked around her desk to stand before Kelly. "I don't. Back in Team Hammerfall, Silva was like our mom, but you were my big sister. You always kept me safe—I…I was the one who let you down."

Kelly rose and stood before Rika.

Their faces weren't so different; Kelly had a bit of a stronger chin, and her hair had a reddish tint, but after Kelly had recovered her face, Rika had been surprised to see how similar their eyes were.

Kelly reached up and touched Rika's face. "I always did think of you as my bratty kid sis, Rika. But you were always the heart of Hammerfall, our moral compass—so much as we were able to have one, with Gunny in our brains all the time."

"Good ol' Gunny," Rika mused. "Got what he deserved."

"Nuclear payback," Kelly grinned.

"We good, Kelly? I know I gave you the 'big, stern talk' back on the field, but the last thing I want is for you to leave the Marauders. Finding you and Silva, and then losing you both again…that would be hard."

Kelly nodded. "I'm not going anywhere, Rika. I feel the same way about you, even if getting your bars has made you into a bit of an asshat."

"Takes one to know one." Rika paused, not sure what to say next, then threw caution to the wind and embraced her friend. Kelly wrapped an arm around Rika as well, and they stood silently for a minute before Rika stepped back.

"I'll talk to Lieutenant Carson about what we can do for the neural laces."

"Carson? Not sure if I want someone with 'Bondo' for a nickname rummaging around inside my head." Kelly's lips twisted to the side, and Rika couldn't help but laugh.

"He's really good. He did your face, and it looks great."

"Rika, brains and faces are two very different deals. Could Niki do it? She neutralized yours, and you seem fine." Kelly winked and gave Rika a light punch in the arm. "Mostly."

<I suppose I could, but I can't really do the whole company. It's not the sort of operation I can perform while Rika is wandering all over.>

"Couldn't you just pop out of her for a bit?" Kelly asked.

<Sorry, but no, Kelly. We all have our insecurities. I rather like being inside Rika; despite all the crazy shit she gets up to, her gut is safer than a lot of other places I could end up.>

"Umm…thanks?" Rika said.

<When we get back to the ship, I'll teach Carson the operation, and we'll do yours together, Kelly. Then he can do it on everybody else.>

"And get your chip removed," Kelly added. "It's creepy knowing it's in your head."

Rika smiled. "You got it, Sis."

DROPPING

STELLAR DATE: 08.10.8949 (Adjusted Gregorian)
LOCATION: *Golden Lark*
REGION: Iapetus, Hercules System, Septhian Alliance

First Platoon's bays looked like the mechs were planning an invasion.

Leslie stood at the entrance to Drop Bay 4 and surveyed her platoon as they hauled gear into the dropships, moved other equipment to the cargo shuttles, and generally did their best to avoid running into one another, the dockworkers, and the pilots.

It was glorious chaos.

So far as she knew, the Genevian Armed Forces had never fielded an all-mech platoon, which meant there had never been a scene like this before. Well, space and time were both huge…so maybe there had been. But this was still a first of sorts.

Seeing the comradery that was blooming between the mechs as they made ready for their first mock-combat drop was inspiring. It almost made her want to be one.

Leslie's tail—inside its armored sheath—waved gently in the air behind her as she nodded to a trio of RR-2s that rushed past, hauling crates filled with charging stations.

The last one reached out to tap the tip of Leslie's tail.

At first, the tradition had bothered her, but she'd grown accustomed to it. Crunch had started it—which was the case for a lot of traditions that were forming in her platoon, and in M Company at large.

He told her he did it to remind everyone in the 'toon that their LT was a mech, too—not a GAF standard model, but her body was better because of the mods added to it, just like theirs were.

As the only non-mech officer in M Company, Leslie fought an uphill battle when it came to gaining the acceptance of the troops. That one gesture from Crunch had changed the entire company's view of her.

Doesn't mean I'm not going to figure out what his name is. However, it did mean that so long as she served under Rika in M Company, the tail would stay.

Chris, the platoon's Staff Sergeant, ambled toward her with a grin on his face. He was a long-time Marauder, promoted from squad to staff sergeant when Rika's company was formed.

"Feels good, don't it, LT?" he asked as he turned and stood beside her. "Combat drop. All mechs."

"*Mock*-combat, Staff," Leslie corrected him.

The AM-2 shrugged, his chitinous armor making a soft skittering sound as he completed the gesture. "Still momentous. May it be the first of many, mock or otherwise. I can't wait for the day we drop a 'toon of mechs on the Niets. The look on their faces will be priceless."

"Right before we blow them to pieces." Leslie savored the thought, as well. This feeling, this excitement in the air, had never been present back in the war. Granted, she'd joined the Genevian Armed Forces after things started going badly. Maybe there had been a more positive attitude at the outset.

Chris chuckled. "The looks on their faces will be just as priceless *after* we blow them to pieces."

"So, how's everything looking, Staff?" Leslie said, shaking her head. "Any hang-ups?"

"Oh, you know; someone always forgets to pack their favorite toothbrush, and has to run back to get it. Someone else tries to bring their special rock collection."

"The usual, then."

"The usual."

Chris cocked his head toward the bow of the *Golden Lark*. "I hear that the major is going to send down a fighter escort with us. Twelve birds?"

"He hadn't committed to a number last I heard. I think it comes down to whether or not the *Perseid's Dream* sends some, too. He's looking at it as an opportunity for a training exercise. The locals haven't been super accommodating, but now that one of our birds got shot out of the sky, they can't push back as much."

"Yeah, I imagine someone in Septhian High Command got a bit peeved that we've been cockblocked so much here," Chris made a fist with one hand and smacked it into the palm of his other, miming his euphemism.

Leslie snorted a laugh and shrugged. "You know how it is. The brass brings in mercs to help bolster the numbers, the regulars resent it and make trouble. Usually when the shit starts flying, no one cares where a merc's paycheck comes from. So long as they're shooting at the same people as you."

"Funny sidenote," Chris added. "Ultimately, a merc's paycheck comes from the same place as a regular's: the people they're protecting."

Leslie raised a hand and wobbled it side to side. "Ehhh, mercs do their fair share of oppressing, too. That's not something the Old Man signs up for—generally speaking—but sometimes we put holes in people to help an individual or a company. Shit like that gives us a bad rep, though."

Chris nodded slowly. "OK, good point. Good thing there's enough Niets to shoot at for a lifetime."

Leslie agreed in principle, but she also knew that the Niets ran a conscription military. They'd be shooting at a lot of people who didn't want to be there in the first place.

Still, it was 'us or them'. Same as it had always been; same as it always would be.

"Looking good, Lieutenant," a voice said from behind

them, and Leslie turned and nodded to Lieutenant Scarcliff, the company's XO.

The FR-2 swept his ever-present scowl across the drop bay as he stood beside Chris. "Wish I was going down with you, but Captain Rika wants me up here to make sure things go smoothly in her absence."

"You've got your work cut out for you, Scarcliff," Leslie replied.

She had an uneasy relationship with the company XO.

Both had been promoted directly from the ranks to First Lieutenant at the same time, and it irked Leslie a bit not to have the XO's job, since she had five years of service on him. Just like she knew it annoyed Scarcliff that she had Rika's ear as much as she did.

Rika had taken the time to explain to them that she felt either could do the other's job well, and their placement was for the good of the company.

"What we're doing here with M Company isn't about anyone's career advancement," Rika had told them. "It's about giving these people a new start with a new outfit that really values them. To that end, we have to make things feel right for our troops. Building a cohesive unit is my goal. Everyone is going to have to make sacrifices to do that, but I won't forget them."

At times like that, it was almost impossible to reconcile the Rika who was now the company captain with that scared and angry young woman Leslie had pulled out of the cryopod less than a year before in that warehouse on Pyra.

Rika claimed that it was Silva's leadership back in the war that had taught her what she needed to know. Silva had claimed it was years of keeping young waitresses in line that taught her how to run a unit.

Leslie wasn't sure if that was all that lay behind Rika's natural command abilities. Though she had kept any concerns to herself at the time, Leslie had worried about the Old Man's promotion of Rika to company commander. Running a team like Basilisk bore almost no similarities to running something like M Company.

But now that they were four months in, she doubted that anyone could do a better job than Rika. Give the girl fertile soil, and she had blossomed like nothing Leslie had ever seen.

She hadn't replied to Scarcliff's statement, and he cast her a curious look. "Cat got your tongue, Leslie?"

Chris barked a laugh, then managed to choke it back before slapping Leslie's tail and walking out into the bay, yelling at the platoon's K1R—a massive T-model affectionately called 'The Van'—to watch where he was going.

Leslie shook her head, and gave Scarcliff a cold look. His eyes widened for a moment, and then she reached up and gave him a light cuff in the back of the head. "Very punny, Scarcliff. Seriously, though, what do you think of Rika's plan?"

"By 'plan', you mean the thing where you take First Platoon down and act like bait?" Scarcliff asked.

"Dangling bait is a perfectly viable plan." Leslie cocked an eyebrow at Scarcliff. "So long as our backup is ready."

"It'll be ready. Whoever is raising shit down there will rue the day they messed with Rika's Marauders."

"We're really going with that?"

"Damn skippy."

"You don't think that it will cause division between our company and the rest of the regiment?"

"I've been in the Marauders as long as you, Leslie. Every unit has to form their own internal bonds. Most of them have their own little names, like Terry's Terrors and Sarah's Scarfaces. Smalls and I put a lot of thought into including 'Marauders' in ours. I think it will be better in the long run."

Leslie hadn't known that Scarcliff and Heather had orchestrated the company name so deliberately, but she had to admit it made sense. She'd be sure to share that logic with the ship's crew, if it came up.

"Well said. I certainly like being in Rika's Marauders more than Ayer's Assholes."

Scarcliff barked a laugh. "I may have been behind coining that one, too."

"Keep dreaming," Leslie said over her shoulder as she walked away. "We all know it was Captain Ayer herself that came up with it."

* * * * *

Leslie settled into the copilot's seat in the pinnace. She'd considered not taking the toon's assault pinnace down in the drop. If there were going to be SAMs chasing them again, the ship she was in would be the first target the enemy selected.

However, it was also the ship best able to defend against incoming surface to air fire.

She glanced at Chief Warrant Officer Charles as he shifted in the pilot's seat. His helmet had a snarling dog painted on it, with the words "Mad Dog" written above. The artwork was impressive; Charles had done it himself.

He'd already painted almost every pilot's helmet in the company, and was pressing Rika to let him paint all the mechs' as well.

"You ready to roll, Chief?" she asked.

"I'm ready with a side of fuck-yeah, Ellll-Tee!" Charles drew out the two letters and gave her a lopsided grin.

"Easy now, Chief." Leslie chuckled at the pilot's enthusiasm before reaching out to Heather. *<Flight Leader, First Platoon is geared up and ready to hit the black.>*

<Board's green here, First. Your fighter escort is in position. You're good to drop by the numbers.>

<Roger that, FL,> Leslie replied and switched her address to

the segregated network with the pilots. *<First platoon, we are green. Drop. Drop. Drop.>*

A siren sounded in the drop bay, and the deck opened up in front of the dropships. The cradles tilted, and in preprogrammed sequence, the ships were accelerated down the ladders and out into space.

"Yeeehaw!" Charles cried out as the well-lit drop bay was replaced by the black expanse of space.

Leslie couldn't suppress the smile that forced its way onto her lips. She'd dropped with Charles on other missions, and his enthusiasm was infectious. It was one of the reasons she'd wrangled him into her 'toon when she heard he was assigned to Rika's company.

Like all the dropship pilots, Charles was not a mech. The cockpits on most ships could barely fit a human, let alone a mech—barring SMI-2s.

Even so, he was heavily modded for piloting a ship, and did it with a grace and skill that few possessed. He had his own customized control suite, a three-dimensional interface that only he could see. He waved his hands through it, turned invisible knobs, and adjusted other controls with gestures that made no sense to Leslie.

Not that she needed to know *how* he flew the ship, just that he had a damn good record and flew the smoothest drops Leslie had ever been on.

She brought up the pinnace's scan data on the holo in front of her and watched as the dropships spread out into a wide pattern, each covered by four fighters. Every vessel was over a kilometer from each other, their jinking patterns loaded and synchronized.

"You think we're going to see action?" Charles asked.

Leslie shrugged. "I hope not. If someone on Iapetus can attack this many ships with impunity, what's to stop them from hitting the *'Lark* or the *'Dream*? We'd be better off finding a new location for our training facility."

Charles laughed as he executed a burn to slot the pinnace into its descent vector. "What better way to train us all than a hostile environment?"

"I can think of a lot of better ways."

"I guess, maybe," Charles said absently as he reviewed the ship's trajectory. "Hey, LT, since this is going to be by the numbers, think you can sing a song for me while we come down? I hear you've got an amazing set of pipes."

Leslie resisted the urge to reach out and hit Charles in the back of the head. "I'll show you pipes. Just fly the damn ship."

* * * * *

Charles kept the pinnace in a holding pattern over the training compound while the dropships settled onto the facility's southern edge, disgorging their troops by the numbers, mechs fanning out, covering corners before moving out to sweep the surrounding buildings.

The structures had once been hangars and repair facilities at a small airport used by light and sport aircraft. On the far side of the buildings were three landing strips for aerodynamic descent.

People got up to strange things in their free time.

For some reason, the airport had fallen out of use, and Barne had been able to secure it for a surprisingly low price.

As Leslie surveyed the facility, she could make out a construction crew on the northern side of the airstrip erecting a simple fence that denoted the edge of Marauder territory, separating it from the half-abandoned commercial district surrounding the compound.

It wasn't a very defensible location, but Leslie approved of Rika's plan. If they were to get to the bottom of what was afoot on Iapetus, they *wanted* to be attacked.

Once the squad leaders declared their assigned quadrants clear, Leslie directed squad two to secure the landing field for the cargo carriers on the northern side of the barracks.

After the compound was deemed secure, and the fighter escort had boosted away, Leslie directed Charles to lower the pinnace from its overwatch position to settle in front of the command building.

She lowered the ramp and stepped out onto the hard surface the moment the ship settled down. Ahead, Rika walked out of the command building, a wide smile on her face as she surveyed the deployment.

"Lieutenant Leslie, congratulations on the drop. A hell of a lot better than mine."

Leslie met Rika's smile with one of her own. "It's easier when no one's shooting at you."

They shook hands, and turned to watch as Staff Sergeant Chris and the squad sergeants oversaw the unloading of the equipment from the dropships—likely receiving direction and chastisement from Barne, who was still back in the command building's CIC.

"The loading go smoothly?" Rika asked as they watched the activity before them. Leslie initialized a HUD overlay showing the scan data from the surrounding terrain and skies above. She was certain Rika was doing likewise. Just because the drop hadn't been hit didn't mean they couldn't be attacked now.

"Without a hitch," Leslie replied.

"Major Tim was surprisingly accommodating," Rika said, and gestured to the contrails the fighters had left in the sky from their thrusters.

Leslie chuckled. "I bet that before we left, the Old Man took the major aside and told him that if anything happened to you, there'd be hell to pay."

Rika looked at Leslie with surprise. "Think so?"

"Well, I didn't see it happen, but I'd be shocked if it didn't. Seriously, Rika. You went from hardware purchased at auction to company commander in under a year. How is it that you don't see how much the Old Man is in your corner?"

Leslie watched as Rika's brow lowered and her lips twisted in thought. "I guess it is a bit of a meteoric rise."

"That's an oxymoronic figure of speech."

"I didn't invent it." Rika shrugged.

"If you're not a part of the solution, you're a part of the problem."

Rika laughed. "Only a day away, and already I'd started to miss you. By-the-by, did you bring those additional items I asked for?"

"What do I look like? Of course I brought them."

"Brought what?" Chase asked from behind the pair.

"Shit!" Leslie exclaimed. "Since when did you become a ninja? That's my gig."

"Learned from the best," Chase said.

Leslie saw Rika reach her hand back and clasp Chase's.

"Leslie and I are going on an excursion into the city tonight," Rika told him.

Chase glanced at Leslie and back to Rika. "Girls' night out, I take it?"

<*Something like that,*> Rika replied over a private connection between the three of them. <*David has spent the last day establishing a connection with a woman in the local garrison commander's HQ. He managed to get her to agree to a private meeting to talk about what they know of the attack on our dropship. We'll find somewhere nearby to discreetly watch the meet.*>

<*You realize that's not the sort of mission the company commander goes on,*> Chase said with a raised eyebrow.

<*I'm aware,*> Rika said. <*But I may take the opportunity to reveal myself and talk with her directly. Depends on how it goes.*>

<*You should take a fireteam,*> Chase advised.

<*Mechs don't blend in all that well,*> Rika said. <*I suppose I could grab some of the SMIs, but they're all in different squads, and I don't want to mess with team cohesion.*>

Leslie considered their options. There were only five SMI-2 mechs in First Platoon. <*We could bring Kelly and Keli. Those two are already thick as thieves most of the time.*>

<*Other than a few short stints on stations, neither Keli or Kelly have been back amongst the general populace yet,*> Chase cautioned. <*I don't know if they're ready for that.*>

Leslie waved her hand dismissively. <*What better time than now? We're in friendly territory—mostly. I brought enough of our handy camouflage robes. Be good for them to get out and be able to blend in.*>

<*I think it's solid,*> Rika said. <*Leslie, you can stay in overwatch, lurk on a roof or something, and the girls can come with me. You know…it'll be the first time since the war that I've worked with a full team of SMIs.*>

Rika got a distant look in her eyes, and Leslie patted her on the shoulder. <*Silva had to go. It was the right thing for her to do.*>

<*I know. Doesn't mean I don't miss her,*> Rika replied.

<*You never know,*> Chase said. <*Maybe after we kick the Nietzscheans all the way to the rim of the galaxy, we can all go and retire with Silva.*>

Rika smiled. <*Sounds like a plan.*>

RECONNECTING

STELLAR DATE: 08.10.8949 (Adjusted Gregorian)
LOCATION: Marauder Training Compound
REGION: Iapetus, Hercules System, Septhian Alliance

Rika lay back on her side of the bed and breathed a long sigh of contentment. "Having a real bed sure is nice. Starships are just not made for couples to get up to shenanigans."

Chase rolled over to face her and trailed a finger through her hair. "We're lucky that the Old Man has a lax attitude when it comes to this stuff. No sane command would let me work under you."

Rika turned her head and smirked at Chase. "Thought it was me that was working under you just now."

"Yeah, well, let's keep that arrangement to our quarters. I like having to salute you."

"Ha!" Rika shook her head. "Nice double entendre there."

"I try. It's hard, working for you."

"OK, easy now. You've proven you can be punny, Chase."

He rose to his knees and swung a leg over Rika, straddling her. A part of her was impressed by how he could maneuver around her body without scratching himself; either that, or he didn't care.

"It always amazes me," he commented absently as he traced a finger down her chest.

"What does?" Rika asked absently, staring up into Chase's dark brown eyes.

"How warm you are."

"I'm cooler than you are. Twenty-eight degrees at rest."

Chase reached down and picked up her hand, placing his palm against what passed for hers. "Yeah, but your hands are warm too. Why is that?"

"Part of our chameleon abilities. We can warm our entire bodies to uniform temperatures. Also tied into our heat dispersal. I could make it warmer." Rika warmed her hand to thirty-four degrees. "There, it matches your hand now."

"Heh, that's hot," Chase said as he reached out and touched the socket on the end of her right arm. Though Rika liked having her GNR attached, she didn't sleep with it. Not after that time when the barrel had whacked Chase during a bad dream.

And Rika often had bad dreams.

"Why don't you keep it this warm all the time?" Chase asked.

"Uses extra energy. Twenty-eight is my average dispersal temperature, when I'm not exerting myself. You're lucky I'm not an FR model; they have these cooling strips on their arms that can get pretty damn toasty. I'd probably burn you during our escapades."

Chase pushed her arm back above her head and leaned in to kiss her.

Rika drew in a deep breath as their lips touched feeling his naked body press up against her carbon-poly skin, his firm pecs pressing into the stiff mounds on her chest.

She had long ago forgotten what real tactile contact across her body would feel like—but given the difference between her face and the rest of her 'skin', she wondered if she would be able to handle the sensations.

"You smell like candy," Chase whispered as he kissed her. "Cotton candy. You secreting some around here somewhere?"

"It's a new facial cleanser Leslie gave me," Rika said with a laugh. "But if I want to hide candy, that's my business."

"So you do have candy!" Chase proclaimed and nibbled at her ear.

Ear nibbles always made her giggle, and sometimes ruined her mood, but Rika didn't care. Being near Chase was what mattered. Being grounded and feeling human was always welcome.

"Do you think the other mechs take lovers?" she asked suddenly, turning her head to look into Chase's eyes.

He shrugged. "Some do, some can't."

"Well, we technically can't make love, either," Rika reminded him—as if she needed to.

Chase leaned down to kiss her. "Rika, I don't need to push inside you to 'make love' to you. Being here with you now, living my life with you, fighting on the battlefield with you—*that* is making love to you. Making love is everything we do."

Rika appreciated the small lie, but she knew he'd like to have real sex. She would too, especially at times like this when it felt like her insides were on fire.

Rika tamped down her urges as much as possible and smiled. "Who would have thought a stone-cold killer like you was such a romantic?"

Chase's smile faded. "I'm not a stone—what would make you say that?"

"I didn't mean anything by it, Chase." Rika frowned, wondering what about her statement had rattled him. "We're all killers. It's what we do."

"I know, but sometimes…sometimes I'd just like to forget that. Don't you want this to end someday? Do something else with your life?"

"Like what?" Rika asked.

It wasn't the first time Chase had made comments like this, but she could never get him to elaborate on his feelings—instead he would just shut down. This time, she tried a different tack.

"I'm a war machine. It's what I do, I'm not in the 'get old with great-great-grandchildren at my knee' profession. I've accepted that."

"What if I haven't?" Chase asked.

"What does that mean? I thought you liked being in the Marauders."

Chase sat up, still straddling her. "I do like being in the Marauders. It's a good job, we seem to be working for the good guys, so that's nice. And I'm with you, which is what I want most. But I don't want to spend the rest of my life in this outfit. We're more than just killers, Rika."

"Of course we are; we're a family. Basilisk, and now M Company. We're saving people, Chase. My people."

Chase nodded. "And after that?"

Rika pushed an errant lock of hair out of her face. "I don't know. I don't think that far ahead. I'm not too sure I can succeed at what's laid out ahead of me now."

"And what's that?" Chase asked.

"I want to drive the Nietzscheans out of Genevia," she replied, her voice lowering. "I want to kill every last motherfucking one of them, scour them from the stars."

Chase's eyes widened, and Rika realized her statement came across with more vehemence than she'd intended.

"Why?" he asked. "What did Genevia ever do for you?"

"It made me this," Rika said, lifting her right arm and rotating her wrist. "It made me strong and powerful. Did it abuse me? Yes. But what would have happened to me if I wasn't turned into a mech? There weren't a lot of survivors from the world where I got convicted. Becoming a mech may have saved my life."

Chase nodded soberly. "Yeah, I looked Kellas up. They got hit hard. But still…why do you love Genevians so much? They aren't that accepting of mechs."

"Chase." Rika reached up and touched his face. "*You're* Genevian. So is Leslie, Barne; stars, everyone in M Company is. The Old Man. We're all Genevian."

"Do you need all of them? Am I not enough?" Chase clasped her hand in both of his. "We could flee deep into the cluster. Past the edge of FTL. Nietzschea won't bother going into the inner empire; it's not worth the effort."

Rika frowned. She couldn't understand why Chase was saying this, he wasn't a coward. She'd seen him in combat multiple times, and he'd never backed down from a challenge.

"What's brought this on?" she asked. "The Marauders are our family, we can't just abandon them."

"A family that's going to get you killed," he replied.

"Is this because we got shot down? Are you worried that I'm going to die?"

"Yes!" Chase almost shouted. "You *did* almost die. If your crazy pilot hadn't dived under the ocean, you'd be toast. Don't you see that?"

Rika shrugged. "I guess…though we might have survived that, too. Stars, people die from all sorts of stupid shit all the time. I won't live in fear just because of what *could* happen."

"What *will* happen," Chase corrected.

"What do you mean?"

"We all die, Rika."

There was a sadness in his voice that told Rika there was some story, some trauma from his past that he'd not yet shared with her.

"What is it, Chase? What's got you thinking like this?"

He rolled off her and lay on his back, staring at the ceiling. "Nothing—other than what we've already gone over and over and over."

Rika rolled onto her side and clasped his hand. "Chase, I want to spend my forever with you, but this is what I have to do right now. It's who I am—I've accepted that. But I promise it won't last forever."

"How can I believe that?" Chase asked. "You've gone from loathing what you are to loving it."

"Because…maybe deep down, where I'm too scared to admit it…I think I want to have my great-great grandchildren at my knee someday."

Chase turned his head and met her gaze. "Mean it?"

Rika nodded, feeling her eyes grow moist. "I think I do. I really do."

THE MEET

STELLAR DATE: 08.11.8949 (Adjusted Gregorian)
LOCATION: Hittis City
REGION: Iapetus, Hercules System, Septhian Alliance

"Nice place David picked for his date with Dala," Kelly said, gesturing out the window as the three SMI-2s settled into their seats at Charlie's Pasta and Chips.

Rika looked across the street to the restaurant David and Dala would be dining at. It wasn't too fancy, simply named Hammurabi, but not having 'chips' in the name took any establishment up a notch.

"Not the sort of place our kind can visit," Keli added.

<*Remember,*> Rika cautioned privately. <*We're regular citizens, we can go anywhere we like. Believe it. Own it. It's the best way to blend in.*>

Keli didn't reply, but nodded as she picked up her menu with gloved hands.

Rika pulled her robe's long sleeves back and did the same. She felt naked without her gun-arm, something that both Keli and Kelly had confessed to as well, but they were all still carrying rifles under their robes. Keli had called them their 'security blankets'.

Rika shifted her weight carefully, keeping one leg extended under her chair to support most of her weight. She wasn't too worried about the seat collapsing, but it wasn't an idle concern for a mech. When they were scoping out a good location, the sturdy steel chairs at Charlie's Pasta and Chips had played a major part in their choice of establishment.

<*You three just better remember to order my takeout. I want a fettucine alfredo, and their lasagna. Plus those fresh kettle chips everyone raves about in their reviews,*> Leslie chimed in.

<*Whatever you say, LT,*> Keli said cheerfully.

<*Stow that glee,*> Leslie retorted. <*If I'd known it was going to rain like this tonight, I would have volunteered one of you for overwatch.*>

<*Would you say it's raining cats and dogs?*> Rika asked with a snicker.

<*Stars, not you, too.*>

<*I can't help it.*> Rika got her mirth under control. <*Scarcliff does it so much that they spring to mind all the time now.*>

<*Well, the next girls' night out needs to involve less of me freezing my ass off out in a storm.*>

<*Noted,*> Rika replied.

The three women reviewed their menus, looking over the options and discussing them casually while each kept half an eye on the restaurant across the street, where David now waited for Major Dala.

"Stars. I think I'll just have the spaghetti and meatballs," Kelly said. "If you count the time I was on ice, I haven't had a good spaghetti in…what, ten years?"

"They had it in the galley just last week," Keli said as she perused her menu.

"Right," Kelly nodded. "I think you missed the part where I said 'good' spaghetti."

"Are you besmirching our ship's cooks?" Keli asked. "Because I'm in love with all of them."

"Points for using 'besmirching'," Rika commented.

"No, no besmirchment—is that even a word?—intended. They didn't have the right sauce, is all. They should have waited for fresh tomatoes before trying it. Their menu here says all ingredients are locally sourced and that they make their sauce fresh each day."

Keli shrugged. "OK, that's good to see. Maybe this place is more than just the joint with the strongest chairs."

<*I swear…I'm going to turn off the comm channel,*> Leslie

groused. *<I'm salivating up here.>*

Rika saw a waitress approach—not human, but an automaton good enough to fool casual observation. She wore a short blue skirt and white blouse with 'Mary' on her name tag. Rika thought her legs were a touch too long for her torso, but not so much that you'd notice at first glance.

<Maybe she's the discount bot,> Niki commented. *<From the defects pile.>*

<How do you make a bot's legs too long as a defect?> Rika asked. *<Seems deliberate.>*

<Well, maybe they were meant for a taller model.>

<Poor waitress-bot, made from spare parts.> Rika shook her head.

"What can I get for you ladies to drink?" the subtly misshapen waitress automaton asked as she set three glasses of water on the table.

"Ohhhhh, drinks!" Kelly proclaimed. "I'll take…one of your cinnamon martinis."

"I'll have this thing you call the cherry bomb." Keli stabbed a finger at the menu.

"Just a glass of your best white bubbly for me," Rika said when the automaton-waitress turned to her.

"OK, you got it. Cinnamon martini, Explosive Cherry Bomb, and a glass of our Atrium."

The three nodded in turn, and Mary gave a nod and turned, walking to the back of the restaurant to prepare their drinks.

"Why make automatons look so perfectly human?" Keli asked. "Everyone can tell what they are."

"Not around here, they can't," Rika said. "Thebans don't mod much—at least not the ones that live on planets. They might not be able to spot a bot like our Mary."

"Weird," Keli replied. "Of course, I haven't seen the inside of a restaurant for about as long as Kelly. Stavros didn't really let us eat out a lot. And by 'a lot', I mean 'ever'."

"I imagine," Rika said with a nod. "Stavros wasn't much of a 'let anyone do anything' kinda guy."

Keli's eyes widened and she nodded in agreement. "Glad you put him down."

"Was actually Barne that fired the shot," Kelly said as she set her menu down.

Keli raised the glass of water that sat before her. "Well, when I get my drink, I'll raise a toast to the Top. May his days of taking out evil dictators never end."

"I'm sure he'd echo that sentiment," Rika said, turning her gaze out the window once more. She didn't really need to watch for Dala's approach. Leslie would let them know when she spotted the Major, and David would confirm when she joined him.

"What was it like?" Kelly asked after a minute of silence stretched between them.

"It?" Rika asked.

"Being out in the world. After the war."

Rika looked at the two women seated across from her and sighed. Both had been injured in the war, and subsequently found by Stavros. Neither saw the end of the fight with the Nietzscheans—saw their leaders surrender or flee. Neither had to live in the shattered remains of their nation amidst a populace that hated them

"It sucked balls," Rika replied. "Lots of balls. All the balls. I guess it would have gone better for me if I'd joined an outfit like the Marauders—or even a gang of some sort. But I was stubborn. I wanted to try to make a go of it as a civilian."

"Now that doesn't surprise me." Kelly grinned, the smile actually reaching her eyes. "You never could let go of an idea once it got into that head of yours."

"Wish I'd been on a team like yours," Keli said. "Kelly's told me all about Hammerfall. You ladies kicked some major ass back in the shit."

Mary returned as Keli spoke, and set their drinks down. "Are you ready to order, or are you still looking over the menu? Oh! I forgot to recite the specials."

<*How does an automaton 'forget' the specials?*> Niki asked. <*Is the NSAI defective, or does someone think this is a clever way to sell the daily deals?*>

<*Beats me,*> Rika replied. <*If folks around here can't tell it's a bot, maybe it does work—or maybe it's randomly variable behavior, or something.*>

<*I guess. I don't usually run into NSAIs managing simple tasks like this,*> Niki replied. <*Usually they're managing things like magnetic fields on a tokamak reactor or something.*>

Keli said she'd like to hear the specials, and Mary began to rattle them off.

<*I would have thought that you talked to NSAIs all the time,*> Rika commented as she half-listened to Mary's recitation.

<*I've spent most of my time on starships. You're only the second person I've been embedded with—though we're not neurally embedded, like a real AI pairing would be.*>

<*I guess there aren't many NSAIs trying to sell you on the Chicken Bolognese on a starship.*>

<*Not so much, no.*>

<*What's it like to be neurally embedded?*> Rika asked, as Mary finished the list, and Keli hemmed and hawed.

<*For the human, it's not that much different. For the AI, we get deeper insight into the logic behind our partner's decisions.*>

<*We use logic?*> Rika chuckled. <*I wouldn't have thought AIs considered many human decisions to be logical.*>

<*Well, for the most part, humans **believe** that their reasoning is valid. If this, then that, and therefore logical. Most of the time, the truly illogical things you humans do are for entertainment—which makes them something that you enjoy. Therefore, it's logical for you to do illogical things, because gaining amusement is healthy for your*

minds, and thus logical.>

<*Huh. You used the word 'logic' so many times it just became a morass of syllables. Is that logical?* Rika asked, then shifted her attention to Mary to order a plate of spaghetti and chips.

Niki just groaned in response, and sent Rika an image of eyes rolling in exasperation.

<*OK, OK,*> Rika replied. <*I guess it makes sense. I mean, it does to me; I just didn't think it would make sense to an AI.*>

<*Well, that's part of why we spend time with humans. It's not to serve you, but rather because there are some things that are better experienced than taught.*>

"So, what was your favorite mission, Rika?" Keli asked once Mary departed.

<*I'm going to come back to this later,*> Rika told Niki. <*I want to understand more about what you meant.*>

<*Sure, I'm not going anywhere.*>

Rika considered it for a moment. "You know, I really liked our mission on Parsons—I mean, except for the part where you died, Kelly. I could barely think about it for years afterward. But now…now it's one that I can actually look back on. We kicked some major ass."

"You saved my life twice on that mission, Rika." The corners of Kelly's eyes glistened, and she gave a short sniff before shaking her head. "I'll never forget you standing atop that K1R, firing your rifle into it until it let me go."

Keli's brow lowered. "A K1R? Why were you fighting one of our own?"

Rika pursed her lips, and Kelly replied. "Fucking Niets turned it against us. Bastard—"

"Was a poor bastard," Rika interrupted. "He didn't ask for what happened to him. I gave him a good death."

No one spoke for a moment, and then Kelly laughed. "And *those* are the 'good' memories."

Rika stretched a hand across the table and took Kelly's,

then grabbed Keli's as well. "No, the good memories were times like this. Sure, we didn't have Mary bringing us the best chips this side of the cluster, but we *did* have each other. That was the *real* 'best part' about Hammerfall. And now we have the Marauders."

"*Rika's* Marauders," Keli said with a silly grin. "Shit, Captain, why you such a big sap? Don' you know we rust if we cry?"

"You might have to see Bondo about that," Kelly smirked as she wiped a gloved hand against her cheek.

<I love listening to the three of you bond as much as anyone,> Leslie interrupted, *<but I thought you'd want to know that Dala is approaching the restaurant.>*

Rika looked out the window to see Dala, exiting a ground car and rushing through the rain to the restaurant across the street.

<I see her. Looks damp.>

<That dress doesn't look like any sort of uniform, either,> Keli commented.

<I guess David made more of an impression than we thought.> Rika nodded appreciatively. *<I'll admit, I hadn't given him that much credit—at least, not that specific type of credit.>*

<I guess Dala likes 'em smart,> Keli added.

<Could be that she's going to spill the beans and wants to make this look like a date, in case anyone is following her,> Leslie suggested.

Rika wondered about that. It would be an interesting twist. Or it just could be that Colonel Zim was as much of a hardass as Rika suspected, and Dala was happy for any excuse to get out.

<She's here,> David advised on a separate channel. Rika hadn't segregated him as a slight, she just didn't want to distract him with their banter—though with his mods, he probably could focus on what was necessary well enough.

Still, he'd confessed to being a poor actor, and Rika didn't want to tax him. <*Remember. Ease her into sharing. Don't force her. If things go well, broach the subject of talking with me. Doesn't have to be now. I'm here for a 'just in case' scenario.*>

<*You got it, Captain,*> David said, a waver in his voice belying a measure of uncertainty.

<*I'll be listening, so if anything comes up that I can help with, I'll offer a suggestion. But I'll keep my chatter to a minimum.*>

The rest of the team was listening in on the conversation, though Keli and Kelly kept up some verbal chatter about the weather on Iapetus so that it didn't seem like the entire table fell silent for no reason.

David provided a feed from his eyes on the team's net, and Rika tapped into it, overlaying it on the right side of her vision.

Dala approached his table, and he rose to greet her. She was wearing a grey dress that had a patina of dark spots on it from the rain. Her pink hair was pulled back into a clip, from which it fell down over her shoulders. Her lips were colored to match her fuchsia eyes, and her smile seemed genuine as she took David's hand and gave it a single shake.

"Very nice to meet you in person, David," Dala said as she sat. "And even nicer to do it at a place like Hammurabi's. I hear their roast chicken is superb."

"I really don't know the local establishments in Hittis that well," David replied. "But no one seemed to complain about this place, so it seemed like a safe pick."

"Weren't you worried that I might be a vegetarian?" Dala asked. "Hammurabi's is mostly known for their meat."

Rika imagined that David must have shrugged or given a smile—though she couldn't tell from his visual feed.

"I looked over your activity on the public feeds. You often post about the types of foods you prefer. It made my selection a bit easier, though it also told me that I needed to be discerning."

Major Dala raised an eyebrow, though a smile toyed at the corners of her lips. "Did *you* check up on me, David of the Marauders?"

"I'm a P-COG. I check up on everything. It's what we do."

Dala's smile faded. "We are all what we're made to do."

"That seems fatalistic," David replied. "What have you been made to do?"

The major shook her head. "Nothing sinister. I was just thinking about how our parents shape us, then school, then our jobs."

"Ah, and especially more so if your job is the military."

"Doubly so, yes."

David and Dala's conversation moved to more trivial topics as they reviewed the menu and ordered their drinks. Rika listened with half an ear as they spoke of the Theban integration into the Septhian Alliance.

Dala was circumspect, but Rika could tell that she resented the change, though she did agree that it was likely a necessity in the fight against the Nietzscheans. Before the attack on the Albany System, the Niets moving into the Praesepe Cluster had been a worry for another day. Now it was history, and no one could argue that Thebes was in the Nietzscheans' crosshairs.

On the public feeds, debate raged as to whether or not the Niets would strike the same target twice, but Rika knew they would. If there was one truth about the Niets, it was that they hated to lose.

If they lost an attack on a world or system, they would return again and again, throwing more and more resources into the conflict until they won.

During the war, Rika had often heard officers speculating about where the Niets were getting their seemingly endless resources. Though their empire was vast, there was no evidence that they had the economy to support the war they waged.

The prevailing logic was that they were being supported by the Trisilieds. That kingdom was the dominant power in the Pleiades Cluster, and had massive mining operations collecting both the dust permeating the region, and the exotic matter that streamed off the massive B-class stars that dominated the Pleiades.

Rika had kept her ear to the ground over the years—something made easy by working in places like Hal's Hell. From what she'd heard, there was little to no chatter about major trade with the Trisilieds. Wherever the Nietzscheans had gathered their resources, it didn't appear to be from there.

Maybe someday she'd be in a position to find out.

Across the road, David and Dala were sipping their drinks. On Rika's side, Kelly and Keli were tucking into their meals, with Kelly letting out more than a few moans of delight as she ate her plate of spaghetti.

<Don't forget to order my takeout,> Leslie reminded Rika at one point.

<Oh, you were serious about that?>

<Rika. It's freezing up here, and I can feel my stomach gnawing a hole in my liver. Listening to Kelly moan about how much she loves pasta is about to push me over the edge. You're damn skippy, I'm serious.>

<You volunteered for overwatch, you know.>

Leslie growled. *<Um, no,* ***you*** *volunteered* ***me.*** *So help me, if you don't have my order placed in five minutes, I'm going to come down there and kick the tar out of the three of you.>*

<OK, OK, I'm signaling our synthetic waitress to come over.>

<You do that.>

Rika followed up on her promise, and Kelly added five more orders, apparently planning to live on leftover takeout for the next week.

Across the street, David and Dala's meals also arrived, and they began to eat in relative silence.

Thus far, Dala had not said anything noteworthy, though they *had* spoken of the attack in general terms. Rika was starting to wonder if Dala had led David on, simply interested in a date with no intentions of sharing anything about the attack.

Or maybe she plans to extract additional details from him…

<*David—*> Rika began, but David stopped her.

<*Busy, Captain. We're having a chat over a direct Link connection. She's telling me about how the ATC and Link were disrupted.*>

<*Well, that's good. Was starting to think she just may want you to go over to her place afterward.*>

David snorted. <*Who says that can't happen, too? I'm bundling up what she's said thus far and sending it to Niki. Going to try to get more details on a few things.*>

<*OK.*>

<*Getting a transmission from David,*> Niki said over the group's connection. <*Oh ho! Would you look at this. On the night we were attacked, the Link towers for five-hundred kilometers just happened to all go through a diagnostic cycle at the same time…one that triggered a core instruction-set update that required a full re-initialization.*>

<*Seems…unlikely that was an accident,*> Keli observed. <*I worked Link relay maintenance before conscription. We had carefully orchestrated rolling update patterns. Different ones all the time, so that they were harder to exploit.*>

<*Maybe they're just dumb here,*> Kelly smirked around a mouthful of spaghetti.

<*You saw how the feeds lit up with people who were bullshit over the outage. If that sort of thing happened regularly, you wouldn't have seen them so upset over it.*>

<*ATC went down as a result of the Link outage,*> Niki added.

<Looks like it's supposed to fail over to proprietary backup communication systems, but it didn't.>

<And why did satcomms go offline at the same time?> Rika asked. *<That has to add to the suspicion.>*

Niki responded without pause. *<The official word from the providers is that the satcomm network got overloaded when the terrestrial one went down. But that's not what Dala's division thinks. They believe that someone hammered the satcomms with bogus data when the ground systems went offline.>*

<This isn't news worth freezing my ass off for,> Leslie interjected. *<The fact that the attack was well orchestrated is evidenced by the attack itself. It's the 'who' that matters.>*

<I'm getting there,> Niki replied. *<Trying to sift through and corroborate as much of what Dala is telling David as I can. OK. Dala says she doesn't* ***think*** *it was orchestrated by anyone in the military, but she also said that some of the people who attacked us* ***were*** *former Theban Alliance soldiers. All discharged before the Septhian takeover, though—which stands to reason. No one's getting discharged from the SAF right now—unless it's dishonorable.>*

Rika wanted to pass a dozen questions over to David for him to ask Dala, but he knew the objective as well as she. There was no point messing up his train of thought.

<Well, that's…> Leslie began. *<Oh shit! Rika, you need to get over there. We've got company!>*

Rika rose from her chair. *<We're live, ladies. Kelly and I will go in the front. Keli, you go around back and secure egress. Chase will pick us up at the park four blocks east.>* She looked at the pair and they both nodded before exiting Charlie's Pasta and Chips.

Rika sent a payment over the Link so they wouldn't have to worry about Mary chasing after them, and moved a dozen meters down the street before crossing. Kelly mirrored her route, bracketing the restaurant. Once across the street, Rika stopped under an awning and reviewed the data Leslie was feeding them.

Leslie was positioned atop the ten-story building that housed Charlie's Pasta and Chips at street level. From her vantage, she had eyes on armored figures atop the next building over, setting up on the roof. That building was only two stories high, and would provide a clear shot through the windows of Hammurabi's.

Leslie hadn't spotted any others, but if there were two, there were more.

<*Think it's capture or kill?*> Kelly asked as she leaned against a post in front of Hammurabi's, obstructing the shooter's line of sight into the restaurant.

<*Capture,*> Leslie replied. <*I see a spotter in a parked ground car thirty meters past your position, Rika. And there's a van approaching. It's staying low, but its flight-capable.*>

<*I'm almost at the alley,*> Keli reported. <*Nothing here, yet.*>

Rika reached out to David. <*We have company coming. Looks like a grab team with an option to terminate.*>

<*Me or her?*> David asked, surprisingly calm.

<*No way to tell,*> Rika replied.

<*Use a pair of drones, triangulate the shooter's aim. Their spotter will be looking at both of us, but the shooter won't. They'll be on their primary target.*>

It made sense; Rika felt silly for not thinking of it herself. It wasn't a foolproof way to tell, but David was probably right.

Rika loosened the scarf around her neck, and two of her miniscule drones flew out, rising through the rain to track the aim of the shooter's rifle.

The sniper had just moved, taking up a new position where Kelly wasn't in the way, and when he settled into place, Rika had her answer.

<*It's on her, David. Not wavering at all. So either the shooter thinks Dala's hot, or she's the primary.*>

<*Could be. I, for one, really dig all the pink she has going on.*

Should I get her out the back?>

Rika checked on the incoming van. It was halfway down the block. Keli hadn't yet made it around the back, but if the van was up front, it was likely that few—if any—enemies would be at the restaurant's rear.

At least Rika hoped that would be the case.

<*We should have brought a bigger team,*> she said privately to Niki.

<*Or at least made Keli hang out in the alley at the back.*> Niki gave a mental nod. <*Mind you, she would have complained about you and Kelly getting the nice meal.*>

<*This is what I get for worrying about people's feelings,*> Rika replied as she drew her left arm within her cloak and unslung her JE-84 rifle. Kelly—who was still clearly visible to the sniper and spotter team—didn't yet make a move. Reaching for a weapon was a telltale motion the enemy would spot in an instant.

<*I'm halfway down to them,*> Leslie said. <*Just one more floor, and I can jump if needs be.*>

<*Kelly. Move into the sniper's line of sight again. David, get moving, take her to the back. Leslie, jump only if they fire—or if you really want to.*>

The team followed her orders without hesitation. Within the restaurant, David rose and held his hand out to Dala, who was still seated, giving him a confused look. Rika hoped he could get her moving without trouble, but couldn't offer any help, as the van arrived in front of the restaurant and its side doors opened up.

A man in powered armor stepped out and raised a chaingun.

Shit!

<*Not a grab op!*> Rika yelled as she fired a trio of rounds from her JE-84 at the enemy. He spun toward her, and his chaingun spun up at the same time as a muffled crack

sounded.

The restaurant's sign exploded in a shower of sparks, struck by the sniper's weapon.

<*Got him!*> Leslie called out

<*Nice timing,*> Rika responded as she leapt into the air to avoid the chaingun's spray of bullets. She grinned as Kelly moved into view, her cloak thrown open, JE-87 spraying kinetic rounds into the back of Rika's attacker.

Without hesitation, Rika added her own hail of bullets, and the man went down, the chaingun cocking up into the air and tracing a line of destruction across the storefronts.

Rika hoped no civilians had been injured, but had no time to worry about it, as two more enemies spilled out of the van and took cover behind it.

A shot rang out from the rooftops, and one of the new foes fell.

<*Nice gun, this,*> Leslie commented. <*The biolock was disabled, though. Bad form.*>

Rika leapt onto the van and fired at the second enemy, before a second shot came from Leslie's position. The soldier's neck exploded, and he crumpled to the ground.

Rika jumped off the van and looked into the restaurant to find David and Dala gone. Behind her, the van took off racing down the street, nearly colliding with two other cars before it turned the corner.

<*Got them. Safe and sound,*> Keli reported.

<*Good, we're coming 'round to meet you.*> Rika motioned for Kelly to follow her. <*Stay in the alley 'til we get there.*>

<*Aye aye, Captain.*>

Rika rolled her eyes at Keli's weak humor and reached out to Chase. <*You coming to give us poor women a ride home?*>

<*Am I to leave poor David behind?*> Chase asked

<*Er…us poor women plus David.*>

<*I'm hanging out above the park now. Just waiting for some guy*

to finish chasing his dog that got away from him, then I'll set down.>

<*OK,*> Rika replied. <*We might be coming in hot, so stay frosty.*>

Chase laughed. <*Hot and frosty. Got it.*>

Rika led the way around the block while Kelly covered her six. They met Keli, David, and Dala around the corner. The look on the Major's face was a combination of anger and worry. Possibly mixed with a little annoyance.

"Should have expected to meet you out here," Dala said when she spotted Rika. "You seem to attract trouble."

Rika looked further down the street, then looked back behind them. So far, there were no signs of pursuit. "Their weapons were aimed at your pretty pink head, Major. Someone didn't like that you were sharing intel with us."

Dala opened her mouth to reply, but she closed it and nodded before asking. "So what's next?"

"We get you to our compound, and then you figure out who you can trust and reach out to them—but not before we arrive. For now, you need to go EM-silent."

Dala worked her jaw, then nodded. "Lead on."

They turned toward the park where Chase was landing and approached the next intersection, when a shadowy figure appeared at the corner, holding up a hand. Rika recognized Leslie's silhouette, and stopped. Nobody moved for eleven seconds, then Leslie's fingers curled up, and her thumb rose. Then she was gone again.

Leslie appeared once more to halt them, but otherwise, their route to the park was clear—as much as it could be, with local cops closing on the scene in front of Hammurabi's.

After the final row of buildings was behind them, Rika led the group through the park's twisting pathways to the clearing where Chase waited in the assault pinnace. Rika passed him the signal, and the ramp lowered.

A half-minute later, the ship was lifting off into the brisk, night air.

Once they were settled into the two rows of seats, Dala's cold gaze found its way to Rika. "Do you want to tell me what's going on?"

Rika looked down at her right arm and moved her fingers, sad to see them and not her GNR's long barrel. They were so ineffective when it came to doing what she needed to do.

After a few seconds' consideration, Rika looked up and met Dala's gaze.

"I was rather hoping you would tell us. Those wonderful visitors we just met appear to be the same folks who paid us a visit the other night."

"They've expanded their acceptable target list," Kelly added.

"And they have the toys to get the job done." Leslie hefted the sniper rifle she had purloined from the enemy. "This isn't Theban standard issue, but it does resemble the Septhian KM-171—the markings are all removed, but it could have been SAF issue."

Kelly leant over and looked at the weapon. "Well that doesn't make any sense. We know from what you said, Dala, that it's likely to be former Theban military elements who went after Rika. Does that mean we have two enemies? Thebans *and* Septhians?"

"Could just mean there was a good sale on stolen goods," David supplied. "With the military build-up that Septhia is undergoing, they're practically bleeding weapons onto the black market."

Dala nodded. "That's true enough. That's one of the things that Colonel Zim oversees: the tracking down of stolen military hardware. The stuff is everywhere right now."

<*That's convenient,*> Niki commented privately.

<*Niki! Was starting to wonder if you were still in there.*>

<*I was helping digest all that pasta you wolfed down.*>

Rika started. <*What? Really?*>

<*No, Rika. I was monitoring local feeds to see when the cops were going to show up. Then I was scrubbing you and your team from the local surveillance systems. Following that, I removed all traces of you ever being at Charlie's Pasta and Chips. Do I need to go on?*>

Rika laughed softly. <*No, I suppose not. Anyone looking askance at our pinnace right now?*>

<*'Askance'? Look at you, getting all fancy. No, Chase has us registered as a sight-seeing tour. Given our stealth capabilities and this rain, we don't look too different from the executive shuttles that are common here.*>

Rika rose from her seat in the main cabin and walked to the cockpit's entrance. "Clear skies?"

Chase glanced back at her. "Yeah. Taking a circuitous route, though."

"Niki told me that we're a sight-seeing tour. Not much to look at out there." Rika peered through the window at the dark night. The rain had picked up, turning into a torrential downpour so thick it was almost impossible to see the city lights below them.

"Yeah, but a great night to ease our way back to the compound—speaking of which, you have to pick a name for the thing. I can't keep calling it 'the compound' and 'the facility' anymore." Chase glanced back at her and winked. "Makes it feel like a prison or something."

"No one has come up with a good name yet," Rika replied.

"What about Fort Hammerfall?" Chase asked. "Sounds badass, has great connotations."

Rika pursed her lips, considering what it would be like to use her old team name like that. "I think that could work. Maybe people will mess with us less if it means taking on 'Hammerfall'."

"It's a—aw, shit, so much for free and clear."

Rika looked at the scan console and saw a contact

shadowing them, three kilometers back. The contact flickered in and out as lightning flashed around the pinnace, then another one appeared, moving up on their port side to bracket the ship.

"Does ATC have them on its boards?" Rika asked.

Chase shook his head. "Nope. According to the towers, those ships aren't there at all."

Rika checked the pinnace's loadout, hoping that not all its cargo from the *Golden Lark* had been unloaded before Chase left the base.

"Booyah," Rika whispered. "The SkyScream is still in the bay," she informed Chase.

"What? Have you looked at this storm? You going to risk it in a SkyScream?"

Rika grinned and leant over to kiss Chase on the head. "You're sweet, hon. That's exactly *why* I'm going to do it."

"Stay safe," he called back, but didn't add anything more.

<*Always,*> she said privately as she walked back through the main cabin. <*I've been thinking about that thing we talked about, grandkids and all. I do want it someday.*>

<*I love you, Rika.*>

"Where you going?" Kelly called out as Rika rushed through the passenger bay to the cargo hatch.

"We have company," Rika replied.

"Company?" Kelly rose.

"Don't worry, we also have a SkyScream."

"Shiiiiit," Keli swore. "I love flying those! Just the one?"

"Yup, and it's the captain's prerogative," Rika said as she ducked into the pinnace's small cargo bay. It was empty except for the SkyScream, and Rika couldn't help a grin as she approached the ship.

The light attack craft was a special weapon that the GAF had produced in the later years of the war. They were made to fit RR and SMI mechs, and were pure joy to fly. When Rika had found seven of them in Stavros's hangars, she ensured that the Marauders secured them.

She climbed up the back of the craft, past the two large engines, and activated the SkyScream's pilot integration procedure.

A slot opened up for her arms, and she sank both limbs into the ship. The vessel detached her limbs and then opened another set of holes for her legs. Rika set them into the ship, and it detached her lower limbs.

Two armatures reached out and attached to Rika's arms and pulled her forward, settling her into the pilot's pocket.

Connections attached to her legs, and then the vessel was still for an instant.

<*Neural connection ready in five,*> Niki said.

Rika nodded and drew in a deep breath as the ship sealed itself around her head, and folded its layered armor over her body.

One moment she was Rika, with a bipedal body—albeit one whose limbs were stored back between the engines—the next, she was a SkyScream: a light attack craft equipped with missiles, chainguns, four electron beams, and one mean railgun.

It was a heady feeling, and Rika swallowed before calling up to Chase. <*If you would be so kind as to open the lower doors.*>

<*Doors open in ten. They've closed to within two klicks. No comms or overt aggression, yet. Once you're out, I'll ping them to see if I can distract and delay.*>

<*You're the best, Chase. See you back at Fort Hammerfall.*>

<*See? 'Hammerfall' sounds perfect.*>

Rika laughed as the pinnace's bay doors opened below her, and the docking clamps released the SkyScream—her.

In an instant, the relative calm of the bay was replaced by the storm's rage. Rika tilted her wings up and pulsed the SkyScream's engines, pushing herself up and back.

<This thing keeps trying to imprint a new identity into your mind,> Niki commented as Rika fell back toward the pursuer that was closing on the pinnace's starboard. *<It wants you to think of yourself as SSRika.>*

Rika nodded absently—as much as she could. *<I remember that from the few times I got to fly these things in the war. Someone figured we'd be more effective if we thought of ourselves as new beings, like birds of prey.>*

<That seems silly,> Niki replied disdainfully.

<I kinda liked it. I'm not sure if it was the imprinting, though. I feel about the same right now as I did the other times I flew a SkyScream.>

Niki chuckled in her mind. *<Well, that's because I let it do the physical imprint, just not the part where you think of yourself with a new name. The physical imprint is necessary—without it, you'd probably kill yourself trying to fly this thing.>*

<Oh…so I'm not a natural flier?> Rika asked while leveling her wings and adjusting their trim, which felt as natural as rolling her shoulders.

<Well, you're good, but the ship is a part of it.>

Rika dropped behind the starboard pursuer, staying just above its engine wash. The vessel wasn't much larger than the SkyScream, ten meters wide and fifteen long. Stubby wings held an array of armament, and a pair of tailfins rose above the fuselage, twisting side to side in the gale-force winds.

No running lights were visible on the ship, and if her own scan systems were not military-grade, Rika doubted she would have seen the fighter until she was right on top of it.

<Any reply, Chase?>

<None, and the ATC still doesn't show them at all—though it caught a ghost of you for a second.>

<Shit…I should have been invisible.>

Niki spoke in a strange voice. *<Probably rain sleeting off you. The SSRika doesn't show up, but her rain shadow does.>*

<Stop it, now it feels creepy.>

Rika felt Niki nod in her mind. *<Good, it should. That was a test.>*

<And there it is,> Rika said as the enemy aircraft powered up its weapons systems, new EM signatures lighting up along its wings.

<Should we shoot first?> Niki asked.

<I'm leery,> Rika replied. *<If we can wait another minute, we'll be past the city, and I won't have to worry about dropping a fighter on some apartment building full of people.>*

Rika charged her railgun anyway. The weapon stayed tucked within the nose of the SkyScream until fired, so she didn't have to worry about the enemy aircraft picking up on her EM signature.

She took a number of slow breaths, calming herself before the inevitable fight. Then movement at the rear of the vessel caught her attention.

<Shit!> Rika called out, and dove down below the enemy ship as rounds from a point defense chaingun described an arc toward her. Rika fired her railgun at the enemy ship, but it dove as well, and her shot missed.

Rika dropped through the clouds after the aircraft, lining up to fire once more. She was tempted to use her electron beams, but that would point her out to the other vessel, and one foe was enough for now.

Rounds flew from the rear of the aircraft, and Rika spun through the air in an erratic corkscrew as she followed after her target, waiting for the right moment to fire.

She was finally charged and lined up when the aircraft fired all four of its missiles. They streaked forward, and then rose up toward the Marauder pinnace.

<Like hell,> Rika whispered aloud and in her mind as she pulled up and fired her chainguns at the missiles.

Two exploded within seconds, but the others were out of

range.

<Incoming!> Rika cried out to Chase.

<I see 'em, beams and chaff are firing.>

Rika knew the beams would be of little use in the storm, but the chaff should create a highly reflective cloud, mixed with the rain.

One of the missiles detonated in the chaff cloud, but the other swung wide and closed in on the pinnace.

<I got this,> Chase said, and Rika saw four detonations behind the pinnace. She knew those bombs would fling explosive rounds out in every direction.

A moment later, the other missile detonated.

Rika drew her attention back to the ship she was chasing, and saw that it had pulled up, slowing to come behind her.

No chance.

She twisted in the air and fired her thrusters on a collision course with the enemy craft, spinning again and firing her engines right above the enemy ship at the last moment.

The blast melted part of the canopy, and Rika extended the SkyScream's 'feet'. They latched onto the aircraft and tore the rest of the canopy off before ripping the forward half of the craft off.

The pilot ejected, and Rika gave a cry of exultation as she fired her engines again and pushed off from the falling wreckage, streaking through the air toward the second ship.

As Rika approached, she saw the pursuit craft fire two missiles at the pinnace. She tried to fire her electron beams at the missiles, but nothing happened.

<You took damage from the rear chaingun,> Niki advised. *<It missed the engine, but one of your e-beams is offline. The control systems were damaged, too. Trying to fix them to get the beams back up.>*

<Calculated risk,> Rika lied.

She'd forgotten about the chaingun, she just wanted to tear

that ship apart. For a moment, she wondered if it was a part of the predatory flight imprint that the SkySkream used. Then something ricocheted off her left wing, and she dove to the side as bullets followed her through the air. She jinked up, then down, and saw an electron beam flash through the night a meter from her right wing.

Rika gritted her teeth. *Not tonight, assholes.*

Her railgun was fully charged, and Rika boosted up, then slewed to the left, tracing a straight line behind the enemy craft. Right as she passed behind its engines, Rika fired.

The rail-accelerated pellets closed the distance between her and the aircraft in a fraction of a second, tearing clear through the enemy ship. One of the stubby wings exploded, and a moment later, nothing was left but a falling ball of flame.

Rika pulled up, twisting through the air and scanning the surrounding airspace for any more interlopers.

<Nice shooting, Rika. Scan's clear. Oh, and somehow ATC missed all that. Not a blip on the public feeds.>

<Damn, I guess whoever is taking pot shots at us still has enough of a chokehold on local systems to do whatever they want.>

<Seems like it,> Chase's voice was laced with worry. *<You OK back there? Uplink shows that you took a few hits.>*

<Nothing serious. SkyScream Rika has a few dents. Rika Rika is just fine.>

Chase laughed over the Link. *<Well, SkyScream Rika does have to keep Rika Rika from crashing to the ground, so I'm glad they're both OK.>*

<Me too. I'd forgotten how exhilarating it is to pilot these things.>

<So I take it you'll escort us back rather than dock?>

<Damn skippy.>

* * * * *

Rika set the SkyScream down beside the pinnace on the hard pack in front of Fort Hammerfall's command building. While the ramp lowered from the pinnace, she triggered her craft's disengagement protocols.

Her sense of self shrank back down to her human form as the SkyScream lifted her out of the pilot's pocket and set her back into her legs. Then she reached forward and sank her arms into the sockets, feeling the ship drive the rods through her arms and legs.

"Shit, Rika!" Kelly called out as the rest of the team walked out of the pinnace. "Next time, I'm calling dibs on that thing! I watched your feeds, it was ridiculous!"

Rika jumped down off the SkyScream, and sent a command for the craft to fly to a nearby hangar. "We'll have to see about that…we don't have many of those birds."

Kelly's face fell, and Rika laughed. "Relax, I was kidding. You'll get a chance. We don't have many of them, but there aren't many SMI and RR mechs, so everyone who wants to will get a turn."

Rika climbed the steps to the command building, and Major Dala caught up with her. "I need to contact…well, someone. I have to report on what happened here tonight."

"Who can you safely call?" The doors opened, and Rika stepped through, walking over to one of the drying stations. Warm air whipped across her body, blasting away moisture and leaving her perfectly dry—though in dire need of a hairbrush—in seconds.

Dala availed herself of a dryer as well, and the device lowered its output for a standard human. Rika wondered if it would have blown the uptight major's dress off if it had remained on full power. That would have been worth a laugh.

<That was an uncharitable thought,> Niki commented.

<How would you know? You can't read my thoughts, and I didn't have any physical tells.>

<No, just the daggers you shot at her with your eyes.>

Rika snorted. *<Daggers are not something you can shoot with your eyes. You should know that.>*

<I beg to differ.>

<Now, ***lasers****…>*

Dala stepped out of the drying pod and approached Rika. "I can't imagine this goes too high, but to hit you with fighters like that, it must. But I would have seen a sign, wouldn't I?"

Rika felt a stab of guilt for her prior attitude toward Dala. The woman *was* trying to do her job, but people she trusted were clearly working against her—and now trying to kill her.

"Core be damned, I have no idea." Rika softened her tone before she continued, tamping down the adrenaline still rushing through her from flying the SkyScream. "I've been on the horn to my liaison with the SAF, and he's stonewalled me at every turn. And I sure as hell don't trust your CO right now—no offense. If Zim himself isn't rotten, his HQ is full of leaks. Who else do you have?"

Dala adjusted the hem of her dress and glanced at David. "I was telling David—right before he rushed me out the back—that we might have to go up the chain to General Adam."

Rika cocked an eyebrow. "The five-star who runs Hercules Command?"

"Yeah. Scuttlebutt is that he's not happy that we've joined Septhia, but he has given a few speeches on how unity is our best defense against Nietzschea. I don't know for sure what he thinks of you, but nothing I've seen has made me think that he actively dislikes the Marauders."

<Not actively disliking is a long way from viewing us favorably,> Niki commented privately.

Rika agreed. It wasn't a ringing endorsement.

"General Mill referred to General Adam as a fair man," David interjected as he stepped out of a dryer. "And nothing I can find in his public information gives me concern."

Rika sighed and stretched her arms over her head, half-wishing she could hop in the SkyScream and fly away from all this political nonsense.

She felt an itch in her right hand and tried to ignore the dysphoria she always felt when her GNR wasn't present. "Even so, I have a suspicion that attempting contact with the general will be tricky—and may get intercepted before we can get in direct communication."

Dala tapped a finger against her lips as she watched the others step out of the dryers. "I *may* have a way to reach him. But we'll have to move fast. If I don't show up for duty tomorrow, people are going to start asking questions—and I was last seen with one of your people." She nodded to David at the end of her statement.

<Well, if they get eyewitness accounts, that's what they'll find,> Niki replied. *<But the city and restaurant feeds all show you dining alone.>*

"You hacked *all* those systems?" Major Dala asked.

<You don't sound happy about it,> Niki replied. *<You want those men to know where you are?>*

"I'm pretty sure they know where Dala is," David said with a slow shake of his head. "If they showed up to stop you from telling *me* something, then it's no great logical leap to assume they'll know where I went afterward."

"Here," Rika said.

"So how do we reach out to General Adam?" David asked.

Major Dala gave him a worried look. "Well, my sister plays rollerball with his daughter sometimes—on opposing teams."

Chase whistled. "That's a tenuous thread."

"We'd better start working it, then." David drummed his fingertips together. "I assume, Dala, that you have proof of the things you were telling me? You'd have to, otherwise they wouldn't be going to such lengths to stop you."

"I have a few purchase orders and a money trail. They're

for equipment that matches what was used against you and your dropship. I've put in a request at the garrison's depot to do eyes-on verification that the inventory is where it's supposed to be, but it hasn't come back yet."

Rika grunted. "What are the chances that our friends back at the restaurant had no idea who David is? Maybe they're just trying to take you out because you got too nosy."

"You three were cloaked, Rika," Chase added. "Maybe they won't have realized that it was Marauders who spanked them."

"A lot of supposition here," David muttered. "I need to spend some time with all the pieces."

"And we need to get a message to your sister," Rika said to Dala. "Very carefully."

"Which is tricky," Dala said, her fuchsia eyebrows lowering. "She's off-world right now."

<Well, Dala.> Niki sent a devious smile into their minds. *<Then we're lucky that we have my handy ability to engage in felonious Link activity. Send me your sister's public tokens. You guys figure out what to say to the general's daughter, while I become…Madaline. Huh. Dala and Ma*__*dal*__*ine? Your parents weren't too original, were they?>*

Rika saw Dala's jaw tighten, and shot Niki an admonishing scowl. *<Be nice, Niki.>*

<You weren't. I'm just taking cues from my CO.>

<Yeah, well, I'm not always the best example. Do as I say, not as I do.>

<You're the boss, boss.>

VISIT FROM THE GENERAL

STELLAR DATE: 08.12.8949 (Adjusted Gregorian)
LOCATION: Fort Hammerfall
REGION: Iapetus, Hercules System, Septhian Alliance

"Well, his eminence, General Adam, will be here in an hour," Rika said to Chase as she sat across from him in the commissary. She looked down at her food. "Man, I really want to send someone to get takeout from Charlie's. That pasta was amazing. I bet it was made from real angel's hair."

"That was fast," Chase said, then quickly covered his mouth as he chewed on a salad. "Sorry, I don't know why I've started doing this lately. I never used to be this slovenly."

"Stress eating," Rika replied. "We've got a lot on our shoulders. Are we even adults? I don't feel like an adult most of the time. Pretty sure I'm not old enough to run a company of lemonade salespeople, let alone of mechs."

Barne set his tray next to them and let out a single laugh. "No, no you're not. Luckily you have me to help. And by 'help', I mean do all the work while you just flit about, getting in dogfights, wrecking our SkyScreams."

Rika grinned at Barne. "Jealous?"

"Fuck, yeah! I'd halfway consider being mech'd just to fly one of those things."

Chase gestured at Barne's prosthetic arm. "Well, you're on your way. I'll use you for a shield at some point, and we'll see if we can get a few more limbs shot off."

"If I was standing in front of you in a firefight, it would be to keep you safe while you were pissing your pants," Barne shot back.

"I don't think that armor counts as pants."

"Dribbling out of your waste reclamation system?"

"Dude!" Chase glowered at Barne. "Eating, here!"

No one spoke for a minute, then Rika said, "That's one hell of an ethical question, though."

"What is?" Barne asked. "Whether I should protect Chase while he wets himself on the battlefield?"

"No. Whether or not we make more mechs."

Chase's eyebrows lifted, and he nodded slowly. "That's a tricky one. With the stuff we got from the Politica, we have everything we need to make mechs...but anyone who *wants* to become one may not have their head on straight."

Rika laughed. "I think I might be a little bit offended by that."

"You know what I mean," Chase said quickly. "Most people don't *want* to have their limbs chopped off. Anyone who does probably has body dysphoria issues, which means there's more trouble beneath the surface."

"But you could make it an option for soldiers who get injured in the battlefield," Barne added. "I hated mechs, back when I lost my arm. But now? If I lost my legs or something, I'd consider it. Not like I'm ever leaving the Marauders."

Rika caught Chase's eyes at that, but neither spoke.

"Well," Rika said at last. "I'll flail my way across that bridge when we get to it. Chances are it'll be the Old Man's call, anyway."

Barne shrugged. "Maybe."

Rika wondered what Barne meant by that, but didn't press the issue, as Leslie came to sit with them, followed by David and Dala.

<*Just the whole group. Yay.*> Rika said privately to Niki.

<*You really don't like Dala, do you?*> Niki replied.

<*I...yeah, I guess not. Her 'mercs are bad' routine got us off on the wrong foot.*>

<*You said it before; she's just trying to do her job. She's in a tough spot.*>

Rika eyed the pink-haired major. For someone so colorful, she certainly was a wet blanket. <*I suppose.*>

<*And she's doing her best to help us,*> Niki added. <*She put her life on the line to meet with David.*>

<*Well, she didn't initially think that it could get her killed.*>

<*Sure, but she could have been dishonorably discharged, if it was seen in the wrong light—which it still might be. She never complained about it, either. She's a good woman. A grumpy woman, but a good woman.*>

Rika considered that. Niki was right, Dala was putting a good face on the fact that someone in her government was trying to kill both her, and the very people she was taking refuge with. Or, at the very least, trying to kill Rika.

"David informed me that General Adam reached out," Dala said after taking a drink of her orange juice. "I was really starting to worry that his daughter hadn't passed the message along—or that the General had missed the encoded portion."

"I was starting to wonder, too," Rika replied. "But he'll be here in an hour, so that puts those particular worries to rest. For reasons he did not elaborate upon, he's hitching a ride with a produce shipment we have coming in today."

"Seriously?" Leslie asked. "Stuff must be totally sideways here if he's doing that. Think even General Adam is at risk?"

Heads nodded around the table, and Rika shrugged. "Either that, or he just doesn't want whoever is taking pot shots at us to know he's onto them. It might escalate this whole thing to another level."

"Could be a combination," David added. "Or there are other, entirely different rationales."

"Care to enlighten us?" Barne asked.

"No," David shook his head. "Trust me, if you had to listen to me rattle off all the things that *could* be going on, your head would explode. Mine nearly does, half the time."

"Good thing it's reinforced, then." Barne laughed, but

everyone else just stared at him and shook their heads.

"What?" Barne asked. "Really? Sorry, David, but we were all thinking it."

David shrugged and grinned. "So was I."

* * * * *

An hour later, Rika waited with Dala and David in a small room off the receiving warehouse near the east gate. Rather than have the general travel across the compound—where he'd be visible to satellite surveillance—Rika decided it would be safest to meet with him where the trucks came in.

She monitored the security feeds, watching as the two trucks passed through the compound's security gate, and drove down the perimeter road to the non-secured goods warehouse.

Across the table, she saw that Dala was clenching and unclenching her hands.

"Nervous, Major?"

Dala snorted. "He could be coming here to charge me with half a dozen crimes. You too, for that matter. Of course I'm nervous."

"Do generals often sneak into mercenary training facilities to deliver charges to captains and majors around here?" Rika asked.

Dala sighed and pressed the heels of her hands into her face. "No, don't be ridiculous. But that doesn't mean it's not an added bonus."

"The fact that he's coming here like this means he's looking for allies. If he were pissed at us and demanding your head, there'd be a battalion outside our gates. Not two trucks, half-filled with lettuce and tomatoes."

The major didn't respond, only drew in a deep breath and let it out slowly.

Rika decided to let the matter drop, and returned to watching the feeds as the trucks backed up to the warehouse.

Within the loading bay, fireteam one/one waited to escort the general to the meeting. The rest of squad one was also placed in and around the warehouse, ready to defend against any attacks from without or within.

The other three squads of First Platoon were nearby, performing drills and working on maneuvers around Fort Hammerfall—all armed with live ammunition, ready for what may come.

The back of the first truck opened up, and the loading bots rolled forward, grabbing stacks of produce and moving them aside. Once a space opened up, a man and two women exited the truck.

Sergeant Aaron greeted them, and then led the trio across the warehouse toward the room where Rika and the others waited.

Rika switched through several surveillance angles, examining the visitors.

The general was a tall man, older, but not showing any significant signs of aging. His hair was dark, almost jet black, and he walked with an easy gait.

The woman on his right bore a colonel's insignia on her collar, and Rika identified her from the public records as Colonel Judi. The other woman trailed behind them, the badge of a command sergeant major on her shoulders. She wore her beret low, and it took Rika a second longer to identify her. Sergeant Major Rene.

A moment later, Sergeant Aaron opened the door and nodded to Rika. "Captain Rika. General Adam and his retinue are here."

"Thank you, Sergeant. Show them in."

Rika, David, and Dala all rose, Dala saluting sharply as the general entered.

His presence filled the room, and he surveyed those in attendance before returning Dala's salute. "At ease, Major." Then he turned to Rika. "Captain Rika, I presume."

He held out his right hand to shake, but Rika raised her left. She'd considered swapping out her gun-arm for a regular one—she knew how much it angered some people to shake with their left—but if the shit hit the fan, she wanted to be ready.

General Adam didn't miss a beat as he extended his left hand and shook Rika's.

"It is very nice to meet you," Rika said. "Though I'm a bit surprised you came out to see us."

"Well, you may not be, soon enough. Allow me to introduce Colonel Judi and Sergeant Major Rene."

Rika shook their hands and introduced Chief Warrant Officer David. Once the greetings were over, they all sat at the table. Rika didn't take the head, and was glad to see that General Adam did not either. He sat across from her, his pale blue eyes boring into hers.

"It's been an eventful few days since you first came down here, Captain Rika. You seem to have attracted no small amount of trouble."

Rika nodded. "It's a talent. Though it seemed like the trouble was lying in wait for me."

"Perhaps," General Adam replied, his tone even, revealing nothing. "And Major Dala. I must admit that it is quite interesting to find you here. Your message was light on details, but high on urgency."

"Yes, General Adam," Dala replied with a small waver in her voice. "I wasn't certain how much information I should transmit, but you were one of the few people I felt confident that I could reach out of band, so to speak."

"But the fact that you have come here means something *is* going on at Iapetus," Rika added. "Something you already know about."

General Adam nodded slowly. "I have suspicions. Suspicions that have solidified over the last few days. Dala's reports regarding the data blackout that engulfed the city of Hittis the night your ship was attacked were quite interesting. Especially the omissions."

"Omissions, sir?" Dala asked.

"Your report felt incomplete," Colonel Judi spoke up. "You seemed to be working toward certain conclusions, and then never made them. It read like a redacted report, but without the redactions noted."

Dala frowned. "Someone altered my reports?"

"I believe so," Judi replied. "I assume you have the originals? Could you transmit them to me—provided we're secure?"

"The room's network is segregated," Rika confirmed. "No one will know if you make a connection here."

General Adam nodded, and Dala closed her eyes for a moment. "There you are, Colonel."

Colonel Judi pursed her lips and sighed. "Yes, these are demonstrably different. Stars, even the damage assessments are—wait, there were survivors?"

Dala nodded, and Rika spoke up. "At least ten; maybe more, if the wounded all came through."

General Adam rose and walked to the sideboard where water and coffee waited. "Then it's as we feared. Subversive elements are operating with impunity on Iapetus."

" 'Subversive elements'?" Rika asked. "That's nebulous, to say the least. Who do you think it is?"

"Who do *you* think?" General Adam asked.

"Hmm…" David began tapping his chin in earnest. "After the first attack, we considered that it was someone who was personally upset at Rika for the part she played in the events on Pyra. After they tried to kill Dala, we widened our scope.

It's certainly someone with means—"

"Kill Dala?" Colonel Judi interrupted. "What are you talking about?"

"None of that reached you?" Rika asked and received negative head shakes in response. "Last night, we saved Dala from an assassination attempt. There was a significant attack in downtown Hittis. Afterward, I took out two fighter craft over the northern edge of the city."

General Adam blew out a long breath. "Stars, I wish I could just purge the whole lot of them. There must be more rot than I expected, to cover up something like this."

"Sir? What is going on?" Dala asked.

General Adam didn't respond at first. Instead, he prepared his cup of coffee and stirred it for a moment before turning to the group. "It's the Nietzscheans, of course. They're here in Iapetus."

"The Niets, sir?" Rika asked. "How?"

The general sat at the table and stared at Rika. "Hard to believe you started all this."

Rika wondered where he was going with this new tack. "Me?"

"When you attacked our president—yes, yes, I know you didn't *really* start it. But you breached her bunker and had her in your sights."

"But I didn't do it," Rika replied. "I got the order to stand down."

General Adam shook his head and smiled. "The order to stand down came almost twenty minutes after you breached. You had plenty of time to kill the president. Plus, I saw the feeds. You couldn't bring yourself to do it."

Rika shook her head. "For whatever good it did. The Niets still killed her."

"It did *a lot* of good," General Adam replied. "Marauders would have had the worst time of their lives in Theban space, if one of theirs had killed our president. Septhian merger or no."

"What does this have to do with there being Niets in Iapetus?" Rika asked.

"Nothing…and everything. There's a reason why Septhian High Command decided to place your training facility here—a *Marauder* facility, engaged in training the Niets' most hated and feared enemy. They wanted to make this system a lightning rod for whatever was to happen next."

"No," David interjected. "It's too fast, sir. We only selected this location three months ago. That's too fast for the Niets to infiltrate so many branches of your military. It's not their strong suit."

"You're right about that, Chief." The general nodded, then took a sip of his coffee. "Which means they were already operating here, and you pulled them out into the open—too tempting a target. Which is what we hoped for; we just didn't expect them to have their hooks in so deep."

"How do they have their hooks in at *all*, sir?" Major Dala asked. "They're the *Nietzscheans*! How is it that anyone is willing to work with them?"

"There's a group of people who think the Niets will win. They figure being a part of Nietzschea is no worse than being absorbed by Septhia. I imagine there's money involved, as well. Lots of money."

"So you need to clean house," Rika replied. "How can we help?"

General Adam chuckled. "Well, for starters, keep doing what you're doing. We wanted a lightning rod, we got one. We need to get these bastards to overextend themselves. Then, when they do, we crush them with extreme prejudice. There's no mercy for traitors."

"Then we need to lure them into attacking this base," Rika replied. "It would take a nuke to dislodge us, maybe not even then. They'll have to hit us hard, and then we catch them with their pants down."

General Adam nodded slowly. "How do you plan to do that?"

Rika looked at David. "How tempting a target will we have to be?"

* * * * *

<*You want us to do **what**?*> Major Tim asked, the exasperation in his mental tone almost a corporeal presence in the room with Rika.

<*It's the best way to make us look exposed and vulnerable,*> Rika replied, surprised at how upset the major was over this idea.

<*Yeah, because you **will** be exposed and vulnerable.*>

<*Well, bait has to be believable. But the General will have ships covering us from orbit. We'll be fine.*>

Major Tim grunted, and Rika could imagine him pacing in his tiny office. <*And you trust this man with your life—with the lives of your mechs?*>

Rika had wondered about that, as well. For all she knew, General Adam was playing her. Getting her to weaken her position so that he could destroy Fort Hammerfall with impunity.

<*What do you suggest, Major?*> Rika asked. <*I'm open to other ideas.*>

<*Here's one. We pack up and leave. Cleaning up this system's internal politics is not our problem.*>

Rika hadn't expected an answer like that from Major Tim. <*What about our mission here?*>

<*What 'mission'? We're here to train. This was a nice spot, but we can do it anywhere.*>

<*And the Nietzscheans?*> Rika asked. <*You know the Old Man's goal as well as I—better, probably. What would he think if we*

ran from the chance to stop the Nietzschean advance? Worse, what if we leave, and the Niets invade?>

Seriously, Major, Rika scolded herself mentally as she rose from her desk and paced across the room. *How is this man so cowardly?*

<*Rika, the general didn't go to all the trouble of setting up your company, just so that we can piss it away in some heroic gesture against the Niets—who may not even be in this system.*>

<*He has a point,*> Niki commented. <*There are a lot of unknowns in this equation.*>

Rika clenched her teeth and drew in a deep breath before responding to Major Tim. <*Other than running away, do you have any suggestions?*>

<*You're determined to stay down there, aren't you?*>

<*I am, and I need an option that we can both work with.*>

Major Tim didn't respond, his silence deafening.

Rika clenched her jaw, willing her heart rate to slow. <*Niki, do you have any ideas?*>

<*I have one, but it's going to take a leap of faith from you, Major Tim. And we'll need General Adam's help to pull it off.*>

SETTING THE TRAP

STELLAR DATE: 08.13.8949 (Adjusted Gregorian)
LOCATION: Fort Hammerfall
REGION: Iapetus, Hercules System, Septhian Alliance

Rika climbed into the ground transport, a vehicle the locals called a Swampfox. It wasn't the prettiest…van-thing she'd ever seen, but Barne had picked up a gross of them for a steal. Corporal Stripes—the lone mech in the repair and maintenance platoon—had pronounced them sound enough for the mission they had in mind.

Rika smiled to herself at the memory. 'Sound' wasn't the word Stripes had used. He had said something more like, "Not gunna fuck themselves to pieces, but they might fuck you with all the rattlin'."

"Surprised Stripes isn't coming along, Captain," Sergeant Karen said as she pulled herself into the driver's seat, seeming to read Rika's thoughts. "He exhibited a special fondness for these things."

Karen settled into place and grasped the controls—not that anyone needed to *drive* the Swampfox. It may have looked older than the invention of spaceflight, but it was Link capable, with a rudimentary comp that was guaranteed not to run over animals or humans.

Rika wondered at the order of the items in that guarantee, but considered that it may have been imported, and the translation might be off.

"If by 'fondness', you mean a strong desire to send them all to the scrap heap, you might be right," Rika replied to the sergeant.

Karen chuckled and pulled her cloak around her armor, ensuring her profile looked natural before leaning around to check on Kelly and Keli.

"Four SMI-2s on a mission together. Think that ever happened in the war?" Keli asked as she settled into her seat.

"Sure," Kelly replied. "Team Hammerfall had four SMI-2s at one point—back before Rika joined up."

"Had four later on, too," Rika added. "Took two mechs to replace the amount of lip you gave all the time, Kelly."

"I didn't have lips back then," Kelly retorted.

"And yet you still got twice the discipline as Silva and I."

Kelly grinned. "Not one to roll over."

"So, what's on the agenda for our little outing?" Karen asked. "Anything you're looking to pick up? Some beer? Fried chicken? Kitty litter for the LT?"

Rika cast Karen a hard look. Knocking the LT was a time-honored tradition, but one usually had the sense not to do it in front of the LT's commanding officer.

Karen blushed. "Shit, sorry, Captain. I'm still getting used to being able to speak again…I keep saying things with my *out-loud* voice that are supposed to stay in the noggin."

"It's OK, Sergeant, I won't tell Lieutenant Leslie. So long as you actually set up a litter box at some point."

"Really?" Karen asked, turning to look at Rika with wide eyes.

"Well, if she figures out who did it, you might die horribly, so it's up to you."

"Damned if you do, and damned if you don't," Karen said as she punched in the destination on the manual console.

Kelly and Keli were doubled over with laughter in the backseat, and Rika smiled as well. It felt good to be able to relax, even if this wasn't going to be a nice, weekend drive.

"Corporal, Private," Karen called back. "Shut your core-damned mouths back there."

"Yes, ma'am!" Keli called out, while Kelly added, "*Now* the sergeant knows when to use rank in address."

"Stars, some days I liked it better when none of us had mouths," Karen said with a sigh. "Things were a lot less catty back then."

"Oh! Good one!" Keli crowed. "I'll have to tell Lieutenant Leslie you said that."

"Seriously, you two," Rika said, suppressing a laugh. "We're not on a grade school field trip. Don't make me come back there."

The Swampfox reached the compound's gate, and the guards looked over the vehicle and its occupants for a minute before waving them through.

"Sucks being the boss," Rika said and sighed. "No one ever gives you the quick once-over. They want you to make sure to notice how good they are at their jobs."

"Hard being an officer, we know," Kelly said with mock compassion.

"You're doing the best you can," Keli chimed in, her tone soulful and appreciative.

"OK, seriously," Rika growled. "When I said we need to act casually, I didn't mean for you to mock your superiors for the whole trip."

"Huh," Keli said then turned to Kelly. "This is most of what we do in our free time. How *else* do we act casually?"

"Beats me," Kelly shrugged. "You follow sports?"

"I don't even know if they *have* sports here."

"Read any good books, watch any good sims or vids?"

Keli shook her head. "Nope. Our hard-assed CO doesn't give us a moment's rest. I am completely without hobbies."

"Well, then." Kelly laughed. "Looks like mockery is the only pastime we have."

"I can think of a few extra pastimes for you two," Rika grunted.

The pair continued their banter as the Swampfox drove for a few kilometers through the commercial district surrounding the old-airport-turned-Marauder-base.

Eventually it passed into a tunnel that ran under a series of maglev tracks. Once they were hidden from any external view, Karen slammed on the brakes, and the four women bailed out of the vehicle. Four other women—some of General Adam's trusted SAF troops—wearing armor under cloaks to approximate the look of SMIs, rushed into the vehicle to take their places.

Rika led the others behind a column and into a maintenance tunnel that ran below the tracks. It was a tight fit, and half the reason Rika had selected SMI-2s for the mission.

They navigated through the tunnel, slipping around conduits and access ladders until they came to a cross passage where Rika took a right. From there, a short twenty-meter walk brought them to a steel door.

It was unlocked, and Rika checked her cloak over, shaking any dust off before raising her cowl and activating the camouflage.

"Ready, ladies?" she asked.

The banter had faded in the tunnel, and the others maintained the silence, each giving a single nod.

Rika sent out a single ping, waiting for the all-clear response before pushing the door open and stepping out into Iapetus's warm, afternoon light.

Forty-seven meters ahead lay their destination—a low warehouse, rented by the Marauders for secondary, low-security equipment storage. A pair of mechs were stationed at the warehouse, guarding its contents.

Rika crossed the distance at an easy pace, careful not to kick up excess dust. A minute later, she stepped inside the warehouse and smiled as she gazed at the other reason why she'd selected SMI-2s for the mission.

Within, lay six SkyScreams.

"Oh, baby," Kelly rubbed her hand against her GNR's

barrel, then stopped. "OK…that gesture doesn't work without two hands."

Keli snickered. "Especially not when saying 'oh, baby'."

An RR-2 walked into the room through a door on their right and snapped to attention, quietly saying, "Ma'am."

Rika nodded to Yiaagaitia. "How's everything look, Corporal Yig?"

"We're secure, Captain. Though CJ thinks she spotted a surveillance vehicle in the area, and there are definitely drones making the rounds, though they're staying back a ways from Fort Hammerfall. Keeping out of range of ours—or so they think."

"How sure are you that no one spotted us coming in here?" Karen asked.

"Pretty sure, Sarge. CJ has their pattern mapped out. She has that upgraded sensor suite some RRs got; can track a mayfly at a thousand meters."

"Good," Rika said and turned to eye the SkyScreams. "We stay mobile while we wait. It's still an hour before Chase and Leslie take squads two and four out on the training exercise."

Everyone nodded in response, and Rika resisted the urge to make a quick Link connection to check up on the platoon's status.

Of course, that would blow everything.

Right now, her Link presence was still registering as being inside the Swampfox, which was trundling alone on a long drive through Hittis.

The other mechs inspected their SkyScreams, and Rika contented herself with watching the surrounding area through the drones that CJ had sent out.

As the drone flies, they were only three kilometers from Fort Hammerfall. Between them lay a swath of warehouses, miscellaneous commercial buildings, then finally, a half-kilometer of open space before the fence that surrounded the former airport.

After what felt like forever, Rika saw a convoy of Swampfoxes pull out of one of the hangars, followed by a flatbed truck. AM, RR, and FR mechs piled into the Swampfoxes, while a K1R-T climbed up onto the flatbed.

The K1R, a corporal named Oosterwyk-Bruyn, was more than capable of keeping up with the Swampfoxes on foot, but the locals had complained about the damage AMs did to their roads. A K1R would pound them to gravel, so a flatbed truck was his chariot.

The flatbed pulled out first, and Rika felt a smile pull at her lips. Everyone thought that Oosterwyk-Bruyn bore the nickname 'The Van' because he was massive—which he was. Or that his real name was hard to say—which was also true.

In reality, he had earned the name 'The Van' because he always insisted on being in the vanguard of a fight. His joke was that a formation didn't need a vanguard. It just needed him.

Through the drones' eyes, Rika saw The Van raise a massive fist in the air; she imagined him crying out "Roo-ah!" as the convoy pulled out of Fort Hammerfall.

"The trap is set," Rika said with a predatory grin. "Now it's just part of squad one and three left at the compound."

Kelly snorted. "Anyone who thinks that twenty-odd mechs is 'just' anything is going to be in for one hell of a surprise."

"Not to mention that our surprises have surprises," Karen said, nodding to the SkyScreams.

DEFENSE OF HAMMERFALL

STELLAR DATE: 08.13.8949 (Adjusted Gregorian)
LOCATION: Fort Hammerfall
REGION: Iapetus, Hercules System, Septhian Alliance

<*I've got movement on the southern edge of our grid,*> CJ reported over the combat net. <*A few cargo haulers moving in.*>

Rika pulled up the feed and saw seven haulers entering the area from different directions. They weren't the only vehicles in the area, but they bore the markings of companies that Dala and David had identified as being tied to other suspicious activity over the past week.

None were headed straight for the former airport, but as they closed the distance, their ultimate destination became clear.

<*I see more activity on the east and the north as well,*> CJ reported after another moment.

Five minutes later, the only area where there were no suspicious vehicles in the area was to the west, where the mech convoy had disappeared into the hills for their training exercises.

<*Based on what I see, they'll set up here, here, and here,*> Rika said over the combat net, highlighting points on the shared map. <*Not sure if they'll mass at those points, or drop troops from those trucks along the way.*>

<*I still don't get how they think that we won't spot this.*> Kelly shook her head and drew a line on the map. <*Once they cross this far, there are no other cargo haulers anywhere nearby—hardly any traffic at all, for that matter. Their movements will be totally obvious.*>

<*The cat will be out of the bag at some point, no matter how they do this,*> Rika replied. <*Remember, it's only via our intel from Dala*

that we even know to look for trucks from these holding companies. If we didn't, they'd blend in with the other ground traffic until the last minute. That's not a lot of warning.>

<*Don't forget, too, whoever is running this op is deeply stupid,*> CJ added. <*I mean, they're attacking mechs. Not just any mechs, either. Rika's Marauders.*>

Rika appreciated the team's confidence, but those trucks could hold hundreds of enemies—maybe even a thousand. She had to assume they were all in heavy powered armor—the only thing that could go toe-to-toe with a mech.

She was certain that whatever the number, the enemies in those trucks were not all they'd face today. Whoever was attacking them on Iapetus was too smart to show their entire hand at the outset of the battle.

This was just the first wave.

Rika had to admit that, for all her bluster, she felt naked knowing that the *Golden Lark* and the *Perseid's Dream* weren't overhead.

She'd become accustomed to knowing that, in the Marauders—unlike the GAF—when starfire was needed, it would fall. Hopefully General Adam would be just as willing to fire on the planet he was sworn to keep safe.

"Let's get suited up," Rika said aloud, signaling CJ to fall back into the warehouse.

The mechs climbed onto the backs of the SkyScreams, each undergoing the same process Rika had the day prior.

"Shit, forgot how weird this feels at first!" Kelly exclaimed as the ship pulled her body into the pilot's pocket, and folded its armor over her.

<*Feels goooood,*> Keli said over the link. <*I'm a fucking warbird, gonna rain beamfire down on my enemies.*>

<*Keep sharp,*> Rika said. <*I mean it. Niki hasn't had time to go through these things with a fine-tooth comb…they're programmed to make us hyper-aggressive in aerial combat, but we have to stay*

frosty. Tonight at the commissary, we're all gonna talk about how awesome this was. No one's eating dirt. Got it?>

A round of 'yes ma'ams' and 'aye, Captains' came back.

Rika drew in a deep breath as her SkyScream activated its systems and imprinted her new physical form into her mind.

She was terror, she was might, but she also had to coordinate a defense against a superior enemy while in the midst of combat….

<*One of the trucks has slowed,*> Niki announced. <*It just dropped off a fireteam, one klick from Hammerfall's south gate. Make that two fireteams.*>

Rika pulled the feed and saw that it was as she suspected. The enemy was in unmarked, powered armor. It didn't offer them the versatility of a mech—living in your powered armor made you a lot more comfortable with it than just wearing it periodically—but they wouldn't be easy to take down.

She hoped the mechs' comfort in their own skins would be enough of an edge. Now that she could see the enemy's loadout, Rika estimated that they could pack forty soldiers in each of the haulers. That put the attackers' number at over a thousand.

Against half a platoon at Hammerfall.

Or so they think.

Rika saw that Barne had pre-configured the combat net with designations for the different units. The enemies were labeled as 'Cockroaches', his nod to how they kept turning up everywhere. However, at this scale, the name beside each of the enemy was abbreviated to only show 'Cock'.

<*Oh, that's classic,*> Kelly snickered.

<*Cocks it is,*> Karen added, and Rika couldn't help but laugh.

She reviewed the enemy deployments and guessed at where the rest of them would disembark. <*Looks like the Cocks are massing at the gates, but they're also going for the corners.*>

<*With that many troops, they probably think they can just march right in,*> Keli added.

<*Well, they do think there are only about thirty-five mechs at Hammerfall,*> Rika replied.

Kelly snorted. <*Thirty-five of Rika's Marauders are worth a thousand Cocks.*>

<*Thousand's not even close.*> Rika put on a brave face for her team. <*Let's try to keep them outside the fence. I don't want our new base getting trashed.*>

<*That's for sure,*> Karen said. <*I just finished decorating my quarters.*>

The SkyScream mechs fell silent as they waited for the Cocks to finish deploying. Though it felt like forever, the enemy was more efficient than Rika had hoped, disgorging their forces from the cargo haulers in just under three minutes.

<*OK, Ladies and Gentleman,*> Rika said. <*You ready to kick some Cock?*>

<*Roo-AH!*>

<*Ouch!*>

* * * * *

Leslie stood in Fort Hammerfall's small CIC, watching the feeds of the enemy's deployment—'Cocks', thanks to Barne's sense of humor. She'd changed the shortened description to 'Roaches', but it had been too late; the mechs had all started using 'Cock' in their communications.

The four fireteams, one at each of the four gates, took cover behind the plascrete barriers, and weapons protruded from the bunkers at each of the base's four corners. Not that there were any mechs within those bullet-magnets, only sacrificial combat drones.

If there was one thing that decades of combat had taught Leslie, it was that mechs did their best when highly mobile.

The brass had often treated them like mechanized infantry, but in reality, even the smallest mech was more like a main battle tank.

A battle tank that could leap a dozen meters into the air, land on your actual tank, and tear the guns off.

Leslie drew in a slow breath, let it out, and then repeated the process twice more before calling out to the mechs under her command. <*Squads one and three, all fireteams ready. We wait for them to fire first. Your quadrants and targets are marked. Potter is assigning priorities, keep your eyes on those, and make sure we give our angels any cover they need. They're gonna be doing the same for us.*>

Acknowledgement lights flashed across the holotank, and Leslie smiled, wishing she was out there with them.

Her placement in the CIC was due in part to their need for the SkyScreams to be piloted by experienced mechs. They only had six of those at present, and Rika was amongst their number.

That put Leslie in the CIC.

Granted, a large, open field was not her ideal area of operation. Leslie knew her style was better suited to dense, urban combat—a battlefield where she could skulk and hide.

When this fight was joined, it would be no place for a squishie, the name her 'toon affectionately called her behind her back.

On the holotank, Leslie watched the Roaches close in around Hammerfall. Their smallest grouping was to the north, where there were only a few outbuildings stretched along the fence line. Beyond lay the landing strips and landing cradles.

Commensurately, the majority of the enemy was grouped at three points along the southern side of the base, where the majority of the structures lay. They closed to within five hundred meters, and then stopped at the edge of the warehouses.

From there on out, nothing lay between the Roaches and the base but tall, waving grass and a narrow road that ran to the gate.

Leslie overlaid an optical view of the terrain on her vision, selecting Sergeant Aaron's helmet cams for her vantage. He'd proven his valor when Rika took down the Politica, and she had no doubt he'd do so again.

Gazing out over the half-kilometer of space between the forces, and seeing well over a hundred Roach tags hovering in and around the distant buildings, she worried that bravery may not be enough to take down so many enemies.

Stop that thinking, Leslie. No one has ever seen a massed mech formation like this before. It's going to be amazing.

The world seemed to pause for a moment, and everything grew still. It was as though Iapetus knew that hell was about to descend, and was bracing for impact.

Four electron beams lanced out from the enemy positions and struck the plascrete barrier on the left side of the gate, then another four struck the barrier on the other side.

Aaron and the four mechs of fireteam one-one returned fire erratically, shooting at targets of opportunity before falling back behind a secondary barrier, this one thicker, with a lead core plus a grav-shield.

Twenty Roaches rushed forward into the grassy plain, holding CFT shields and using the covering fire from their compatriots to enable their advance. Another group repeated the maneuver, then another.

A minute later, there were one hundred enemies leapfrogging one another across the field.

Leslie looked at the eastern and northern gates. The Roaches were using the same tactic there, as well. They hadn't advanced on the bunkers at the corners, but they would soon, once they determined the response the mechs would bring to bear.

Only, it wouldn't be mechs that they met.

Leslie activated their first line of defense, and aracnidrones—twenty on each side of Fort Hammerfall—dug themselves out of the ground behind the advancing Roaches and opened fire.

At the south side of the base, six enemies went down in the initial volley. The Roaches still in position at the edge of the plain tried to take shots at the aracnidrones, but most of the bots were between them and their teammates, making clean shots impossible.

The drones, however, had no compunctions about unleashing suicidal fury on the Roaches, taking out another dozen in the next ten seconds, firing missiles and chainguns, and tearing limbs off with wild abandon.

Several of the enemy's CFT shields fell to the ground, and others turned to face the aracnidrones as the advancing Roaches suddenly found themselves surrounded.

At the southern gate, Aaron and his fireteam took the opportunity to lay down heaver fire on the enemy, slinging depleted uranium slugs and rail-accelerated pellets.

In a minute, fifty of the Roaches had fallen. Similar scenarios were playing out at the other gates, and Leslie wondered if the enemy commander would call a retreat. Losing over ten-percent of your force in the first few minutes was not a good sign.

Despite the tactic's success, casualties were not one-sided. Several mechs had taken damage as well, but unlike purely organic humans—even ones in powered armor—the mechs could take a lot of punishment before going down. They felt no pain when losing a limb, nor did they fear that level of damage, and it gave them a distinct advantage when under heavy fire.

Just when Leslie thought the enemy would in fact fall back, they rose up and rushed Fort Hammerfall from three sides.

"Shit!" Leslie whispered glancing at David, who was standing silently on the far side of the holotank.

"This is good," he said, nodding slowly. "We *need* them to overextend. We have to give Dala time to do her part."

Leslie nodded in return. "It's just nuts for the enemy commander to commit his full force like this."

"Yes." David was drumming his fingers on the edge of the holotank. "If our forces were what they appear to be, then a combined assault with his troops would be enough to overwhelm us."

"He's a fool to think this is all we have," Leslie replied. "Same thing as nuts, in this case."

On the holotank, six blue markers lifted out of a warehouse, three kilometers southeast of the base, splitting off into pairs, each headed for the gates that were under attack.

As Leslie watched the SkyScreams streak toward the onrushing enemy, Lieutenant Travis pinged her over the command net.

<Should we go?>

<No,> Leslie replied. *<We wait for them to hit the bunkers or breach the fence line.>*

<We're going to lose mechs if they breach,> Travis insisted.

<Travis,> Rika's voice came over the command net. *<Hold your position. We don't know if they have anything else up their sleeves. We need our reserves.>*

And our reserves' reserves, Leslie thought.

The feed from Aaron's helmet picked up an earsplitting scream, and two airborne shapes flashed over the enemy formation, each firing all four electron beams, raking them across the ground, slicing through the second wave of attackers, followed by the Roaches out on the field—who were still under attack from the aracnidrones.

David chuckled, a grim look in his eyes. "That's a lot of dead Cocks."

Leslie groaned. "Not you, too. The after-action reports alone are going to make me cringe for days."

Even with Rika's SkyScreams raking the enemy lines, the Roaches still continued their advance. Pockets of enemies set up gun emplacements protected by shields and began to spray anti-air fire at the SkyScreams, pushing them back.

"Potter, tap those guns," Leslie ordered.

<*With pleasure,*> Potter replied.

Guided mortar fire burst from three of the nearby hangars, arcing high in the air and jinking side to side before falling on the AA emplacements.

The Roaches' guns took out most of the incoming mortar fire. Leslie had anticipated that and didn't even need to give Potter the word; the AI launched a salvo of groundhuggers, missiles that flew a mere dozen centimeters above the terrain, masked by the tall grass.

While the Roaches were firing into the sky, the groundhuggers struck, blowing away four of the AA guns and flinging enemies in all directions.

"Nice shooting, Potter," Leslie said grimly as the enemy continued to advance, now within only a hundred meters of the southern fence.

* * * * *

Rika watched four of the six AA emplacements at the southern gate explode, and twisted in the air, diving toward the fifth, as it remained focused on incoming mortar fire.

She kicked a round out of her railgun and cried out in triumph as it struck true, taking out the gun.

The Cocks below turned their weapons on her, and Rika fired her engines at max burn, boosting back into the sky, jinking left and right to avoid incoming fire.

While the Cocks were aiming at her, Karen swooped in

from the south and fired a pair of missiles into clusters of the enemy, flinging armored bodies across the battlefield.

Rika smiled with satisfaction, but then saw a group of Cocks rush out of one of the buildings to the south of the battlefield, and fire shoulder-mounted missiles at Karen.

<*Karen! You've got buzzards on your six!*> Rika called out.

<*See 'em! Firing chaff!*>

Rika dove toward the missiles, firing her chaingun at them and taking out two before she had to pull up to avoid enemy weapons fire.

One of the missiles switched targets and locked onto her. Rika swore, twisted in the air, and released chaff before banking hard to port, bringing her chaingun to bear on the missile. The weapon flung hot carbon shards at the missile, ripping it to shreds.

With that threat neutralized, Rika turned her attention to the Cocks who had shoulder-fired the missiles at the SkyScreams. She directed all four of her electron beams at them, and the enemy fell under her withering beam fire. There was no time to revel in the small victory, as a red light flashed on her HUD.

Karen had been hit.

Rika twisted in the air and boosted toward her teammate. The sergeant's SkyScream had been hit in the port engine, and was wobbling, barely maintaining altitude.

<*Grav systems got hit, too,*> Karen reported. <*I'm going to set down in the compound, cover me.*>

Rika launched two missiles at the enemies below, clearing a path for Karen to set down. The sergeant's SkyScream came in low and fast, digging a long furrow into the grass within Hammerfall's fence line.

Her breath catching in her throat, Rika boosted higher, seeking a better vantage and the relative safety of altitude. Relief flooded her upon seeing Karen slide out of the pilot's pocket on her SkyScream far below, the craft's armatures setting her back into her legs.

Good, she's still in the fight.

She banked left and saw Aaron's fireteam falling back to their third barrier, the first two nothing more than smoking ruins. They were nearly flanked; another minute, and they'd be surrounded.

<Leslie, Travis coming soon?>

<On it, Captain. Any moment now.>

Three days ago, when First Platoon had made their mock-combat drop to Fort Hammerfall, a flotilla of cargo ships had dropped from the *Golden Lark*. Those ships had carried supplies and equipment, but they'd also contained the mechs of Lieutenant Travis's Second Platoon.

The crates containing the reinforcements had been transferred to the hangars, where the mechs had begun to dig.

The Cocks continued to advance on Aaron's team at the south gate, no doubt certain in their victory over the five beleaguered Marauders. Then the ground exploded in two places a scant, dozen meters from the flanking Cocks.

On the eastern side, a massive figure lumbered out of the ground—a K1R-M that everyone in the company simply called 'Bitty'.

Bitty carried two large caliber chainguns loaded with HE rounds, and they were already spinning when the six tons of mech hit the ground.

The front ranks of the enemy were torn to shreds before the rest of Second Platoon's squad four even finished breaking through the surface of the field.

<Incoming missiles!> Potter called out over the command net, and Rika spun in the air, picking up the incoming ballistic weapons.

There were twelve of them, only three kilometers out and coming from the east. Rika targeted four with her electron beams, taking out two on her first salvo.

<*I got your back.*> Kelly's voice came into Rika's mind, and a rail shot, followed by four electron beams, lanced out, destroying another three missiles.

Five seconds later, they were in range of the base's three AA turrets, and the guns rose from the ground, firing on and destroying another four of the air-breathers, leaving only three.

The guns pivoted to track the missiles, when a trio of rockets streaked out from the enemy lines, hitting one of Fort Hammerfall's AA guns. A fireball rose up from the weapon's wreckage, even as a quartet of electron beams lanced into the second AA gun, tearing it to ribbons.

Hammerfall's third AA gun took out one more of the missiles, but the final two were closing fast. Rika steadied her trajectory, trying to get a lock on the incoming weapons while still jinking herself to avoid groundfire.

<*Could really use some starfire!*> Rika called in to Leslie.

<*I've ordered a strike, but General Adam's ships are under attack from other SAF cruisers!*>

<*Well, shit!*> Rika cursed. <*That tears it.*>

The missiles were within seconds of striking the mechs at the southern gate, when Bitty casually raised both arms and fired both chainguns into the air, creating two cones of destruction that the missiles had to pass through to reach their targets.

Which they did not.

The HE rounds tore through the air-breathers, and the missiles exploded a hundred meters above the ground, raining shrapnel down on the enemy.

<*Portable AA battery at your service,*> Bitty grunted before turning his guns back to the enemy.

Rika watched the K1R-M from above, grateful for his quick thinking.

The enemy had singled out Bitty as priority number one, directing more fire on him, tearing away his ablative armor bit by bit. Rika was raking more beamfire through the lines when she spotted the Cocks bringing a four-meter-long, crew-served railgun to bear on Bitty.

It fired once, catching the K1R in the shoulder. Carbon plating and steel exploded from the impact, and Bitty staggered back. He swung his left chaingun around to fire at the enemy, but nothing happened.

Rika wasn't sure if it was out of ammo or jammed, but before Bitty could bring his other weapon to bear, another shot from the railgun hit, this one tearing his left arm off entirely.

Bitty froze, and Rika feared that something in his control systems had broken.

The K1R jerked side to side, and the enemy aimed the railgun at the mech's head.

Time slowed as Rika dove toward the enemy's weapon emplacement, firing wildly. Try as she might, her angle was no good; one of her shots was blocked by a CFT shield, and another by an enemy soldier.

She estimated that the rail would fire again in one second, maybe two. Bitty seemed stunned, or had suffered a failure, and was unable to move.

Then Rika saw a blurred shape leap out of the mech ranks, arch through the air, and land atop the crew-served railgun, firing wildly at the surrounding enemy.

Rika's HUD tagged the figure as Staff Sergeant Divinar—an AM-3 they had rescued from the Politica.

The Staff Sergeant killed two of the Cocks, but then took a shot in the shoulder that blew his right arm off. He switched to his shoulder cannons, and took out another Cock before the gunner pivoted the railgun and fired at Divinar.

Rika watched, cold determination flooding her veins, as the rail-fired shot tore Divinar in half, flinging his body in two directions, spraying blood and steel across the surrounding enemies.

A second later, Rika had a clean shot—but she didn't take it.

Instead, she swooped down into the enemy lines, grabbed the gunner and his rail in the SkyScream's talons, and lifted them into the air.

She bent the gun and flung it back down at the enemy before tearing the gunner to pieces, throwing his remains onto the Cocks below.

* * * * *

"Southern advance is halted," Leslie muttered as she watched the massed mechs from Second Platoon overwhelm the front lines of the enemy, driving them back across the fence line.

A few turned and ran from the mechs' advance. Once the Roaches saw their comrades fall back, more and more of them turned and ran for the relative safety of the warehouses and commercial buildings half a kilometer distant.

Leslie turned her attention to the eastern gate, where Staff Sergeant Chris had slowed the Roaches' advance, and was now bolstered by Second Platoon's squad three.

Thirty seconds after the enemy at the southern gate began to flee, the Roaches at the eastern gate began to fall back—albeit in a more orderly fashion.

Leslie couldn't help but smile as Kelly streaked overhead and fired her last two missiles at the retreating enemies, sending half of them into a full run.

Well, about as orderly as they can, with two SkyScreams harrying them.

The defense of the northern gate had not fared as well.

There had not been enough time to dig tunnels to the

northern fence, though two fireteams from Second Platoon had hidden in the outbuildings near the fence line.

The defenders at the gate had been overrun and fell back to those buildings, where the fighting was fierce as mechs fought the enemies in powered armor in close quarters—sometimes hand-to-hand.

<*Any time now would be nice,*> Leslie called out to Barne.

<*Almost there. These Swampfoxes are pieces of shit.*>

<*And here you were* ***so*** *glad that they were a great deal,*> Leslie shot back.

<*Whatever. In range in less than a mike.*>

Leslie watched the two dots north of the base close on the former airport at top speed. At first, she thought the mechs were still in their vehicles, but when she got a visual, she realized that the foremost signal was The Van, out ahead of the rest of his team. The AMs and FRs were trailing behind in a second group.

The Roaches had maintained a reserve as they advanced into the northern end of the base, and The Van tore into them, killing with both his weapons and his swinging arms. The rest of the Marauders accompanying him spread out around The Van and swept toward the base, driving the enemy into the other mechs within.

"Damn, that northern bunch may be forced to surrender," David said in awe. "This is unheard of. I've never seen such a small force take out so many so fast—not when the enemy was armored almost as heavily."

Leslie couldn't stop the grin that was spreading across her face. "Just think of what would have happened to the Nietzscheans if the GAF had let us fight like this."

David met her smile with one of his own. "Believe me, I *am* thinking of it. When we get the second wave of mechs from the Politica, we're going to have the beginnings of an army like no one has ever seen. Then we'll get to see how the

Nietzscheans deal with it, outside of our imaginations."

Leslie watched the other elements of First Platoon's second and fourth squads sweep in toward the enemy. The only place the Roaches had available for retreat was east, toward the city of Hittis.

ATTACK ON ATLANTIS

STELLAR DATE: 08.13.8949 (Adjusted Gregorian)
LOCATION: Fort Hammerfall
REGION: Iapetus, Hercules System, Septhian Alliance

Rika could have cried for joy as she saw several of the Cocks signal their surrender. They were going to win this fight with exceptionally light casualties, and they'd have more than enough prisoners to interrogate.

Her only hope was that General Adam had managed to track where the enemy was coordinating their attack, though the attack on his ships in space—which they knew little about—may have disrupted that goal.

She circled the battlefield once, then swept to the south, firing warning shots and trying to push the enemy back from the east and into the force that Barne and Chase had returned with.

At first it looked like the tactic was working, but the enemy began to form up into groups and offer more resistance. Rika was worried they would disappear into the commercial district and take days to flush out—or worse, escape entirely.

<Are you seeing this?> Rika called in to Leslie. *<Are we going to get any help from the SAF?>*

<I just got a message from General Adam. They're moving ground troops in to help corral the Roaches, but that's not our biggest concern. There are long range attack craft coming in from the west, over the ocean. I've managed to get a feed from space; he's in no position to help. We're going to need our ace in the hole.>

<Do it,> Rika replied. *<Call in the Major.>*

Rika gained altitude, seeking a clear visual on the ocean, ten kilometers to the east. She caught sight of a blast of steam erupting from the waves, and then water began to slough off of a large oval shape.

A few seconds later, the *Perseid's Dream* was visible, rising from the waves within its shield bubble, its six-hundred-meter hull gleaming in the afternoon light.

A few kilometers further out into the ocean, the *Golden Lark* surged out of the water, over a kilometer of starship rising up into the skies.

The *Golden Lark* fired on the incoming fighters, its beams cutting into the enemy ships. The attack craft tried to avoid the *'Lark*'s beams—and some did—but moments later, the ship's complement of fighters burst from its bays, and gave chase to the enemy fighters, driving them back the way they'd come.

While the *Golden Lark* moved east over the ocean, the *Perseid's Dream* moved inland and stopped a kilometer east of Fort Hammerfall. Beams lashed out at the Cocks scurrying about on the ground below, while Third and Fourth Platoons dropped from the ship to the choke point, between the commercial district surrounding the old airport and the rest of Hittis.

<*Someone call for an exterminator?*> Lieutenant Michael of Fourth Platoon asked as his mechs engaged the enemy near the maglev tracks that Rika had snuck under earlier in the day.

<*You got pests, you call for the best,*> Third Platoon's Lieutenant Wilson chimed in.

Rika watched the remaining enemies begin to surrender in droves.

<*We did it, Niki. The battle is won.*>

<*Well, it is down here. General Adam has one hell of a fight on his hands above us.*>

Rika was about to offer the SAF assistance when Major Tim contacted her.

<*Rika, looks like the enemy launched those fighters from a wet-navy carrier, two hundred klicks out to sea. I'm in contact with General Adam, and he requested that we neutralize the target while*

he cleans house upstairs. I can hit the carrier with fighters, but it may be better to drop Fifth Platoon on it.>

Rika reviewed the data Major Tim sent and agreed with his assessment.

<Do you have any details from him on what's going on up there?>

<Just a little bit of an attempted coup,> Tim replied, his voice dripping with disdain. *<From the looks of it, General Adam has the upper hand now. I think the enemy was expecting success on the ground to bolster their odds in space, but when Dala took out Zim, and Adam shot down their flagship, things went sideways.>*

<Starshit!> Rika exclaimed. *<All that's been going on while we putzed around down here?>*

<Seems like most of the space battle was on the far side of the planet,> Niki supplied. *<I'm glad Dala is OK, as well.>*

Rika had to admit that she was, too. They hadn't even known if Zim was involved, but if Dala took him out, then that question was answered.

<OK, Major, take the fifth out to the carrier,> Rika replied to the *Golden Lark*'s captain. *<I'm on my way to join them.>*

Rika fired the SkyScream's engines at max burn and streaked over the *Perseid's Dream*'s bow and out over the ocean. She raced after the now-distant shape of the *Golden Lark*.

Once within tight-beam range, Rika Linked to the *Golden Lark's* CIC and pulled up the data on the enemy ship they were approaching.

She had never understood why some worlds still operated wet navies, especially something the size of a carrier. Submarines made sense—they were sneaky, and made for interesting strategic options—but a carrier was just a big, slow, moving target. Maybe it was nostalgia, or maybe some people just liked to be sailors. Maybe both.

As she drew closer, Rika got a visual on the carrier and

revised her opinion. The thing wasn't as much a *carrier* as it was a floating spaceport.

<*Much more practical than I expected,*> she said to Niki.

<*What were you thinking? Some sort of ship with a landing strip attached to the top?*>

<*Nevermind what I was thinking,*> Rika shot back with a laugh.

The carrier-spaceport was four kilometers long and two wide. The *Golden Lark* was holding off ten kilometers to the west.

The data from the *'Lark*'s CIC tagged the carrier as the *Atlantis,* and Rika watched as a trio of railguns atop the floating behemoth fired shots at the Marauder cruiser.

Because both ships were in fixed positions, the *Golden Lark*'s defense beams melted the railgun shots before they hit. It was still a spectacular sight though, the rail shots exploding over the ocean, each one a brilliant display of energy, brighter than daylight.

Above, the Marauder fighters were engaged in an aerial fight with the *Atlantis*'s attack craft. Rika was tempted to join in the fray, but tamped down her enthusiasm. Chances were that this vessel was the staging ground for all of the attacks on her and her mechs.

There would be answers within.

<*Any ideas for how we're going to land on that thing?*> Rika asked Major Tim.

<*Well, I was thinking that I'd swoop in close, and your mechs could just jump out of the bays.*>

The Major's voice was entirely deadpan, and Rika couldn't tell if he was kidding or not. <*Umm…OK.*>

<*Glad you approve,*> Tim responded. <*Tuck in under the* 'Lark*'s hull and you can ride in inside our shields.*>

<*OK, then. Crazy-ass jump, it is,*> Niki commented privately.

Rika connected with Lieutenant Crudge, and they planned

out Fifth Platoon's breach points. Fifth was the smallest platoon in the company, with only sixty-six mechs. A pittance against the hundreds that could be on the *Atlantis*.

However, sixty-six mechs against a six-kilometer square floating spaceport was a walk in the park after what they'd faced at Hammerfall. Especially with a starship as backup.

The *'Lark* pulsed its engines, and pushed in toward the *Atlantis*. Rika stayed close to the cruiser's hull, but didn't go underneath like the major had suggested. She could only imagine what getting between a starship and its grav column would feel like.

As the they approached the *Atlantis,* the carrier increased its rate of fire, adding short-range missiles and anti-air to its defense. All of which splashed harmlessly against the cruiser's shields.

The *Golden Lark* was one of the Marauders' most powerful cruisers. It would have taken a nuclear warhead to breach its shields, and that would have destroyed the *Atlantis* as well.

As they eased up to the *Atlantis,* Rika signaled the SkyScream to disconnect her from the vessel, passing control of the fighter over to Niki. Once out, Rika quickly reattached her limbs, keeping her arms tucked inside the storage slots until the last moment.

To her right, the carrier loomed large, towers, cradles, and landing strips forming a jumbled mess on its surface.

Her HUD noted the *Atlantis*'s shields with a dim glow. It had a defensive barrier as powerful as the *'Lark*'s, but in twenty-two seconds, the Marauder ship would brush its shield against the carrier's, and the two graviton-driven shielding systems would nullify one another.

Rika timed her countdown with that of Fifth Platoon, and slowed her breathing, forcing herself to grow calm and get ready for whatever was to come.

Her timer hit zero, and Rika leapt off the SkyScream, which

Niki then flew up into the *'Lark'*s open bays on her left.

She fell the thirty meters to the deck of the Atlantis and immediately came under fire from a group of soldiers to her right.

Rika fired a depleted uranium round at them, then dove behind a low structure—some kind of venting system—and unslung her JE-84.

She released two drones and saw that her shot had killed two soldiers, and that the remaining three were falling back.

Run, little cockroaches, run!

She synced with the platoon's combat net, and saw that she was close to her intended position near squad four.

<*Sergeant Jynafer, all accounted for?*> Rika asked the squad leader.

<*Hale and whole, Captain. We're moving to link up with you. Do I read correctly that our target is the ship's CIC?*>

<*Smart cookie,*> Rika replied. <*We're going to see if we can lop the head off this snake—or at least find out where the head is.*>

<*I'm all about killing snakes,*> Jynafer replied with a grin.

Rika saw fireteam four-two approach from her left and signaled to them that there were three enemies on the far side of the vent. They nodded and spread out to flank them.

She joined in their formation, and they found that the soldiers had fled below deck. Rika was tempted to rush after them, but she and the mechs could cover ground more quickly on the surface of the carrier—even if it incurred more risk of being flanked or surrounded.

As they moved toward the location of the CIC, a tower near the center of the carrier, more and more enemies appeared, attempting to stop the fourteen mechs.

Behind them, the *Golden Lark* had backed off again, lest the *Atlantis's* railguns shoot it where the shields were negated.

<*If we fight them all, we'll be here for days,*> Rika said to Sergeant Jynafer. <*We need to push through.*>

<You got it, Captain. Run and gun, it is.>

Jynafer reformed her squad into a spear, and they took off at a run, the forward fireteam bringing maximum fire to bear on the targets directly in front of them, and the trailing mechs shooting at anyone who attempted to close in behind them.

Rika imagined that anyone observing the surface of the carrier would see a straight line of destruction pointed at the CIC tower.

It telegraphed their intent, but she couldn't think of a better way to reach their target in a timely manner.

<I've gained access to their general net,> Niki announced. *<There's no sensitive data on it, but I do know what the lunch special is today.>*

<Is it pasta?> Rika asked. *<I **still** have a craving for it after Charlie's the other night. I want to get back there before long.>*

<For someone who lives off batts more than food, you sure think with your stomach a lot.>

Rika laughed as she leveled her GNR and fired an electron beam at an AA gun that was pivoting to fire at the deck where the first half of the squad was advancing.

The AA gun exploded, and Rika picked up her pace, moving to join the forward fireteam.

*<I went **years** without eating. It's possible that I might be hungry for the rest of my life.>*

<At least you have the metabolism of an ox. Would be a shame if you couldn't fit in your skin anymore—oh, here we are, a nice little network port that got left open by someone trying to connect to…an illegal sim site. Nice.>

Rika fired her JE-84 at a pair of enemies in light armor, half-curious what the Roaches had been thinking, advancing on mechs in light armor, and half-wondering what passed for illegal sims on Iapetus.

<What's the word?> Rika asked.

<There's a submarine being prepped in a bay below the CIC. I

think they're evac-ing whoever is in charge.>

<Over my dead body, they are.>

Rika passed updated orders to Jynafer's squad, and ahead, an AM-3 tore a hatch off its hinges before dropping a grenade down the hole.

<Boys and girls,> Jynafer announced to her four fireteams. *<We're going in!>*

Fireteam four-two went in first, pushing ahead and making room for the other mechs. Within a minute, all were within the *Atlantis,* pushing down, deck after deck, toward the bowels of the carrier.

In close-quarters fighting, the never-ending stream of enemies began to wear them down. An AM-3 lost an arm, while one of the RR-2s had a damaged leg lock up. Another AM-3 took a rocket to the chest while they were advancing through a mess hall.

<We can't keep up the pace, Captain,> Jynafer said to Rika. *<Not with the wounded.>*

Rika had to admit that Jynafer was right. *<OK, take four-three and work your way back up. Second squad is moving to our position and can clear the way for you.>*

<Got it, Captain Rika. Good hunting.>

<Oh, it will be.>

Rika and the remaining mechs pushed on, descending another two levels. Rika consulted the schematics that the SAF had provided, and saw that they were only one level from the submarine bay.

A ladder at the far end of the corridor should take them down to a gantry above the bay.

<You're almost out of time,> Niki announced. *<The sub has signaled that all personnel are aboard and is sealing its hatch.>*

"Shit," Rika swore. She rushed ahead and jumped down the ladder, landing on a catwalk overlooking a bay occupied by four submarines. Two were active, and Rika took aim at the first while asking Niki, <*Which one?*>

<*I don't know! They didn't file manifests.*>

Rika figured the VIPs would go for the closest, and fired a sustained burst from her electron beam, followed by her last depleted uranium round. The shots connected with the submarine's hull one meter forward of the main access hatch.

The electron beam heated up the hull and melted away a few centimeters of steel, creating a cavity for the DPU to strike. When it hit, the uranium rod punched right through, smashing a half-meter hole in the sub's hull.

A second later, more shots came from the catwalk as the other mechs fired on the bow and rudders of the two submarines.

Confident that neither vessel could get away, now that they were no longer watertight, Rika leapt over the railing to the dock below.

As she dropped, Rika considered that the subs could have grav shields. It was risky, but a desperate person may try to brave the seas with a hole in the hull, trusting their shields to keep them safe.

She'd just have to make sure they didn't try that.

Rika sprinted across the dock, firing her JE-84 at several enemy soldiers who tried to slow her down, before she jumped across the widening gap between the dock and the ship.

By some miracle, the submarine's shield hadn't come online yet, and Rika slid through the hole she'd blown in the hull, fell through a gash in the first deck, and landed in the ship's command center.

There was a man with an admiral's stars on his lapel screaming for the submarine to dive, while another with a colonel's leaves yelled something about capture. Two sailors at the ship's navigation consoles were working furiously, one reporting that they couldn't dive, as the grav shields had failed.

With all the commotion, none of them noticed Rika until she stepped forward and called out, "Is this a private cruise, or can anyone join in?"

All four turned to face her, and Rika's eyes narrowed as she looked into the colonel's.

"I know you…."

REVELATIONS

STELLAR DATE: 08.14.8949 (Adjusted Gregorian)
LOCATION: Fort Hammerfall
REGION: Iapetus, Hercules System, Septhian Alliance

The local SAF command center in Hittis was in shambles after Major Dala's attack, and the closest base was on lockdown, still undergoing scrutiny from General Adam's investigators.

The *Atlantis* was in similar condition, a thousand SAF soldiers working their way through the carrier, deck-by-deck searching for intel on the full scope of the attempted coup.

Surprisingly, that made Fort Hammerfall the safest place on Cassini's eastern seaboard for the meeting with the SAF command.

Rika stood in her quarters and drew a deep breath. She'd faced down a president—and made a friend of her—and challenged and killed a despotic dictator. A planetary governor, General Adams, and their staffs were *far* less imposing.

She could do this.

Besides, she'd captured the prize on that submarine. No matter how upset any of them may be at how the prior day had gone, they were now one step closer to cutting out the cancer that had festered on Iapetus, and in the Hercules System in general.

Rika walked out of her quarters and almost ran into Chase in the hall.

"Chase! Sorry!" Rika exclaimed. "I was lost in my own head there. What are you doing here?"

Chase smiled and slid an arm around Rika's back, pulling her in close for a kiss. "I wanted to find you before you went into the lion's den to wish you luck. You've got this…whatever 'this' turns out to be."

"Well, it'd better turn out to be a big fat 'thank you'." Rika's eyes darted in the direction of the command building. "If I get reamed out after saving their planet, I'll be pissed."

"No one's gonna ream you," Chase gave Rika another kiss. "You're the one that'll—nevermind, this metaphor is going to fail me fast. Look, you'll do fine. Let me walk you over."

Rika stilled her mind and enjoyed the few minutes of peace as she and Chase walked out of the officer's housing and across to the command building.

Outside, activity thrummed all around them, and the bulk of the *Perseid's Dream* loomed over the buildings from its resting place between the landing strips to the north. The *Golden Lark* was back in space, maintaining a geosynchronous position over Fort Hammerfall.

Rika ignored all of it, simply glad to be alive and to have lost so few of her mechs—only five fatalities, though Lieutenant Carson and his R&M platoon were up to their necks in repairs.

The sun was rising in the western sky, and Rika took a deep breath as its warm light struck her face. "You know, you're right. It's going to be a good day. I can feel it."

"Damn straight, it is," Chase replied with a grin. "We kicked bad guy ass yesterday. Once the mess down here gets cleaned up, we're going to drink ourselves stupid and party for a week."

Rika snorted and laughed at the same time. "Damn…you made me snorgh!"

" 'Snorgh'? Where'd you grow up? Everyone knows that's a 'lort'. Way easier to say."

" 'Lort', my hard, steel ass. It's a snorgh!"

Chase shook his head as he held open the door to the Command Building—it had taken a hit from stray fire in the fight, and the automatic actuator was broken. The glass had been shot out as well, so Rika wasn't certain why he bothered to open it at all.

She stopped and turned to him. "Wish me luck."

"You don't need luck, you're Rika."

Rika scowled at him. "Wish me luck anyway. I like to feel lucky."

Chase leant forward, and his lips met hers. Half a minute later, he pulled back. "Good luck."

"Got one of those for me, too?" Leslie asked as she walked past with Captain Penny.

Penny raised an eyebrow. "Fraternization with the enlisted?"

Rika rolled her eyes at Penny. The captain of the *Perseid's Dream* frequently gave Rika a hard time about her relationship with Chase. She did it in good fun, but sometimes Rika suspected there was something behind the jokes.

"You bet. It's how we roll in the Ninth Battalion. If you can't screw your underlings, what's the point?"

"I'm an underling now, am I?" Chase laughed and gave Rika a final peck on the cheek. As he walked out of the command building, he called out over his shoulder, "Well, this underling has a massive mess to help clean up, while you uppity-ups all talk about things that have already happened."

"Zing!" Rika called back and joined Leslie and Penny.

"So, who all is coming now? The list changes every time I check," Leslie said.

"Governor Hengch is already here, along with two aides. Major Tim is on his way down. General Adam, his retinue, and Dala will be in attendance, as well. Plus some Admiral named Irah."

"I guess Dala is doing Zim's job now," Leslie replied. "What, with him being as dirty as a hog on a steaming hot day."

Rika nodded. "I find myself wondering if Dala was always doing Zim's job—at least the part that he was *supposed* to be doing, not the illegal, insurrection-supporting part."

It didn't take long to reach the conference room, and Rika steeled herself before stepping inside. *Remember, you've faced worse,* she told herself.

She pushed open the door to find Governor Hengch sitting at the table, reviewing information on a personal holo. Her two aides stood behind her, and while the governor did not immediately make eye contact, they did. One seemed dispassionate, and the other clearly did not like what he saw.

Rika decided to ignore them.

"Governor Hengch." Rika reached her left hand across the table.

The governor looked up, and her eyes narrowed as she took Rika in. "Captain Rika, good to finally get to meet you."

Rika laughed nervously. "Had you been anticipating this for long?"

Hengch shrugged, her long green hair bouncing on her shoulders. "Well, when a mercenary operation sets up shop on your soil, one does become curious—especially if it's run by a soldier as famous as you. I wanted to come out for a visit sooner, but never got the chance. Seemed like a priority now."

By the governor's expression, it was hard to tell whether or not Hengch meant 'famous', or would have preferred to say 'infamous'.

"Well, I'm glad things turned out better than they could have," Rika replied with a warm smile. "This is Captain Penny of the *Perseid's Dream,* and Lieutenant Leslie. My XO, Lieutenant Scarcliff, will be along shortly, as well as Major Tim of the *Golden Lark*. One of our Company AIs, Potter, is in attendance as well, as is Niki, the AI that resides within me."

<*Thanks for the intro,*> Niki said privately and placed a large winking eye in Rika's mind.

Governor Hengch nodded to Penny and Leslie as they sat. "Good to meet you as well. Iapetus owes the Marauders a debt of gratitude that we will do our best to repay."

"It's what we're here for," Rika replied. "Well, not exactly, I suppose—given that this was supposed to be a training mission. Either way, kicking folks like the Roaches in the teeth is what the Marauders do best."

"I heard you had named them that." Hengch gave a perfunctory smile, but then her expression grew troubled. "But I don't think this was the work of some separatist group, or an element of angry, ex-military patriots."

"Yes, that much is—" Rika was interrupted by the door opening, and another group filing in.

Lieutenant Scarcliff was the first through, followed by Major Tim and Major Dala. General Adam and Sergeant Major Rene followed after. Lastly came a man who Rika did not recognize, and she assumed it must be Admiral Irah.

The introductions were brief, and a minute later, everyone was seated at the table—excepting General Adam, who stood at the head and appeared to be chewing on the inside of his cheek.

After a moment, he spoke. "Well, people, we survived. Exactly what we survived is just now becoming clear, but the colonel Rika captured on the *Atlantis* has turned out to be our best evidence."

Rika nodded. Though she'd recognized the colonel, it took a bit to remember where from. He looked different in an SAF uniform—not at all like the last time she'd seen him.

No one spoke up, and the general continued. "That colonel is named Fallon, and he's a known entity in Nietzschea's Coreward Regional Command."

<Come up a ways since I attacked his platoon back on Laras,> Rika said privately to Niki.

<That's for sure. Nietzschea's CRC is the command that's

focused on expanding the empire coreward.>

General Adam's statement was simple, but the implications were vast. Until now, there had been no hard evidence that the Nietzscheans were running subversive ops in Thebes. Speculation was one thing, but now there was proof. Incontrovertible proof.

"This certainly changes things." Hengch ran a hand through her green hair, the long locks shimmering and sparkling around her head. "It's confirmed, then. These were not misguided men and women resisting the Septhian takeover; they're traitors."

"We don't know that for sure," Admiral Irah spoke for the first time, his voice marred by a strange rasp that hinted at a recent illness, or perhaps an injury. "We know that *some* were traitors—like that pile of shit, Admiral Fergus, on the *Atlantis*—but the rank and file had no idea they were fighting for the Niets. From what I understand, even the force that attacked Fort Hammerfall here had no idea who was behind this."

"Still criminals, though. They knew they were part of a coup." Governor Hengch's eyes were hard, and her lips drew into a thin line—a strange contrast to her still-sparkling hair. "I assume they'll all face charges and a long time in the stockade?"

"Perhaps," General Adam replied without elaborating.

Rika wondered at Adam and Hengch's relationship. She had learned that while Adam was a native Theban, he was put in command of the Hercules System's armed forces by Septhian High Command *after* the takeover, likely displacing someone less committed to unity. Hengch didn't seem to dislike Adam, but she seemed wary of the man in some way.

"That's not a significant concern," Admiral Irah added. "There are far more pressing issues."

"Major Dala," General Adam gestured for Dala to take the

floor as he sat across from Rika. "Tell us about what you found when you took Zim down."

Dala rose and walked to the head of the table. "When we stormed the colonel's HQ, we found him actively coordinating the operation against Fort Hammerfall. We put a stop to that and managed to keep a reserve force he was holding onto from entering the battle."

"Thank you for that," Rika replied, and Dala gave her a smile and a nod before continuing.

"Once in custody, Colonel Zim was convinced to surrender his personal tokens, and I dove into his records on the insurrection. What I found took some confirming, but careful passive scans have corroborated what his records had revealed: a Nietzschean fleet."

"What?" Governor Hengch exclaimed, halfway out of her chair. "Where? How long do we have? Stars, why the hell are we here? I need to be in the command bunker!"

Governor Hengch wasn't the only one to react to Dala's statement. Everyone around the table had tensed, as though ready for Niets to storm through the door at any moment.

Admiral Irah raised his hands, "They're not moving to attack—not yet, at least. It's a small fleet, and I think they were counting on Admiral Fergus's coup to succeed."

Dala summoned a holo above the table, and a view of the Hercules System appeared before them.

"They came insystem a few weeks ago, as best we can tell. Ten ships in total; six cruisers and four destroyers." Ten red dots appeared sixty AU from the Hercules System's star as Dala spoke. "They were using some sort of stealth tech that we've not seen before. It wasn't perfect, but they were bracketed by a trio of bulk haulers that were running dirty. The whole area was hard to scan, and no one was looking for stealthed Niets mixed in with the cargo haulers."

"So where are they now?" Major Tim asked. "Even

stealthed, you can't just float around in a system for weeks…well, not inside of sixty AU, at least.

The view of the system zoomed in on Armens, a jovian, gas giant planet thirty-two AU from the star.

"They're in here. They snuck in when a solar flare's EM wave passed through the area. We've not picked up all ten ships, though—not all at once. But the freighters that were masking them are still at Armens, so it's reasonable to believe that all ten Nietzschean ships are still there, as well."

Rika leant back in her chair and considered the implications of what Dala had told them. Ten Nietzschean ships were not enough to cause the SAF any trouble—normally.

But right now, General Adam's fleet was in disarray. Over a third of the system's ships had been involved in the coup, and there was reason to believe that many of the vessels that had not participated in the attack still had dissenters in their crews.

If the Niets made a move, it was hard to say how the SAF fleet would respond.

A slow smile spread across Rika's lips. "General Adam. I do believe that you want us to hit these Nietzschean ships."

The general nodded, his expression grim. "Yes. Right now, the group of people who know about the Nietzschean fleet is not significantly larger than what is present in this room. Irah and I are in agreement: if we mount a concerted attack, the Niets will run. It would take us days to get a fleet out there, and it will be plain as day what our goal is. Armens only has a few ships nearby, and the Niets can cut a swath of destruction on their way outsystem."

"Either that, or we'll end up fighting a second coup attempt," Irah added. "We need to crush those Niets and show our people what we're really fighting. Septhia and Thebes have been close allies for centuries. Things are tense right now, but Septhia is not an anathema to our way of life. Nietzschea is. People need to remember that."

"Trust me, I've been working on that." Hengch sighed and shook her head. "It's not easy. People are too quick to blame Septhia for what happened in the Albany System—even though it was actually the Nietzscheans behind it. The Septhians were the ones who saved the day."

"Sorry for our part in it," Rika apologized.

Governor Hengch shrugged. "Not your fault…well, sort of, but it would have happened anyway."

"We all seem to have been underestimating the Nietzscheans' guile," General Adam said.

Major Tim folded his arms across his chest. "Let's get down to brass tacks. How do you propose we take out ten Nietzschean ships? I'm sure you remember that we have just two in the Hercules System."

General Adam nodded to Major Dala once more, and she continued with her presentation.

"As far as we can tell, the Niets are in a relatively close formation, roughly a hundred kilometers beneath Armens' cloud tops. There are a few mining rigs scooping around Armens, so their orbital paths are limited to this band." A band lit up in the planet's northern hemisphere as Dala spoke.

"The plan we've worked out would have you heading to Formax, a dwarf planet nine AU beyond Armens. We'll spin that it is a safer alternative training site to use while things calm down insystem.

"A slingshot around Armens is a logical flight path to reach Formax right now. If we time it all right, you can fly around the gas giant while the Niets are on the far side. During your closest approach to the planet, you'll release your dropships into the cloud tops. Your two starships carry on, while your assault teams close in and breach the Nietzschean ships."

Major Tim was shaking his head, and Rika had to agree

with his general sentiment. She pursed her lips, then spoke first.

"I don't think this is a job the Marauders are willing to sign up for."

Admiral Irah sighed, and General Adam chuckled. Major Dala just frowned at Rika, but held her tongue as the general said, "I had a feeling you'd say that."

Stars, I'm sitting in a room with a General, Admiral, and Governor, telling them 'not good enough'. This is surreal.

Rika drew a deep breath to steady her nerves, and looked up and down the table. "Don't get me wrong. There's nothing Marauders like more than kicking Nietzschean ass; it's a life-calling for us. But we're not suicidal. Breaching starships a hundred klicks below a jovian's cloud tops sounds like the very definition of insanity."

"Not to mention that we don't have enough mechs to take out ten ships."

"You have nearly four hundred," Major Dala replied.

"Three-fifty that are combat ready," Rika corrected. "That's thirty-five a ship, though we'd hit the cruisers with more."

"You cut through the *Atlantis* like it was made of butter with just one squad," General Irah pointed out. "The Nietzschean cruisers have far less mass and volume."

"I had three other squads distracting the enemy on *Atlantis*," Rika reminded him. "And though it was bigger, starships are harder—more sectioned, easier to lock down. Vent atmo, kill grav, whatever. No way we can do any more than five."

"Five won't work." Irah shook his head and glanced at Dala. "We need to hit all ten at once."

<Rika, may I offer a suggestion?> Niki said privately. *<I think I might know of a way we can do this.>*

"Niki has a suggestion," Rika said, curious what the AI had in mind.

<*Thank you, Rika. Through contacts I'd rather not share right now, I have knowledge of a number of viable backdoors into Nietzschean command and control systems. As you all know, Nietzscheans do not use sentient AIs in their military operations, only NSAIs. These NSAIs have a logic loop that can cause them to suffer degraded performance, and there are a number of ways to trigger this logic loop. It shouldn't be hard to keep it going for five or six minutes—depending on processing power.*>

"Leaving aside how you have this information, five or six minutes is not long," Major Tim replied.

<*Correct, it is not,*> Niki's tone seemed positive, despite the limited use of her intel. <*However, once the NSAIs' performance is degraded, there is a multi-pronged attack we can make that will shut them down entirely. Then we can assume limited control of the ships.*>

"Propulsion?" General Adam asked.

<*Yes, so long as we can get to their engineering section and ensure no one can perform direct overrides.*>

Major Tim was running his finger and thumb along his chin. "I see a hole in your plan, Niki. Correct me if I'm wrong, but you're going to need nine more AIs capable of this sort of work to take the field with you."

<*Very astute, Major. You are correct. And I'll only share this information with free AIs. I won't take to the field with slaves.*>

The humans at the table shared a series of looks between them. Rika knew that the governor had an AI—though she'd failed to introduce her, and General Adam had one as well. Rika wondered what those AIs were saying.

"Don't you have more AIs in your company, Captain Rika?" General Adam asked after a moment. "I see a Potter and Dredge on your roster."

"We do," Rika nodded. "However, they're not free AIs. They're owned by the Marauders."

<*Rika, what are you playing at?*> Major Tim asked privately.

<*I'm not playing at anything. I'm building allegiances. Valuable allegiances.*>

"And I assume you don't have the legal authority to free them," General Adam said from behind steepled fingers.

<*No, she does not,*> Niki replied. <*Technically, I'm not free either—but those proceedings are in progress.*>

"It may be that you could help with this." Rika spread her hands and smiled "I've spoken with some lawyers on behalf of our AIs to grant them asylum under the same provisions Septhia enacted for the mechs we rescued from the Politica. They are interested in pursuing it, and have filed preliminary paperwork—but they warned me that it could take months, maybe even years...."

Rika let the statement hang, ignoring the look of surprise on Penny's face and the barely contained anger on Tim's. Leslie was smirking, and Scarcliff appeared bemused.

"I see those filings," Governor Hengch said after a moment. "There are seven separate AIs listed in the plea for asylum. I thought you only had two in your company."

"Seven?" Major Tim nearly shouted as he turned to Rika. "You filed on behalf of *my* AIs?"

"*Your* AIs?" Rika met the major's rage with her own steely gaze. "Do you believe in owning sentient beings, Major Tim?"

The major worked his mouth for a moment, but then clamped his jaw shut. <*We'll speak of this later,*> he snapped at her privately.

The governor's brow was raised as her eyes danced between Rika and Tim. When it was clear there would be no further outbursts, she spoke up. "I have it within my authority to provide temporary asylum. Jira?"

<*The governor is correct,*> Hengch's AI said. <*I'm surprised I didn't think of this myself. I'm not under indenturement, but once this goes through, we may see a number of AIs availing themselves of the provision,*> Jira paused and chuckled. <*Sorry, got carried*

away. Regarding this case, because Iapetus is a full member province-world of Septhia, the governor can grant an executive asylum. The regular process still has to be followed, but this grant provides instant status. Persons, human or AI, are granted immediate freedom. However, there are limits on legal proceedings they can undertake, as well as caps on property ownership.>

"How does that strike you, Potter?" Rika asked.

<*Strikes me just fine,*> Potter replied. <*How long does it take?*>

<*We could have it done within the day,*> Jira replied.

Potter laughed. <*Sign me up!*>

"This is all fine and dandy," Irah said, his rasp more pronounced. "But you only have eight AIs total, and I imagine you can't send them *all* on this mission."

"Not if we want our ships to fly," Major Tim shot Rika a cold look. "Granted, once they get their freedom, they may not want to remain our ships' AIs at all. Then this mission will become a lot harder."

<*Maybe you should ask them,*> Niki suggested over the Marauder's private connection. <*I bet if you act like you support the idea of their freedom, they'll be a lot more likely to stay on. Maybe a big signing bonus, too. That always helps.*>

<*Shit, I need to hire my own AI?*> Major Tim asked.

<*Moshe is already onboard,*> Penny said with a wink. <*I'll help you with Cora and the rest, sir.*>

Rika held back a smirk and looked at the general and admiral. "From what I can understand of our AI configuration, Jane, Frankie, and Lauren can come on the mission—if they want. This is a volunteer op. That means we need four more AIs. Know of any?"

General Adam nodded. "I just may."

* * * * *

Once the guests had departed, Major Tim slammed a fist on

the table. He glared at Rika before kicking his chair back and rising to pace across the room.

Rika had been waiting for this outburst, and stared impassively at the major as he worked off his anger. Leslie was giving the man a sour look, Scarcliff's expression was carefully neutral, and Penny wore an expression that Rika couldn't quite quantify. It seemed like a cross between '*grow up*' and '*relax, already*'.

Finally, Major Tim stopped pacing and turned to Rika, his finger pointed in accusation. "When the general learns of this—"

"He'll, what?" Rika asked. "Fire me? Re-enslave the AIs? Good luck keeping this company of mechs in the Marauders if he does—not that I think he would."

"It doesn't matter what you think, *Captain*. This is the general's regiment. You can't just free the AIs; it's above your paygrade."

"*I* didn't free the AIs," Rika replied. "They filed their own requests for asylum. I just helped the ones under me, and they shared the information with the others. It's the Septhians, our primary benefactors, who freed our AIs."

"It has good optics," Captain Penny added. "It looks like the Iapetan governor did this to help us out. We come off looking even more like the defenders of freedom and liberty. Probably help with recruitment, too."

<*It **will** help,*> Niki added. <*You're going to get AIs flocking to you in droves. You've never seen what free AIs can do, but you're going to.*>

"Seriously, Major Tim," Rika said. "Listen to us. This is a *good* thing. Look at how amazing free mechs are when they're fighting for themselves and their teammates. A lot of people thought massed mechs was a terrible idea. But a hundred and fifty mechs took out over a thousand heavy infantry, with a casualty ratio of less than two hundred to one. That's never been done before."

Major Tim ran a hand through his hair, and Rika could tell that he was trying to get his emotions in check. When he did speak, his voice was hard and edged. "You'd better be right, Rika."

"I *am* right. A free AI, Niki in this case, has given us the key to taking out *ten* Nietzschean ships. I don't know if you looked at the contract General Adam sent over, but the payment is *huge*. Worth the cost of hiring a thousand AIs. I don't see any scenario where General Mill will dislike what we've done here."

Major Tim groaned and closed his eyes before nodding. "Then we'd better pull this shit off."

DEPARTURE

STELLAR DATE: 08.15.8949 (Adjusted Gregorian)
LOCATION: Fort Hammerfall
REGION: Iapetus, Hercules System, Septhian Alliance

"So how does it feel, Chief Warrant Officer Second Grade?" Rika asked Niki as she looked at herself in the mirror after brushing her hair.

<*It feels weird. Weird but good,*> Niki said. <*It's nice to be formally recognized for my contributions.*>

"How do Potter and Dredge feel?"

<*You could ask them yourself, you know.*>

Rika ran a hand through her blonde hair, reveling in its feel before pulling it tight and wrapping it into a bun. "I have asked them, and they're almost too effusive in their gratitude. I'm seeking other opinions."

<*Well, rest assured, they're not being disingenuous.*>

"And it looks like the ship AIs are going to accept, as well. Major Tim managed to get his head out of his ass and negotiate a good deal with Cora."

<*Will wonders never cease. Granted, the wording in his offer to Cora smacked of Penny's influence.*>

"Well, got his head *mostly* out of his ass, at least."

<*Trust me, Cora was still happy to have it, even if the major is having mixed emotions.*>

"She is? I got the impression from you that her signing on wasn't a guarantee."

<*I may have painted their continued enlistment as less certain than it was. I wanted to know that you'd do the right thing even if the outcome wasn't ideal for you.*>

"Seriously?" Rika's brow lowered, her face darkening as it scowled back at her in the mirror. "You think you need to play me like that, Niki? After all we've been through?"

A strange feeling of anxiety came from Niki. *<I…you're right. I shouldn't have done that. Trust comes hard for me.>*

"Trust begets trust, Niki. I've trusted you with my life, and I know you've placed yours in me, too. Let's not ruin that by allowing doubt to creep in."

<OK, Rika. You're right.>

Rika wondered about Niki's answer. It was too pat. She hadn't forgotten about some of the things that the AI had hinted at when talking about the AI rebellion.

Still, it was like they always said: fear and doubt were the mind killers. She couldn't dwell on concerns like that before the mission.

Rika grabbed her helmet, slotted it onto the anchor on her hip, and exited her quarters. The halls were empty, and a minute later, she walked out of the officer's housing into a veritable wall of sound.

Squads of mechs were double-timing it across the fields to their dropships, loading up for the trip to the *Golden Lark*. Others were crossing the airstrip to directly board the *Perseid's Dream*, which was still resting on the planet's surface. Cargo haulers were dropping down, while others lifted off.

It was glorious, organized chaos.

"This is one crazy shit-ball you've signed us up for," a voice growled from Rika's left.

She turned to see Barne scowling at the scene before him. "You ready for it? It's going to be a tough run for a squishie. No one will fault you if you hold back."

Barne coughed and scowled at her. "Seriously, Rika? Might as well tell everyone about how I got a piggyback ride from you that one time. Top is first in and last out. Doesn't matter what my body's made of."

Rika reached back and slapped Barne on the shoulder. "I didn't expect you to take me up on the offer. Especially since

Chase and Leslie are going, too."

"Of course they are. Who would miss the chance to kill so many Niets and then steal their starships?"

"Good point."

Rika gave one last look at Fort Hammerfall, which would be staffed by a skeleton crew of Marauders from the ships and mechs not recovered enough for combat.

I'll be back, she thought while walking down the steps. *We all will.*

BRIEFING

STELLAR DATE: 08.15.8949 (Adjusted Gregorian)
LOCATION: *Golden Lark*
REGION: Hercules System, Septhian Alliance

Five hours later, Rika walked through the *Golden Lark* on her way to M Company's briefing room.

The *'Lark* and the *'Dream* were boosting hard for their slingshot around Armens, and the ships thrummed from the reactors running hot and grav systems dampening the *g*s for the crews.

She believed that the Niets hiding within Armens' clouds would grow suspicious as the two Marauder ships approached for their slingshot maneuver. But there were no other SAF ships on similar vectors, and no one would expect two ships to attack ten. Of course, the Marauders weren't attacking with their ships….

Rika had scoured the archives over the prior day, looking for similar missions performed deep within the clouds of a gas giant. She'd only found a few, and most were on stationary platforms hanging down into the clouds. Rarely had there been attacks on *ships* inside gas giants, let alone ten well-armed military vessels.

And absolutely none with mechs involved.

Nevertheless, she gathered what she could, looking at the pitfalls, failed attacks, ineffective strategies.

There were only two reasons to hit a ship in such a dangerous location—capture or kill. Most of the successful missions had 'kill' as their objective.

Tucking a ship into the gravity well of a gas giant was far simpler than capturing it and pulling it out.

While Rika was aiming for capture, she'd take kill if they

had to. David had worked out a very favorable contract with the Septhians: the Marauders could keep half the cruisers they saved, and all the destroyers.

Bringing General Mill new additions to his fleet, along with a handsome payout, would help mitigate any wrath he may feel at knowing his AIs were all going to be freed very soon.

She reached the briefing room's door and walked in without hesitation.

Inside were thirty-five Marauders; with the exception of Chase, Leslie, Barne, and Dala, all were mechs. It was quite the sight, and Rika felt a smile form on her lips.

As she stepped up behind the podium, ten holographic figures appeared along the side of the room. Some appeared as people, others simply as columns of light.

They were the ten AIs who would make this mission possible. Each would be placed within a mech, who would make guarding that AI their top priority on the mission.

Few mechs had the internal mods to accept an AI, and of those, not all were comfortable with having an AI inside their bodies. As a result, a few privates were in the room to hear what their part in all this would be.

The four additional AIs who had signed on all ended up being civilians, not members of the SAF. Rika had found herself glad at that outcome. It meant that there would be no conflicting loyalties, and each had temporary contracts with the Marauders.

Even better, all of the new AIs—Carter, Airin, Nedly, and Willa—were formerly from Genevia, displaced by the diaspora years ago. All had a bone to pick with the Nietzscheans, and all understood the risks.

Rika grasped the podium with her left hand and nodded to the assembly. "Some of you know what we're up against, others have only heard through scuttlebutt. I'll give it to you straight. This is a volunteer op. Every Marauder will have the opportunity to sit this one out—not that I expect any to."

Rika saw many heads nod in agreement and felt a sense of pride well within her as she continued.

"There are ten Nietzschean ships in this system. Six cruisers and four destroyers. They're hiding like the cowards they are, tucked deep within the clouds of Armens, the jovian planet we're on course for. SAF has worked to plot their positions, and we're going to drop in during a slingshot maneuver. From there, we'll come around the planet and breach their ships.

"Sensors will be shit in the clouds, so we're going to depend on a coded relay coming from the SAF to be our eyes. However, the Niets are laying low, so they won't be running active scan. We should be able to hit them all simultaneously."

Rika looked at Lieutenant Heather. "Your pilots are going to have to pull out all the stops. They'll need to find solid grapple on the surface of those ships, and hold on tight. We may need to evac any ships that we can't pull out of the clouds."

Heather nodded somberly. "They can do it. What're the details on the Niets' shields?"

"Low power is the guess," Rika replied. "Major Dala?"

Major Dala stood, her pink hair making her look like a flower, rising above a field of black and grey.

"We're not running active scan, either," she said. "Not 'til the last minute when you're closing on the Niets. However, we're certain that their shields are on low power—just enough to hold the atmosphere back. Any more, and we'd see the grav waves rippling through Armens' atmosphere."

"How dense is it where they're hiding?" Heather asked. "And how are you sure they're running shields?"

"They're in one of the belts, where the gases fall back down into the planet. The second one up from the equator," Major Dala replied, gesturing at the holodisplay of Armens next to

Rika. "Where they're situated, it's a little over five times Iapetus's surface pressure. Not too dense, but enough that a ship's hull can't take the pressure without running shields."

"OK." Heather's eyebrows were pinched, the way they always did when she was running equations. "Given their ship's mass, structure, and those numbers—which I'll review in more detail—I can make a guess at their shield strength. Our dropships can pass through them, but the Niets'll know when we do. Can't hide it."

"I expected as much," Rika said. "I've worked up squad configurations. Some rejiggering was necessary to get the AI-bearing mechs on each assault team. Single squads are going to hit the destroyers, while we'll bulk up with extra fireteams on the cruisers."

Rika pulled up diagrams of the ships, using data that the Marauders and SAF had on the vessels they believed they were facing.

From there, Barne rose and began discussing the ideal breach points on the ships. Of all the Marauders in the company, only he and two others had ever been aboard Nietzschean ships as anything other than captives.

Several of the platoon leaders posed questions about what they should expect to find inside the ships, and Barne answered them to the best of his abilities.

"Remember, people," Rika said when Barne was finished. "Primary objective is to get your AI to the closest network access point, and then hold that point while they breach the security. Once the NSAIs are down, you should have the ability to go wireless. From there, you take engineering to ensure no local helm bypass. If you cannot take engineering, scuttle the ship and get off."

"What happens if we can't go wireless on the hack?" Lieutenant Travis asked.

Rika drew a deep breath. "That's one of the points where

you make the scuttle-or-not decision. On the cruisers we'll have multiple teams at different breach points, so holding the physical network access point will be doable there. On the destroyers, you'll have to make the call. However, we don't need martyrs; if you can't take engineering, and you can't scuttle, do as much damage as possible, and then get off. Even if we take half the ships, the rest will have to come out and surrender, or spend the rest of their lives down there."

"Where will the *'Lark* and the *'Dream* be?" Heather asked.

"Once we breach, there won't be further need for subterfuge. They'll boost back. There are also two SAF cruisers on patrol near Armens, and they'll make for the planet, as well.

"Oh," Rika laughed and looked at the AIs. "Don't forget to change the ship's broadcast when you pull above the clouds. Don't want friendlies shooting at us."

Rika fielded several other questions before no more hands rose. "OK, people, get your mechs in the sims and start running your breach points. I want everyone in the company to be able to walk backwards blindfolded to any place on those ships."

She dismissed the company leadership, barring her HQ team.

"So, what do you think?" she asked. "Defending Hammerfall was just the warmup."

Barne chuckled as he leaned against the bulkhead. "You can say that again. The destroyers alone could carry as many troops as we faced at Hammerfall."

"Though they probably don't," Heather added.

Lieutenant Scarcliff nodded. "Smalls is right. The destroyers *could* carry a thousand, but a lot of those will be crew, not ground troops. They also won't be armored up when we hit."

"But they could be within minutes," Tex, the company's

gunnery sergeant, added. "But I bet they won't use the same level of ordnance we will."

"Careful of that," Leslie advised. "Don't forget, the goal is to have these ships functional enough for the AIs to fly them out of Armens' atmosphere. If we shoot them to shit, chances are we'll blow away their network access, and this'll be a waste of time."

Tex grinned. "Well, we'll be sure to be all discriminate when it comes to what we shoot the shit out of. I bet it'll still be a hell of a lot more than they will."

"Granted." Scarcliff nodded. "I don't know about the rest of you, but I feel like I should be worried, yet somehow I'm not. Those Niets are going to shit themselves silly when they see a mech breach team hit their ships. Stars, I wish I was on The Van's assault team. Can you imagine seeing a K1R come around the corner on a starship?"

Barne barked a laugh. "It's gonna be classic. I'll be sure to record their expressions for you."

"Can't help but think you planned the assignments that way, Top."

Barne gave Scarcliff a roguish grin. "Who says I didn't? And who said you can call me 'Top'?"

"Barne, I'm the company's XO."

"So?"

GOODBYE BASILISK

STELLAR DATE: 08.19.8949 (Adjusted Gregorian)
LOCATION: *Golden Lark*
REGION: Approaching Armens, Hercules System, Septhian Alliance

Rika stood in her office and couldn't keep her face from wearing a big, stupid grin. "You three mean so much to me…can you believe that we met just a half a year ago?"

Chase raised a finger. "I met you further back than that."

"Yeah, but not *too* much before that—minus my stint in cryo."

Chase shrugged. "Was over two years ago, actually."

Rika rolled her eyes. "I'm trying to be all poignant, here."

"You sure you know what that means?" Barne smirked.

Leslie smacked a palm into the back of Barne's head. Then she looked at Chase and smacked him as well. "Just like the boys, gotta ruin the moment."

"We're having a moment?" Barne asked. "I'm not kissing anyone."

"What about a hug?" Rika asked. "I know you're all badass and everything, but I don't think it would kill you to hug someone."

Chase chuckled and punched Barne in the shoulder. "Not sure about that. It might."

"Sheesh, why's everyone hitting me? And I hug plenty of people. Women. Right before I fuck their brains out."

"Ha!" Rika laughed. "There's the Barne we've all come to know and love."

"No love," Barne retorted. "That leads to hugging. Remember, no hugging unless I get to fuck your brains out, and you're both off-limits." He glared at Leslie and Rika as he spoke.

Leslie sidled up to Barne. "Why am I off-limits?"

"Les! Damn. Stop that! You're like fucking kryptonite. I could die if you touch me."

Leslie took a step back and cocked her head at Barne, then Rika. "Kryptonite? What the hell is that?"

Chase leaned close to Leslie and whispered loudly in her ear. "It means he finds you so damn attractive that he can barely function when you're around."

Halfway through Chase's explanation—which he delivered with a goofy smile plastered across his face—Barne yelled for him to stop, but Chase only raised his voice to carry over Barne's.

When he was done, Barne's face had darkened, and Leslie was staring at him with wide eyes.

"Seriously, Barne?" she asked.

Barne kept his eyes locked on Leslie's. "Well, you're the most attractive woman on the ship, it's perfectly natural to be attracted to a beautiful woman."

"What about the tail?" Leslie asked as her tail rose and touched Barne's neck.

"Leslie! Stop it! Seriously." Barne swatted her tail away. "We have to go on a mission. I can't have your sexy tail in my head the whole time."

Rika wasn't sure if Barne was playing with Leslie or not. He *did* sometimes make comments about how she was always slinking about. But the comments always seemed derisive, or at least critical.

Of course, that's exactly how someone would hide feelings they knew they shouldn't have.

Leslie pulled her tail down, a worried look on her face. *<Is he serious?>* she asked Rika privately.

<Stars, I have no idea. It's Barne; this could be an elaborate ruse.>

<He wouldn't do something so cruel, would he?>

Rika's eyes locked on Leslie's. *<Leslie. It's only cruel if you have feelings for him. Otherwise it's just tasteless.>*

<Uh...yeah. Can we talk about this after we kill a whole bunch of Nietzscheans?>

"OK," Rika said aloud. "Let's table whatever the hell just happened here and get our heads in the game. We have a job to do and a company to lead. We're going to get in there, secure ten core-damned starships, and kick the Niets in the teeth while we're at it."

Barne grunted. "Lots and lots of teeth kicking."

Everyone put a hand in the center of their small circle, and called out at the same time, "Rika's Marauders!"

Everyone except for Rika, who still said "Team Basilisk!"

Barne shook his head. "You really gotta get onboard with that name."

"I...uh." Rika felt a flush rising on her cheeks. "OK, let's try it again."

They put their hands out again, and this time all four called out, "Rika's Marauders!" together.

Rika felt stupid and proud at the same time, but the expressions on her friends' faces filled her with confidence.

"OK, Marauders." Rika struggled to keep her expression stony. "Let's do this."

They filed out of Rika's office. At the first intersection, where Barne and Leslie broke off for their drop bays, Rika and Chase paused, staring intently into one another's eyes.

"Good luck, Rika," Chase said. "I'll see you tomorrow."

"Tomorrow," Rika nodded.

They parted ways, each trying to focus on the mission ahead, but failing miserably.

INSERTION

STELLAR DATE: 08.19.8949 (Adjusted Gregorian)
LOCATION: *Golden Lark*
REGION: Approaching Armens, Hercules System, Septhian Alliance

Rika settled into her seat at the front of the dropship, and clipped the harness onto her hard points. She looked at the mechs seated on the benches, First Platoon's squad one, and nodded to them.

"Ready to kick the door in, Marauders?"

"Rika's Marauders!" Sergeant Aaron called out, generating a *Roo-ah!* from the rest of the mechs.

<*Did some of them just say, Riii-ka, or are my ears playing tricks on me?*> Rika asked Niki.

<*They're not, almost half said some variation of your name.*>

Rika held back a groan and glanced at Kelly, who sat with her helmet on her lap, grinning at Rika. Kelly tapped her chest, and Rika saw that Team Hammerfall's logo was still there, but below it was the Marauder's crest.

Rika gave Kelly a thumbs-up and shared a crazy smile with her old friend.

<*I can't believe we're really doing this,*> Kelly said privately. <*Remember back in the war, we used to say that the GAF should use mechs to take enemy ships? We could decimate them on the ground; on a starship, it would be like shooting fish in a barrel.*>

<*I do recall a few conversations like that.*> Rika nodded, smiling at the memory. <*I guess we'll get to see if we were right.*>

<*Too bad Silva won't be here to see it.*>

Rika felt the same way, but knew that Silva needed to be with her daughter, and her daughter needed to be with her mother.

<*We'll send her a vid. She'll have to live vicariously through our*

ass kicking.>

<Oh, there will be vids. I'll be watching this mission when I'm old and grey—when they've replaced my legs with training wheels.>

Rika laughed, and then Flight Leader Heather's voice came over the Link.

<We're approaching the apex of the slingshot. If you pull up the external feeds, you'll see that we've dipped below the cloud tops. Dropships will begin boosting down the ladders in fifteen seconds. Good luck, Marauders.>

Rika had already given her speeches. Everyone had their orders, and Niki had trained the AIs on the breach protocols. Once they dropped, communication would be minimal. From here on out, she was a soldier in a squad, focused on their one objective.

Good luck, everyone.

The light at the front of the dropship went from red to green, and they fell through the deck and out of the ship.

"Goooood afternoon, squad one. We'd like to thank you for flying Air Shit-Storm; I'm your captain, Vargo Klen. The temperature outside is a chilly 120 degrees kelvin, but we expect to enter a warm band soon, where we'll see things creep up to a nice, comfy 320 degrees.

"If you activate your external feeds, you can see a lovely column of particulate ice off our starboard bow, and to port, it's raining ammonia. The inside of our grav shield is pressurized, so that scraping noise you hear is the planet's frozen atmosphere dragging along our shields."

"Klen!" Crunch hollered up to the cockpit. "Is that supposed to be comforting?"

"Why, thank you for the audience interaction. And yes, it is—at least when you consider that there's no planetary surface below us. If we experience any failures, we'll be crushed *long* before we fall the thirty-five thousand kilometers to Armens' liquid metallic hydrogen core."

Crunch looked like he was going to say something else, but only shook his head and sat back.

Klen continued his speech. "Our current flight path and cruising speed has us looking at a nine-hour and thirty-seven-minute flight time, so may I suggest our inflight entertainment system otherwise known as staring at your teammates' helmets?"

"Man, someone needs to at least get us some good vids on this ride," Private Kerry groused. "If I have to stare at Ben's head this whole trip, it's gonna crack my viewscreen."

"Stow it," Sergeant Aaron grunted. "I don't want to have to listen to your shit the whole ride out."

"Sorry, Sarge," Kerry said, giving a thumbs-up. "Can I talk on the way back?"

"Maybe. We'll see how many Niets you kill."

The mechs spoke little for the rest of the ride, though Rika suspected that they were still chatting over the Link. Some would be reviewing the mission details and ship layout, others would be thinking and talking about anything *but* the mission.

The way the dropship bucked and rattled in the gas giant's winds, she bet a lot of the mechs were pretending to be anywhere else.

Whatever worked was fine by her. So long as when the dropship latched on, everyone got out by the numbers and covered their corners.

Rika had a visual of their progress overlaid on her vision. She kept an eye on it, as the thirty-four dropships slowly crept toward the Nietzschean ships at what felt like an agonizingly slow pace.

The dropships were successfully maintaining their formation, pinging one another periodically on a shifting ULF band. Rika breathed a sigh of relief, as the second check-in passed, and the ships were all still in formation.

Other than a rogue lightning strike, the initial entry was the most dangerous part of the journey. If they'd made it this far, they'd make it to the Niets, no problem.

Then the real fun would begin.

Rika was with the team assigned to the enemy cruiser dubbed 'Big Daddy'. It was larger than the others, nearly four kilometers long, and three whole squads were assigned to it.

Squad one, present in the dropship with Rika, would breach an airlock near the rear of the ship, while squads two and three would land amidships, and break up by fireteams once inside to harass the enemy and disrupt any assistance that may be sent back to engineering.

Rika lost track of time—deliberately keeping her eyes from the countdown. It seemed to work, because when Klen announced that they were on their final descent to the Nietzschean ships' altitude, it took her by surprise.

The message came from Heather's dropship that she'd sent out the signal to the SAF; a minute later, live scan data began to flow in from orbiting military satellites.

The Niets would detect the scan, but Rika would bet her life they wouldn't expect what was coming next.

"We're seven hundred kilometers and closing," Klen announced. "Expect some turbulence as we pass through the enemy's shield, and please make sure you take all your weapons with you and kick some ever-lovin' Nietzschean ass!"

A chorus of shouts met Klen's proclamation, and Rika pulled up the view from the nose of the dropship, hoping for a visual of the Nietzschean cruiser.

Unfortunately, all she could see were the dark clouds surrounding them, punctuated by periodic flashes of lightning.

Then the enemy cruiser pushed through the clouds, and the dropship spun and fired its engines, lurching, and jostling the mechs about.

"Mind the bump," Klen cautioned. "We've just passed through their shield. Bringing us in toward our landing site."

Rika could barely see a thing on optical, but on IR, the ship glowed brightly against the dull red of the surrounding clouds.

"Damn, that sucker's hot," Klen commented, breaking out of his pilot's drawl for once. "They'll have to rise up to higher altitudes soon—seems like they can't disperse enough heat down here."

"We'll see if we can't help them with that," Rika replied. "I hear space is pretty cool."

"Too cool—well, too lacking in matter to transfer energy to. When you guys bring those ships up, you should try to do it slowly, with the cooling vanes deployed all the way."

<*Noted,*> Niki replied.

"I have a visual on the other two ships, they're latching on," Klen called back. "We're touching down in three, two, one."

The pilot's statement was punctuated by a dull *thud,* and then the rear hatch on the dropship opened, mechs rushing into the darkness without hesitation.

Rika was last out, and she felt a wave push her upward, off the ship, a moment before her maglocks kicked in and pulled her back down.

<*Did they just try to push us off the hull with a grav wave?*> she asked Niki.

<*Seems like it. I've advised Klen to activate the dropship's weld-grapple.*>

<*Good call.*>

A burst of beamfire came from a nearby point defense cannon, splashing against the dropship's shields.

<*Better late than never. Must have bled off its charge in the heat,*> Sergeant Aaron said. <*One-one, go take that thing out.*>

Ben and Al—who had both been with Rika that fateful

night when they defeated the Politica—were joined by Harris and Kim. They each took aim, stepped through the dropship's shield, and fired in unison.

Aaron nodded with satisfaction. <*Clear any other nearby turrets, one-one. You're going to keep our exit, and the dropship, safe. One-two, get that airlock open.*>

The airlock was five meters from where Klen had set the dropship down, and one-two set to their task, planting a pair of shaped charges on either side of the door's center seam.

<*Fire in the deep!*> Crunch called out. The explosion flared brightly, and the airlock doors bent inward. Crunch and Shoshin, who had recovered fully from his prior injuries, slammed their feet into the airlock doors, caving them in the rest of the way.

Rika's external pickups detected a high-pitched whistle, and she realized it was the planet's atmosphere, pushing into the ship.

That's a change. Hope they like hydrogen.

Crunch and Shoshin dropped down into the airlock to attach explosives on the inner door, as fireteam one-one took out another surface turret to Rika's right.

Rika tried to reach out to the dropships assaulting the other ships and found that it was as they'd suspected. With the planet's interference, and the Nietzschean ships' shields, the assault teams couldn't communicate with one another.

She did connect with squads two and three; both were already moving into the ship and had pulled some rudimentary data from its network. Foremost of which was that the ship they were attacking was the *Fury Lance.* Rika was tempted to still think of it as the *Big Daddy,* but updated the combat net with the correct name to avoid confusion.

Another explosion shuddered through the planet's thick atmosphere, and she saw its cloudy air rush into the ship. The lock was breached.

Fireteams two and three formed up around the airlock while fireteam four held back, just in case anything untoward happened.

<*Dropping probes,*> Kelly announced over the combat net.

Two tiny probes flew out of Kelly's back and dropped down through the airlock. The outer doors had been smashed inward, and the inner seal—a solid disk that rolled into place—was folded over at the middle, just barely making enough room for the AM-3s in the squad.

Rika was glad that she didn't have to worry about getting a K1R through the ship. The Van wouldn't fit through this airlock, even if they'd opened it without explosives.

Kelly's probes flew into the passageway beyond the entrance, and noted likely locations of auto turrets—though why they hadn't deployed was curious.

The passageway ended in a T, and the probes split up, each travelling to the next intersections and stopping to keep an eye on all approaches.

<*One-two, get in there,*> Sergeant Aaron ordered.

<*With pleasure,*> Kelly said and jumped into the airlock.

The rest of the fireteam followed, and then Aaron leapt in after them.

Rika deployed one of her own probes to keep an eye on the fireteam from the rear. She pulled up feeds from second and squad three, which were relayed from their dropships to Klen's, and then to her.

The other squads had already met resistance, but in the form of unarmored crew, barely even worth reporting.

<*The Niets' reaction is surprisingly slow,*> Niki noted.

<*They weren't expecting this sort of attack. No one does crazy shit like this.*>

<*I get that they had the cannons and turrets powered down, they were cutting back on energy use to keep the ships from overheating, but to have so little crew on duty? It doesn't make sense.*>

Rika considered the possibilities. *<Think maybe they're in cryo? Net energy use when in cryo is a lot less than a person up and about, eating, moving around, whatever…>*

<Plus waste. Ships use a lot of power dealing with human leftovers.>

Rika nodded absently as she watched third and fourth fireteams slip into the airlock. She looked to her right where one-one was ranging across the ship's hull, destroying surface cannons—most before they even came online.

<One-one, keep in visual range of the dropship. If we can't see them, they can't shoot at us.>

<You got it, Skipper,> Ben replied. *<Just one more that could hit the top of the shuttle, then we'll fall back. Probes are out, so we'll see their ugly asses before they see ours.>*

<Good job, Corporal. Keep in cover, two in the airlock, and two in the dropship. They could try to push us off again, or maybe even drop their shields. You don't want to be in the open, if that happens.>

<Shit, no we don't,> Ben grunted. *<We really don't. Double-time it, Whispers. Take out that last gun so we can stop being ants in a windstorm.>*

Rika looked up at the dark clouds surrounding the *Fury Lance.* Though two atmospheres of pressure had seeped through the ship's shields, there was a lot more out there.

Not to mention winds that screamed like howling banshees. Crazy as it sounded, she looked forward to the refuge of an enemy starship.

Rika set the feeds from her squad on the left side of her vision, and the feeds from the other two squads along the right side and bottom. Fifty-six layered squares surrounded the view before her, and Rika set combat detection alerts on them.

Satisfied that she could watch the entire breach with minimal obstruction to what lay around her, Rika jumped into the airlock and joined her Marauders in the storming of the *Fury Lance.*

THE FURY LANCE

STELLAR DATE: 08.19.8949 (Adjusted Gregorian)
LOCATION: ***The Fury Lance***
REGION: Within Armens, Hercules System, Septhian Alliance

Kelly was on point, with Crunch and Shoshin covering her six. She'd killed a dozen Niets so far; four of them had been unarmored, and she'd dispatched them without a second thought.

On closer inspection, two of those didn't even have weapons, but she wasn't going to wait for them to fire at her to see if they had malicious intent.

The only good Niet was a dead Niet.

Her fireteam was on a direct route to the network access point that Niki needed to reach, while the others were taking parallel passages, on the lookout for flanking maneuvers from the enemy.

Kelly's probes rounded a corner ahead and caught a view of several Niets in powered armor—a moment later, the feed went dead.

<EM hit the probes. Saw…six. On the right.>

<We got it,> Crunch said as he passed Kelly with Shoshin on his tail. She turned to cover the rear, letting the heavier mechs do what they did best.

Crunch eased up to the corner, glanced back at Shoshin, and raised his KE-72, toggling the grenade launcher.

He fired a trio of grenades that bounced off the wall and disappeared around the corner, at the same moment that three came back.

Kelly had a moment of confusion, wondering how the Niets had kicked the 'nades back so fast, before she realized they had used the exact same tactic at the same time.

Crunch screamed something and dove to the side as the grenades detonated. The force of the explosion picked Kelly up and threw her back to the last intersection they'd passed.

She scrambled to her feet, sending out more probes while cycling her vision to see through the fire and smoke that filled the corridor.

She made out the shapes of Crunch and Shoshin and rushed toward them, but Crunch waved her off as he struggled to his feet.

<Clear the intersection, we're OK…I think.>

Kelly nodded and walked past, JE-87 in her right hand, angling her GNR-40E on her left arm to get a clear shot at anyone who showed a body part around the corner.

She spared a glance at Shoshin as she passed him. He looked OK, though his faceplate was cracked, and the ablative plating on his right side was almost entirely gone. Poor guy was having the worst luck, lately.

Focus, Kelly!

She didn't want to waste a probe, in case their EM source was still functional. Instead, she drew a deep breath and then leapt across the intersection, firing at any shapes she could discern through the smoke.

Something moved on the left side of the passage, and it got a trio of projectile rounds from her GNR. Another shape got a burst from her JE-87, and then another burst from her GNR hit a third shape.

She landed and ducked behind the bulkhead, waiting for return fire, but none came.

Movement to her right caught Kelly's attention, and she nodded to Crunch and Shoshin as they eased up to the intersection. Crunch had a slight limp, and she hoped it wasn't enough to slow him down.

Crunch was an RR-3, and unlike earlier RR models, the 3s had leg stubs like SMIs—which meant they could suffer injury to their thighs and hips. Unlike Shoshin, who no longer possessed organic limbs.

<*You sure you're good?*> she asked Crunch.

<*Good enough to kill—shit!*>

An electron beam streaked down the corridor and struck something behind Kelly. She spun around to see a Niet in heavy armor fall to the deck, his neck half burned away.

<*Stay frosty, people,*> Rika said as she emerged from the smoke behind Crunch and Shoshin. <*Looks like the Niets are starting to get their shit together.*>

<*Yeah, frosty,*> Kelly said, shaking her head. <*Warn a girl before you do that again.*>

<*You snooze, you get the shit scared out of you,*> Rika replied, waving Kelly on.

Kelly eased around the corner and walked past the six Niets who'd tried to take them out. One was moving, and she fired a round into the woman's head without remorse.

Die, bitch.

With Rika bringing up the rear, the fireteam made it the rest of the way to the network access point without further incident.

Kelly rounded the last corner to see Kerry and the rest of one-three waiting for them at the NAP's entrance.

<*What took you so long? Find an ice cream shop or something?*> Kerry asked.

<*Yeah, your mom was running it, so I got her to make a double-dip sundae. You want one?*>

<*Hey, don't be touching my mom's sundae!*>

<*Cut the chatter,*> Sergeant Aaron growled as he approached with one-four.

Kelly took a corner at an intersection twenty meters from the NAP and nodded to Rika as she passed.

<*Give em' hell, Chief,*> she said to Niki.

<*Always do,*> the AI replied.

Kelly sent a probe down each of the two corridors she was covering and tucked each into corners, hoping they'd stay safe. She only had five more, and this party was just getting started.

* * * * *

<*I like Kelly,*> Niki commented as Rika approached the door to the network access point. <*She's boss.*>

< *'Boss'?*> Rika asked. <*What does that mean?*>

< *'Boss', adjective, meaning excellent, outstanding.*>

Rika stopped at the door and grunted. <*Huh, never heard that definition before.*>

<*You've lived a sheltered life.*>

<*Is that what you call it?*>

Niki laughed. <*Well, I guess not. Drop some nano on the access panel so I can walk through this thing.*>

Rika complied, while Niki muttered, <*Stars, I wish you had better nano. Would make some things a lot easier.*>

<*Better nano?*> Rika asked. <*I guess* ***some*** *people might have better, but this is top-of-the-line stuff.*>

<*Really, Rika? You do know that Praesepe is a backwater, right? In the core, children have better nano than you.*>

Children with advanced nano seemed like a very bad idea to Rika. <*How do their parents deal with that?*>

<*They have even better nano than their kids.*>

Rika was suddenly very happy that she was not fighting against the core worlds. *Thank stars the Hegemony of Worlds is eight hundred light years away.*

<*OK, door opening in one…two…dammit, that's not—*>

The door slid open, and Niki let out a whoop as Rika entered.

<*I thought you were having trouble?*>

<*I was, but I can solve problems a lot faster than I can talk to*

you.>

Rika ignored the jibe and looked around the room…which wasn't a room at all. She stood on a catwalk encircling the center of a ten-meter by ten-meter shaft that dropped deep into the ship.

Rika leant over the edge and saw that the bottom of the shaft lay almost a hundred meters below; the top was another sixty up.

In front of them was a five-meter cube, with conduit streaming out of it to points on the walls around them and stretching down the shaft to another cube far below.

"This is not what I was expecting," Rika said aloud.

<*Quiet, it's listening.*>

< *'It'? The cube?*>

<*Yeah, this is one of the NSAI's nodes.*>

Rika raised her GNR. <*Can I just shoot it?*>

<*No! We need to access it, not blow it up. NSAIs on ships like this are multi-nodal. Take out one, and it just reroutes. We're here to poison it.*>

<*What do you need me to do?*> Rika asked.

<*I need you to take your direct connect cable and plug it into the port on the console over there.*>

<*You want me to plug into this thing?*> She had imagined just connecting to some secure panel somewhere. Connecting to the NSAI seemed like a very bad idea.

<*Yeah, this is what we came here to do; you got that, right?*>

<*I did—do. But this is somehow more ominous than I thought it would be.*>

<*Don't worry, you're triple-buffered from what I'm doing. Remember, Carson added in additional firewalls.*>

Rika drew another deep breath and approached the console. <*What about you?*>

<*Me? It's an NSAI, not a core devil. I'll be fine.*>

<*What's a core devil?*>

<Nothing,> Niki dissembled. *<Just a crazy rumor that never seems to go away.>*

Despite their promise to be open with one another, Niki seemed to constantly have more secrets that she'd allude to and never share. Rika knew the AI didn't make slip-ups, so Niki was doing it on purpose.

Is it just to goad me into something? she wondered.

Rika ignored the feeling and pulled out the hard-Link cable and plugged into the socket Niki had highlighted. The cable was only a half-meter long, so she was stuck here for however long this took.

<OK, starting my game of cat and mouse,> Niki announced.

While Niki did her work, Rika checked over the other two squads' progress through the ship.

Kristian's squad two had taken some hits—only minor injuries, though. They seemed to be drawing the most Niets, likely due to the presence of The Van. Nothing like having a K1R-T stomp through your ship to make you pull out all the stops.

Third squad, which had Staff Sergeant Chris accompanying it, was nearly at the engineering bay. Rika saw that one of the AM-2s, a PFC named Kyle that everyone in the platoon called 'Goob', had taken a hit to the torso. He was still alive, but his armor had initiated an emergency coma. CJ and Yig had pulled his limbs off and were taking turns carrying him.

They were meeting with increasing resistance, and Rika was considering peeling off a fireteam from her squad to assist them, when Niki started swearing profusely.

<Awwww, shitty mcfuckface, this is bad. Fucking bad. Clusterfuck bad.>

<Niki, spit it out!>

<They patched the loop—well, at least the best trigger for it. Without that, there's only a minute to attempt the takedown. It's not long enough!>

<*Then we have to scuttle,*> Rika replied, reaching for the hard-Link cable.

<*No, wait! I might be able to figure something out, but we'll need to get it to the other breach teams.*>

Rika groaned. <*You mean the breach teams on the other ships that we can't currently talk to?*>

<*Yeah, those breach teams. Shut up for a minute, will you?*>

Rika wondered if they could relay the updated data to Klen, or if someone would need to take it up to him.

As she was considering her options, something pinged off the catwalk, and Rika realized someone had fired on her from below. She circled her drone around and saw five Niets on a catwalk, twenty meters below, and moving to get a good firing angle on her.

<*Aaron, I've got Roaches crawling around down below. Can you take them out?*>

The squad sergeant sent a quick affirmation, and a moment later, two RR mechs dashed through the open door and leapt off the catwalk, firing as they fell. Rika watched them take out a Niet each on the way down, then land on two others.

Ten seconds later, the five Niets were dead, and the RRs took up positions on either side of the lower catwalk's door, ready to take out any other enemies.

<*Nicely done,*> Rika couldn't help but smile at the mechs' calm efficiency.

<*Thanks, Skipper,*> one of the RRs, a corporal named Mitch, replied.

<*OK! I got it!*> Niki announced. <*As I'd hoped, their patch solved just one avenue of attack, not the core problem. I was able to leverage another vulnerability and get in. How are we going to get it to the other AIs?*>

<*Can we transmit it to Klen?*> Rika asked.

<*Yeah, it's not a big burst…though if the NSAI sniffs it out and cracks it, the hack won't work anymore.*>

<We have to chance it,> Rika replied. *<Running a datapod up to the dropship will take too long.>*

<OK, sending to Klen's ship.>

Rika sucked in a deep breath and got ready for what she was about to ask the pilot to do.

<Vargo, how's it looking up there?>

<Great, Captain. Kim, Harris, and I are having afternoon tea. Had to fight off a drone attack first, though. How're things downstairs?>

<We had a setback with the NSAI hack, but Niki worked out a solution.>

<Good to hear. Why are you pinging me?> Klen's voice carried a note of wariness, and Rika suspected he already knew what she was about to ask.

<The other AIs are going to need this data. Niki has pushed it up into your comm stack; you need to get out there and deliver the data burst to each breach team.>

There was a brief pause, then Klen replied. *<Understood, Captain Rika. I assume I should kick my guests out?>*

<Yes, I'll instruct them to meet up with us. You need to go now.>

<Aye, Captain. I'll be back for the pickup, don't you worry.>

Rika prayed he would. Once he started broadcasting the signal to the other teams, he'd make himself a target for every Niet ship out there. *<I know you will. See you on the flip-side.>*

<You bet. You're buying too, Captain.>

<Damn straight, I am.>

Klen cut the connection, and Rika pulled a feed from Kim's helmet. The dropship cut its weld-grapple free and lifted from the *Fury Lance*. A beam shot out from a point-defense cannon, but was bent around the dropship by the vessel's grav shield.

Then the thrusters fired, and the Marauder dropship shot out of the relatively calm air within the *Fury Lance's* shields and passed out into Armens' raging storms.

Good luck, Marauder.

Rika briefly ensured that one-one was making their way toward the rest of squad one before returning her attention to Niki.

<The console here is showing errors in the node,> she said. *<I take it that's a good thing?>*

<Yeah,> Niki's response was curt. *<Tight timing, here. Shush.>*

Rika sighed and returned to monitoring her various teams. Second squad had slowed to a crawl, but their goal was to cause chaos—which they were excelling at.

However, squad three wasn't doing much better. They were still fifty meters from the engineering bay, and were fighting flanking attempts by the Niets at every turn. Staff Sergeant Chris was out of commission, a series of chest wounds placing him in an armor-coma, as well.

Rika considered sending one-one to assist them, but they would take too long.

<Crunch, how's the leg?> Rika asked.

<Good 'nuf, Captain. Shoshin is a miracle worker with a brace, though I can't say I'll ever be as pretty as I once was. What's up?>

Rika remembered all too well what it was like to get an internal brace jammed into her thigh. It was the furthest thing from fun she could think of. *<Link up with Sergeant Karen and squad three. They're getting hung up, and we need them in that engineering bay in five mikes, tops.>*

<You got it, Captain. Run and gun is the name of the game.>

<Aaron,> Rika addressed squad one's sergeant. *<I'm lending one-two to Karen.>*

<No problem, Captain. She always did need an extra hand.>

<Be nice, Sergeant.>

Weapons fire echoed down the corridor and through the entrance to the shaft.

<I'm always nice,> Aaron grunted in response a minute later.

*****

Kelly ranged ahead of Crunch and Shoshin, keeping her eyes peeled for Niets and firing indiscriminately at any she saw. She followed her probes around a corner and shot a woman in the head, then slammed a man against the bulkhead, crushing his neck.

A door down the passageway opened, and a Niet appeared with a rocket launcher. He wasn't armored, and would kill himself in the explosion, but Kelly had no interest in dodging missiles. She took aim and fired a uranium sabot round at him.

The round struck the end of the rocket launcher, and shrapnel showered the man, tearing him apart.

<*Nice shooting,*> Crunch said as he came up behind her.

<*Couldn't let you get all hurt again, Corporal,*> Kelly said with a smirk that he couldn't see behind her helmet.

Weapons fire came from behind, and Kelly turned to see Shoshin unloading his chaingun on a group of Niets that had tried to flank the team. The enemy ducked behind a bulkhead, but it wasn't enough to save them.

Shoshin's gun tore through the plas and steel, and Kelly saw blood spray out onto one of the walls.

<*Clear,*> Shoshin grunted.

The team resumed their mad dash through the ship until they came to a broad concourse that ran down the center of the vessel.

It was thirty meters wide, and at least two kilometers long. They stood on a catwalk, seven meters above the deck, with the overhead a broad arch, fifteen meters over their heads.

The center of the concourse was occupied by four maglev tracks, a stopped train occupying one of them.

Two of squad three's fireteams were hunkered down next to the train, trading fire with a group of heavily armored Niets with CFT and grav shields on the far side of the concourse.

Squad three's other fireteam was working their way down the concourse, toward a staircase that led down to the engineering bay one deck below.

Squad three's firing angles were terrible, with the maglev tracks giving the Niets plenty of cover. One-two, on the other hand, had a clear view of the enemy, who had not yet spotted them, thanks to an EM flare that Karen had thrown moments before.

Crunch signaled for Kelly and Shoshin to spread out. When each member of one-two was a dozen meters from the next, they opened fire on the Niets.

Kelly let her electron beam fire on max power, burning away CFT shields, and shorting out grav generators with the bolts of lightning that arced out as she raked it across the enemy line.

Shoshin followed after with his chaingun, filling the air with HE shells that tore through the Niets.

Crunch fired two missiles at a cluster of Niets that had taken cover behind a low bulwark alongside the tracks. Plas and steel flew into the air, exposing the enemy to Shoshin's guns.

Below, the elements of squad three that were behind the train rose up and rushed the remaining Niets, cutting them down as the enemy attempted to flee.

<*Thanks for the assist,*> Karen sent, as she directed two of her fireteams to take the stairs down on the far side of the tracks, while she led her team down the stairs on the near side.

<*No problem. There were only seventeen of you down there, I can see why you needed the three of us to help,*> Crunch said with a coarse laugh.

<*You always have to be such an ass?*> Karen shot back.

<*Umm…yeah, Sarge. It was in my contract.*>

<*Just hold position up there and keep any more Niets off our backs.*>

<*Easy peasy, Sarge.*>

Kelly looked around the concourse for a location with good cover, and her eyes were drawn to the arches that supported the ceiling. <*Going to take overwatch up there,*> she gestured at the nearest arch.

<*Looks good,*> Crunch replied. <*Shoshin, get over to that far catwalk. We'll set up a field of fire on anyone who thinks they can come along for a look-see.*>

<*All teams, be advised. Ship's NSAI is offline. I repeat, the NSAI is offline,*> Niki announced over the combat net. <*I have control of the engines and am initializing warmup. We'll be boosting out of here in t-minus fifteen mikes.*>

<*Knew she could do it,*> Kelly said to the team as she swung up onto a strut and shimmied up to the overhead arch.

<*Well yeah; Captain Rika wouldn't have taken the job if there was any doubt.*>

<*There's always doubt,*> Shoshin said.

Kelly rolled her eyes at the man, then realized he couldn't see it through her helmet, so she sent him an image of her rolling her eyes at him over the Link.

<*Mature,*> he replied.

<*Glad you've noticed.*>

STEALING STARSHIPS

STELLAR DATE: 08.19.8949 (Adjusted Gregorian)
LOCATION: *The Fury Lance*
REGION: Within Armens, Hercules System, Septhian Alliance

<*Engines are warming up, and I have helm,*> Niki announced as Rika leant over the railing and fired at the entrance on the level below, aiding the two RRs down there in stemming the never-ending flow of Niets.

<*Great. Can you lock down parts of the ship? This place is still crawling with enemies!*>

<*I've locked down as much as I can, but they pulled a lot of their soldiers out of cryo—you were right about that, by the way. Nearly everyone was on ice. Anyway, their troops are blowing through everything I close.*>

<*What about grav? Can you try messing up gravity on their decks?*>

Rika got a mental image of Niki shaking her head. <*No, their grav emitters have limits of* 1.2g *relative. It's hardwired into them.*>

<*How many enemies are you tracking?*> she asked.

<*Seven hundred and forty-six soldiers. There are still over two-hundred crew throughout the ship, but the ones that are left are either at duty stations, or hiding.*>

Rika considered her options. Fighting through over seven hundred Niets wasn't impossible, but it would be a brutal slog.

<*Can you get on their 1MC?*>

<*Yeah, but what are you going to say?*>

Rika didn't answer. Instead she turned to Sergeant Aaron, who was reloading in the shaft's doorway.

"Sergeant, there are seven hundred Nietzschean soldiers

out of cryo now. If you were them, what would your main goal be?"

Aaron laughed. "Escape pods. Think they can break free of Armens' gravity well?"

"Seriously, Sergeant."

"They need helm control. They're all going to head for engineering."

That was Rika's summation, as well.

"We need to stop that from happening. If they mass, they could take us."

"Then we should go for the bridge and draw some of their force along with us," Aaron suggested.

Rika nodded. "I like where your head's at, Sergeant."

He fired around the corner and laughed. "Me too."

<*Form up, squad one. We're moving out,*> Rika said before detaching the hard-Link cable from the console.

<*Hey! How did you know that was OK to do?*>

<*Because you didn't say anything about us not being able to go to the bridge.*>

<*Oh.*>

<*Kristian, are you and squad two having fun?*> Rika called the platoon sergeant.

<*Gobs, Captain. It's like my favorite holiday every thirty seconds. Nietsdeadday.*>

<*Clever.*>

<*Thanks, been working on it for a bit. We're running a bit low on ammo, and The Van's taken some serious hits, but he's still kicking.*>

<*Good. I've updated the combat net with the enemies Niki is tracking throughout the ship. Should give us some help, but they can fool their internal sensors just as much as we can, so don't trust it too much.*>

<*Understood. You want us to go somewhere?*>

Rika stepped aside as the two RRs on the lower level jumped back up before replying. <*We're going to push to the bridge—we need to draw as many of these bastards away from engineering as we can. I need you to get to that big, long concourse that runs through the ship. They may try to send trains filled with troops down to hit Karen.*>

<*Or trains filled with bombs,*> Sergeant Kristian added.

<*Yeah, that too.*>

<*Count on us, we'll keep Karen safe.*>

<*Good luck, Sergeant.*>

<*Don't need luck. I have Rika's Marauders with me.*>

Rika groaned and closed the connection. She surveyed squad one's status. Kelly, Crunch, and Shoshin were still absent, covering the entrance to engineering, hopefully with backup before long.

Fireteam one had arrived a minute earlier, and other than a few disabled limbs and minor flesh wounds, squad one was ready to roll.

<*Route's up on the combat net,*> Rika announced. <*Aaron, roll 'em out.*>

<*You got it, Captain.*>

The mechs surged forward, alternating suppressive fire with heavy weapons bursts that cut through the enemy's ranks. Corridor by corridor, one threat-laden intersection after another, they cleared a path toward the bridge.

There were several pitched fights in open spaces where the Niets were able to mass and bring superior firepower to bear, but the enemy seemed ill equipped to deal with mechs that could jump a dozen meters in the air and land behind their lines.

After seven minutes, squad one had made it far enough forward that Rika was ready to let the Niets know what she was doing.

"Nietzschean scumbags, this is Captain Rika of the Marauders," she announced over the 1MC. "We'd like to thank you for hosting us today, and dying so easily. We have engine control and we have helm, but there's still a lot of you pesky bastards aboard. So I figure it's best to work from the top down.

"Ship's logs show captain as a Commander Kiers. Well, Commander, hope to see you soon. Keep your seat on the bridge warm for me."

<*Nicely done. Just enough cocky,*> Niki commented.

<*Cocky? I was being sincere.*>

<*Oh.*>

"I liked it," Aaron grunted as he checked a room on the squad's right. <*Clear. Keep moving.*>

<*Niki, any chance you have scan, yet? I'd really like to see how all the other ships are doing. Getting worried about Klen.*>

<*Not yet, their scan and weapons are on segregated systems. I'm trying to work my way in, but they've initialized some new NSAIs that are slowing me down. They have the same vulns as the other one, so they're toppling one-by-one, but it's taking time.*>

Rika peered up a ladder and fired on a shape above before sidestepping to avoid return fire. <*OK, let me know as soon as you have it.*>

<*Yes, Mom. If you get the bridge, you can hold a gun to some poor Niet's head and make him run scan.*>

<*Good idea,*> Rika set a two-second fuse and tossed a grenade up the ladder shaft.

Flames shot down behind her as she moved to the head of the group. Just seven hundred meters of ship to go, and she'd get to see if Niki's idea would work.

* * * * *

<*I see another group working their way forward,*> Kelly called down to the fireteam.

She sighted down the concourse, watching the group of Niets advance along the maglev track. There were ten of them;

two in heavy armor, three in lighter armor, and five in nothing but cloth uniforms.

Idiots all have death wishes.

The heavies were in front, protecting the others, and Kelly considered her options. She only had two DPU rounds, just over sixty projectiles for her GNR, and enough charge for two electron beam shots—*if* she kept the bursts short—plus a cluster of 'nades, and over a dozen mags for her JE-87.

Second squad better get here soon.

She selected her best option and fired a DPU round at the maglev rail beside the advancing Niets. The uranium rod shattered against the track and sprayed shrapnel into the unarmored enemies.

The heavies stopped and looked back. Kelly watched Crunch peek out from behind a vertical column and fire on the backs of the Niets. Kelly added to his attack, and the two heavies fell.

They made short work of the rest.

<*At some point, they're going to give up, right?*> Kelly asked.

The sound of Shoshin's chaingun came from her left, and she turned to see him firing on a group further aft that was well entrenched behind a derailed train.

<*Karen's going to send up three-four to spell us, but they're taking a lot of fire down there, too. These Niets really are just like cockroaches.*>

<*I don't need spelling, I just need ammo.*>

<*When three-four gets back up here, we should scavenge the battlefield,*> Shoshin suggested.

<*Use Niet guns?*> Kelly asked. <*Might as well throw rocks at them.*>

Crunch laughed. <*Well, at least it wouldn't be any worse than what they're using.*>

<*Cold comfort, Crunch,*> Kelly replied.

Shoshin gave a single laugh. <*Nice alliteration.*>

Kelly spotted something down the concourse, near the end, and cycled her vision, zooming in. It looked as though there was some sort of smoke or fog gathering.

Then she magnified further.

<*Shit! Drones!*>

<*What?*> Crunch called out.

<*The Niets set their space-combat drones loose in here!*>

Kelly tried to count the number of drones, but there were so many and they were moving so fast that she couldn't manage. There had to be over a hundred, though—maybe more.

Crunch fired on the leading wave. <*Damn…those things are coming in fast!*>

Kelly didn't reply, but started taking aim at the drones with her GNR, lobbing her projectile rounds.

<*It's no good! They have shields I can't penetrate!*>

<*Get down from there,*> Crunch ordered, and Kelly obliged by dropping down to the train car below and sliding behind it.

Shoshin was firing on the drones with his chaingun, and Kelly set the timer on a 'nade and chucked it at the incoming bots.

It exploded midair, taking out two of the drones, but that was just a scratch.

<*Having fun?*> CJ said as she crouched next to Kelly and fired a missile at the drones.

<*Where'd you get that?*>

<*From the Niets, they were very accommodating.*>

Kelly didn't have time to be relieved, as the drones opened fire on the Marauders, laying down a withering blanket of beams and kinetics.

The maglev rail beside Kelly was torn to shreds, and to her left, one of the support columns buckled and collapsed. She looked up and watched the arch she had been perched on moments earlier pull free of the overhead and fall toward her.

Shit! I'm not dying again!

*****

The *Fury Lance* had two doors to its bridge, both emptying out onto a broad foyer, which was strewn with the bodies of over two-dozen dead Niets.

Rika looked to her right, where Aaron helped Kim sit up so he could apply biofoam to a hole in her stomach, while she kept repeating that she was okay, she could still fight.

"Of course you can, Private. Once we put your insides back where they belong, I expect you to pull a trigger just like the rest of us."

"Put it in my hand, Sarge, I got it," Kim grunted out between rasping gasps.

Rika clenched her jaw and stepped over a fallen Niet on her way to the bridge. She slammed a fist into the starboard door and called out over the 1MC.

"Better get in your escape pods. We're coming in, and we're gonna grind you to pieces. You're no match for the Marauders."

"Rika's Marauders!" someone called out wearily from behind her.

Rika looked back at her Marauders and nodded before turning back to the bridge. "Surrender, or prepare to meet your maker…or find your star, or whatever you fucks believe in."

<Ready to fire the engines,> Niki announced. *<We'll be out of Armen's atmosphere in five minutes.>*

<Thanks, Niki. Don't pull us out yet, though. I don't want to leave anyone behind. We're last out.>

<Got it.>

No response came from within the bridge.

<Are they still in there, Niki?>

<Yeah, there are…ten of them. They're all hunkered down behind consoles. They have handguns. One rifle.>

Rika piggybacked on Niki's visuals from the ship's internal cameras. *<Damn…maybe I scared them all too much.>*

<Perhaps.>

"Last chance to surrender! We don't kill hostages."

No one on the bridge moved, which was impressive in and of itself.

Not that their bravado would buy them any mercy.

Rika nodded to Ben and Whispers to take the door down.

<As non-lethal as we can,> she advised. *<I'd like their captain and some crew, in case we need them to push some buttons.>*

Acknowledgements lit up on her HUD, and Rika calmed her breathing. This was it. *Take the bridge, force the surrender of everyone aboard, win the day.*

Ben and Al were out of explosives, but two pairs of mech-fingers prised the door open, and then heaved the two halves back, tearing them right out of the frame. Four mechs flooded through the opening, laying down pulse fire and fists. Aaron and another four followed, and five seconds later, the 'all clear' came.

Rika walked onto the bridge and saw that two of the crew were dead, several were down, and Commander Kiers was writhing in Kerry's grasp, his feet a dozen centimeters off the floor.

"Commander Kiers," Rika said in greeting. "I've been looking forward to this for…oh, about half an hour, now."

"Fucking mech-meat. You'll never take the *Fury Lance*!"

Rika glanced at the mechs around her as they secured the command crew. "Does he know something we don't?"

Ben shrugged. "Doubtful. We could still kill him."

"Our drones wiped out the rest of your force. It's just you, now," Commander Kiers raged.

"You mean the drones you sent down the concourse to take

back engineering?" Rika asked.

The commander nodded, but his expression changed to one of worry.

"Yeah, our AI got control of them just in the *nick* of time. It was a close call. Then she used them to cut your troops to ribbons. Thanks for giving us what we needed to wrap this up quickly."

Kiers yelled something unintelligible and began to struggle again.

Rika shook her head. "Restrain him and toss him in the corner over there. I want him to watch while we seize or destroy his fleet."

<*Wait,*> Niki called out. <*Get some nano on him first. I want to see if I can get his command tokens; it would make running this ship a lot easier.*>

Rika complied, then turned to the holotank at the front of the bridge. It was only displaying the crest of the Nietzschean military, but she found it hard to believe that the commander hadn't been trying to communicate with his other ships after his own came under attack. She hit the 'recall command' sequence, and the last scan data appeared before her.

Rika nearly crowed with delight.

Three of the destroyers were already breaking out of the clouds, and two cruisers were hot on their tail. One cruiser was falling deeper into Armens, but two Marauder dropships were visible, flying away from it.

The other ships—four cruisers and one destroyer—were still holding their course, but this data was a minute old.

<*Got it!*> Niki called out triumphantly. <*Scan updating!*>

The holotank flickered, and now two more cruisers were rising out of the clouds, while the final destroyer began to fall. Rika felt her breath catch—it was the ship Chase was on.

She was about to issue the command for Niki to dive after it, when the Marauder dropship detached from the destroyer's hull and began to boost upward.

"Comms?" Rika asked aloud, eyes fixed on that ship.

<Linked.>

<Chief Charles, come in. Are all aboard?>

<Captain! Fucking awesome to hear you. Uh…yes, Sergeant Chase said all Marauders are back aboard, but two are KIA.>

Rika clenched her teeth as guilty tears of relief flowed down her face. She wanted nothing more than to talk to Chase at that moment, but she needed to find out what was happening on the two cruisers that were still holding in the clouds. If she started talking to Chase, she might lose her edge.

<Understood. Tell him I'll see him soon.>

<You got it. Mad Dog out.>

<Have you been able to reach those two teams?> Rika asked Niki.

<Yes, Potter has helm and is a minute from firing engines. Lauren is on the other one; she never got the updated hack, but I'm sending it to her now. She should be good to go in a few minutes.>

Niki sounded relieved, and Rika felt the same way. The entire time they had been fighting through the *Fury Lance*, the fear that the other teams had all failed had lurked in the back of her mind.

One company assaulting ten cruisers with a total complement of over ten thousand, and winning? This would be the stuff of legends.

"Wait…" Rika said as she reviewed the scan holo and the raw data that was scrolling in a panel to the right. "Vargo Klen. I don't see him. Did he make it out?"

<I have a Link to the SAF, let me check,> Niki replied.

Rika glanced at Aaron as he approached and gave his update.

"We are secure, Captain. There may still be some Niets holed up here and there, but based on the numbers that the cryo systems show, all but a few of their soldiers are dead."

Rika clasped a hand on his shoulder as the second-to-last cruiser fired its engines and began to climb out of the clouds.

"Almost there," Rika whispered.

<*They didn't pick Klen up,*> Niki reported. <*I've scoured the logs. He took weapons fire on the way back to the* Fury Lance.>

Niki highlighted the location where Klen's dropship had last been seen, and Rika scowled at the scan display. "I don't see anything."

<*Compensating for winds—it's a killer storm out there…*>

Rika bit her lip. She'd been the one who sent him out there—granted, she'd sent *everyone*…but he wasn't a mech. He couldn't handle what they could.

<*Got him, he's two hundred kilometers down. It's not crush depth…but there's a huge low-pressure zone moving in beneath us.*>

Rika felt her breath catch. "Which means he could fall like a rock."

<*I can take us down. We can grab him with a grav beam, and draw him in.*>

"Do it. We're not leaving anyone behind."

<*He could be dead…*> Niki said quietly, for Rika's ears alone.

<*Niki, no one gets left behind. He saved the day. Armens will not be his grave.*>

<*Aye, Captain Rika,*> Niki replied on the combat net. <*Chiefs Ferris and Tanya, I've opened up a shuttle bay that looks to be clear of Niets. I advise you to get inside.*>

Rika watched the feeds from the two dropship pilots that were still attached to the hull of the *Fury Lance* as they pulled free and eased around the starship toward the bay Niki had indicated.

The moment they were within, the bay's doors began to close. Three kilometers behind them, the *Fury Lance's* engines roared to life, and Rika felt a small shudder beneath her feet.

<*Dampeners are running at low power. Trying to keep things cool,*> Niki said. <*Cooling vanes are all the way out.*>

Rika pulled up a view of the clouds around the ship on the forward display, as they turned and began to fall through the gas giant's atmosphere. All around the vessel, lightning flared, striking the shields and the cooling vanes with increasing intensity.

"Is that normal?" Aaron asked.

"Nothing we're doing is normal. But the ship can take it; she's rated for a lot deeper than this."

"After spending weeks down here heating up like a toaster?"

<*She'll hold,*> Niki replied, her tone filled with more determination than confidence.

A shudder began to run through the deck as they dropped, and then suddenly they all felt a moment of weightlessness as the ship fell faster.

<*Hit the low-pressure zone, compensating. I have a visual on Klen's dropship.*>

The secondary holotank came to life, showing the front half of the dropship. It was spinning wildly, but Rika saw that the cockpit hatch was sealed.

There was a chance.

Niki spun the *Fury Lance* so that its engines were facing down toward the planet core, and let them fall until they were within one kilometer of the dropship.

The shuddering in the deck plates had intensified, and Rika couldn't help but notice that they were now more than five hundred kilometers below the cloud tops.

Lights began to flash on several consoles, and an alarm sounded. The bridge's forward display flashed a warning that the hull of the ship was over 700 degrees kelvin.

<*Got him!*> Niki cried out. <*Pulling him in…same bay as the other ships.*>

Rika turned to the feeds from the other dropships and watched with dismay as the red-hot ruin of Klen's dropship was set on a cradle.

The moment the clamps wrapped around the wreckage, Rika shouted. "Go! Go!"

The deck lurched under them, and Niki cried out. <*All Marauders, hold onto your hats. Dampeners failing!*>

Rika ran to the back wall of the bridge as the dampeners and artificial gravity cut out at the same time. Suddenly the ship's engines were 'down', and 10*g* of thrust slammed everyone into the rear wall.

Commander Kiers fell down the bridge, hit a chair, and then flew out the open door, into the atrium beyond.

Ben peered around the door at what was now a sixty-meter drop. "Oops."

The *Fury Lance* bucked like a wild horse in the gas giant's winds, but Rika could see that their descent had stopped, and they were rising once more.

<*Shit, we're dancing close to thermal shutdown on the reactors,*> Niki warned. <*I'm decreasing our angle and burn.*>

The 10*g* dropped to only 8, and Rika felt a small lessening in the tremendous pressure on her chest. She wondered how the squishies must be feeling. She suspected that their ascent was going to kill as many Niets as the attack had.

The minutes dragged on as the ship crept out of the planet, kilometer by kilometer. Then they passed into the troposphere; the heat warnings began to fall silent, and the shuddering decreased to a mere tremor.

A minute later, the blessed blackness of space filled the forward viewscreen, and the bridge erupted with cheers.

<*Niki, you deserve a promotion.*>

Rika was surprised to hear a tremor in her AI's voice.

<*Tell me about it.*>

<*How close?*> Rika asked.

<*You really don't want to know.*>

CAPTAIN RIKA

STELLAR DATE: 08.20.8949 (Adjusted Gregorian)
LOCATION: ***Fury Lance***
REGION: Within Armens, Hercules System, Septhian Alliance

Rika sat in the *Fury Lance*'s command chair, reviewing the after-action reports and damage assessments that were flowing in from her teams.

All-in-all, it was better than it could have been, but worse than she'd hoped. Twenty-seven of her Marauders had died, and fifty more were seriously injured.

Vargo Klen, by some miracle, had survived—though there wasn't much of him left. Someone had found his last will, and in it, he asked to be turned into a mech if he was seriously injured.

Rika didn't want to think about that just yet. He could be kept in a medical coma for the time being.

There was nothing wrong with prosthetic limbs in and of themselves, and should the receiver be willing, there was no moral dilemma.

But mechs were more than mods and prosthetics—they were made to *kill*. An arm that helped you pick up your cup of coffee or caress your lover was one thing. An arm that was purpose-built to kill everyone in sight was a different thing entirely.

Rika pushed that concern from her mind as a call from Major Tim came in.

<Captain Rika! I have to hand it to you. I…that's quite the victory.>

<He was going to say that he didn't think we could pull it off,> Niki said privately.

<Yeah, that was my suspicion, as well,> Rika said to Niki

before replying to Tim. <*Five ships for the Marauders, three for the SAF, and a whole pile of dead Nietzscheans. It's a good day to be a Marauder.*>

<*Do you think the SAF will let us keep that dreadnought?*>

<*The* Fury Lance*? They'll pry it from my cold, dead fingers. We've saved their bacon twice this week.*>

Major Tim laughed and began to speak, when Cora interrupted him <*Major, Captain! A ship just jumped into the system broadcasting an alert. The Albany System is under attack! Half of it has already fallen to the Nietzscheans!*>

<*What the fuck!?*> Rika exclaimed. <*What about Pyra? How long ago?*>

<*When the ship jumped out, Pyra was still holding on. Intel is three days old.*>

Rika rose from her chair and looked at the dreadnought's bridge before her.

<*Give me all ships, Niki.*>

<*You've got it.*>

<*Marauders. This is Captain Rika. Today, we saved the Hercules System. But now the Nietzscheans are back in Albany. Crews on SAF-claimed ships, get off those vessels and make for the* Fury Lance. *We are boosting for the Albany jump point in thirty minutes.*>

<*Rika!*> Major Tim shouted into her mind. <*What? You can't!*>

<*Major. I am not under your command. In fact, in matters such as this, you are under mine. My mechs are going to need the supplies on your ships; I order you to accompany us.*>

<*Rika—*>

<*She's right, Major,*> Cora interjected. <*She's in charge of where the force deploys. General Mill was explicit in his orders, and made no mention of remaining in the Hercules System.*>

Major Tim didn't respond for almost a full sixty seconds, but Rika could feel his anger spilling across the Link.

Finally, he replied. <*Very well, but I'm in command of fleet formation. I'll provide vector and burn before we depart.*>

<*Understood,*> Rika replied and closed the connection.

"Rika!"

She spun to see Chase entering the bridge, and leapt over the command chair as she rushed toward him. She stopped short when she saw that his left arm was missing.

"Chase! Again?"

"It's OK, Rika. It's just an arm."

She wrapped her arms around him and gave a gentle squeeze. "Seems like a habit. Vargo Klen wants to be a mech; maybe we should just get it over with, and do it to you, too."

Chase raised an eyebrow and gave her a tired smile. "You know, I wonder if that wouldn't be such a bad idea."

"Really?" Rika couldn't keep the surprise from her voice.

"Yeah I'm losing limbs on nearly every engagement. Would be a lot more useful if they could just bolt on a new one."

Rika took a step back and gauged Chase's size. "AM-3?"

"Hell no!" Chase exclaimed. "If—and this is probably just the post-battle adrenaline talking, plus the wonderful drugs my armor is injecting me with…where was I?"

" 'If'," Rika supplied.

"Right! *If* I become a mech, I'm keeping my man-bits. No two ways about it."

Barne snorted as he walked onto the bridge with Leslie at his side. "A mech with a dick. That'll be the day. Then once you get *your* bits back, Rika, you two can finally fuck and make little mech babies."

"Barne!" Leslie exclaimed and smacked the First Sergeant on the back of the head. "That's…I'm not sure what. Inappropriate, at least!"

Rika couldn't help but notice that Leslie's hand had been clasping Barne's before she'd pulled it free to hit him.

"It's OK, Leslie. Asshole is part of Barne's charm."

"He's a man made of ass," Chase added.

Barne nodded. "And I make it look good."

Chase turned back to Rika. "So, what's this about Albany?"

"Niets hit them nine days ago," Rika replied. "We're jumping out there to lend a hand."

"On whose orders?" Leslie's eyes narrowed as she stared at Rika.

"Mine," Rika replied.

Barne sat at a duty station and placed his feet on the console. "Fine by me." He leaned back and interlaced his fingers. "If that's where the Niets are, then we'd best get going. They're not going to die on their own."

Rika grinned and slapped Barne on the shoulder. "I like your attitude, Top."

"Who said you could call me 'Top'?"

TANIS RICHARDS

STELLAR DATE: 08.27.8949 (Adjusted Gregorian)
LOCATION: Jersey City, Pyra
REGION: Albany System, Septhian Alliance

Tanis sagged against the crumbling brick wall, praying it would hold up long enough for her to catch her breath. She looked down at her rifle, shaking her head at the energy readout.

Ten percent.

Her left arm was gone—the flowmetal it was made of long ago consumed to build nano—and a hole was blown clear through her right leg. To top it off, her reactive armor was failing.

Overhead, just beyond the burning towers of Jersey City, another Nietzschean ship drifted into view, beam fire glowing brightly as it fired on…something.

<*Stars, those things just keep coming!*>

Angela sighed, the AI also somehow sounding weary. <*They have at least ten thousand…maybe more.*>

Tanis felt her eyelids droop, the last of her energy nearly gone, when the sound of heavy footfalls came from a nearby side street.

Her eyes snapped back open, and Tanis pushed off from the wall, wincing each time she put pressure on her injured leg. She collapsed behind a pile of rubble and swung her rifle up onto the debris, aiming it in the general direction of the side street. Her breath was loud and ragged in her ears as she waited for whatever was next.

There was no backup to be called, no ship to save them with starfire. They were alone.

<*Is this how it all ends, Angela?*>

<I don't know, Tanis, but I know one thing for sure: we're going to find out together.>

Tanis felt a smile grace her lips. *<Together. That's how we'll always be.>*

Above them, more Nietzschean ships drifted over the city, their beams raking the ground as far as the eye could see.

On the ground, the first Nietzschean soldier came around the corner, and Tanis opened fire.

She'd kill as many as she could before they got her.

THE END

* * * * *

The adventure continues in ***Rika Commander***, coming out April 19th, 2018.

But first, Rika has a date with destiny in the Albany System. Find out how Tanis ends up not far from where Rika was re-united with Chase in: ***Attack on Thebes***.

Read on for details about the different types of mechs, and the members of Rika's Marauders.

MECH TYPES AND ARMAMENTS

While these are the standard builds and configurations documented by the Genevian Armed Forces (GAF), many mechs reached the field in mismatched configuration, or were altered after deployment.

Sometimes these alterations were upgrades, sometimes downgrades, as repairs were often made with whatever spare components were available at the time.

The mechs in the Marauders generally align with the stated configurations, though many have altered themselves over the years.

K1R (Kill Ranger – Generation 1)

This mech is more of a two-legged tank than a mech. The K1R sports a central 'pod' where the human is situated. None of the limbs utilize human material.

K1Rs often had mental issues due to feeling as though they had lost all sense of humanity. When the Nietzscheans won the war, they did not release any K1Rs from their internment camps. It is not known if they kept them, or killed them all.

Until the discovery of the mechs in the Politica, there was only a single K1R in the Marauders (who had been under General Mill's command at the end of the war). That mech has joined Rika's company to assist the four K1Rs Rika freed from the Politica in re-integration.

K1R mechs have a variety of heavy armament, including massive chainguns, railguns, missiles (with and without tactical nuke warheads), electron beams, and proton beams. They also sport a variety of suppression devices, from pulse, to sonic, to portable grav shields.

K1R mechs were not made later in the war, due to their cost and mental instability.

There were rumors that a limited run of K2R mechs were made, but no credible reports exist.

Sub-Models:

All K1R models could be outfitted with interchangeable armament, excepting the base model, which could not carry the tactical nukes.

K1R – The base K1R model was made in the early years of the war, and lacked the coordination and reactive armor of the later models.

K1R-M – The 'M' K1R added in the reactive armor, and included upgraded railguns with more advanced scan and target tracking systems. These mechs carried two missiles in launcher pots in their backs. They could be (and often were) upgraded to support the tactical nuke warheads on the missiles.

K1R-T – The 'T' model was a similar configuration to the 'M', but came standard with tactical nuclear warheads. Instead of the pair of launchers the K1R-M sported, the 'T' model carried as many as twelve missiles.

AM (Assault Mech)

The AM mechs represented the bulk of the GAF's mechanized infantry program. It is estimated that over ten million AMs were created during the war, and over one hundred thousand are known to have survived. Many joined mercenary outfits or the militaries of other nations.

AM model mechs were a 'torso only' design, where none of the human's arms and legs were retained. The original idea was to make their cores swappable with K1R models, but it turned out that the mechanized infantry design of the AM models was generally more effective than the 'walking tank' design of the K1R models.

AM models were versatile mechs which had swappable loadouts. The improvements over time were mostly centered around human-mech integration, armor, and power systems.

AM mechs were often outfitted with chainguns, shoulder-mounted railguns, and electron beams.

Without known exception, AM mechs were always male.

Sub-Models

AM-1 – The original model of AM. Fewer than 100,000 AM-1 mechs were made, and none were known to have survived the war.

AM-2 – The AM-2 mechs quickly superseded the AM-1s, with better armor, more efficient power systems, and superior human-mech integrations.

AM-3 – The third generation of AM mech had upgraded power supply systems, and an artificial epidermis to remove the need for periodical removal and cleaning. Some AM-3s were also AI capable.

AM-T – Design specs for AM-T mechs exist, but it is not known if any were made by the Genevians. The AM-T design utilized two AM-3 mechs working together in one larger body, controlling more limbs and separating motion and combat functions.

RR (Recon/Ranger)

The RR model of mech was the precursor to the SMI model. RR's were based on both male and female humans, though smaller humans were used for RR models than AM and FR mechs.

These mechs were similar to AM models, except they were physically smaller and lighter. This allowed RRs to handle light aircraft/drop deployments.

As a compromise, they had smaller power sources, and could only operate for two to three days in the field.

Their loadouts were swappable with AM models, but they rarely utilized the chainguns.

Sub-Models

RR-1 – This model of mech began to appear on the battlefield around the same time as the AM-2 mechs. They utilized the power upgrade of the AM-2 mechs to have smaller power systems, but they also had a smaller power capacity. In theory, the new batteries of the AM-2 line should have worked, but they had overheating issues in the field, and more than one RR-1 suffered from battery detonation when utilizing multiple firing systems.

RR-2 – The RR-2 mechs were rolled out around the same time as the AM-3s, and had few significant changes other than improved armor, and marginally longer-lasting power that no longer suffered from overload issues.

Second gen RR-2 mechs were also skinless, like AM-3 and SMI mechs.

RR-3 – The RR-3 mechs reached the field shortly before the end of the war, and were different in that they had partial legs, like SMI mechs. This was done as a cost/component-saving measure.

FR (Force Recon)

Force Recon mechs were mechs that had the lighter drop capabilities of the RR mechs, with the additional power and armor of AM-3 models. All FR mechs were skinless.

Sub-Models

FR-1 – The first generation of FR mechs were limited run, and had both weight and power load distribution issues.

FR-2 – Second generation FR mechs solved many of the issues from the first generation, and were well regarded for their effectiveness.

XFR – The XFR model is not known to have been widely produced. This model had additional power and carrying capacity to utilize shoulder mounted proton beams and chainguns. However, the mech's loadout made it almost has heavy as an AM-3 without the armor.

SMI (Scout Mech-Integrated)

The final mech model produced at the end of the war was built out of a desire for a super-light mech that could be used in place of standard infantry in sniper/recon situations, and bring extreme fire to bear if desired.

SMI mechs were also cost-saving mechs, as they retained more of their human body components, making for fewer prosthetic neural connections. They also leveraged progress in muscle and bone augmentation that had been used in RR and FR mech models.

The mechs were built exclusively from small, lithe women who could fit in the mech armor and still create a small profile.

Unlike other mech models, SMI mechs were never deployed with two functional hands. One was always a weapon mount.

SMI mechs are all skinless.

Sub-Models

SMI-1 – The first generation of SMI mechs had a short production run due to psychological issues. Because they retained more of their human bodies than other mechs, they ended up having additional dysphoria issues.

SMI-2 – Second generation SMI mechs had improved physical integrations and psychological conditioning that caused the mechs to view themselves as less human. However, in the field, it was observed to have the opposite effect, and SMI mechs retained a strong connection to their humanity.

3rd MARAUDER FLEET 4th DIVISION

Fleet Commander: Colonel Argon
Division 4 Complement (2 Ships)

Golden Lark
1200-meter heavy cruiser
64 fighters
Ship's AI: Cora
Other Ship AIs: Jane & Frankie
Captain: Major Tim
XO Commander: Scas
Dockmaster: Chief Ora

Perseid's Dream
650-meter destroyer
24 fighters
Ship's AI: Moshe
Other Ship AI: Lauren
Captain Penny

9th MARAUDER BATTALION 'M' COMPANY

Note, not all personnel in M Company are listed. Full company complement is 380+.

Company HQ

Commanding Officer (CO) – SMI-2 Captain Rika
Executive Officer (XO) – FR-2 First Lieutenant Scarcliff
Flight Leader (FL) – RR-3 First Lieutenant Heather (Smalls)
First Sergeant – Barne
Gunnery Sergeant – Tex
General Council – David
Tactics and Strat AI (1 & 2P) – Potter
Tactics and Strat AI (3-5P) – Dredge
Lead DI – Staff Sergeant Chase

First Platoon

Platoon CO – First Lieutenant Leslie
Platoon Sergeant – Staff Sergeant Chris (AM-2)

Dropship Pilots (6 per platoon)
- Vargo Klen
- Ferris, "Ferryman"
- Charles, "Mad Dog"

First Squad
Squad Sergeant Aaron (AM-3)
4 Fireteams (19 mechs)

FT 1-1
- CPL Ben (AM-2)
- PFC Al, 'Whispers' (AM-2)
- PFC Kim (RR-3-F)
- PFC Harris (FR-2)

FT 1-2
- CPL Crunch (RR-3-M)
- PFC Kelly (SMI-2)
- PFC Shoshin (AM-3)

FT 1-3
- PFC Kerry (RR-2)

FT 1-4
- CPL Mitch (RR-2)

Second Squad
Squad Sergeant – Kristian (RR-2-M)
3 Fireteams (13 mechs)

FT 2-1
- CPL (K1R-T) Oosterwyk-Bruyn, 'The Van'
- PFC Keli (SMI-2)

Third Squad
Squad Sergeant Karen (SMI-2)
4 Fireteams (19 mechs)

FT 3-1
- PVT Kyle, 'Goob' (AM-2)
- CPL Yiaagaitia, 'Yig' (RR-2-M)

FT 3-4

- Carolyn 'CJ' (RR-3-F)

Fourth Squad
Squad Sergeant – Kara (SMI-2)
4 Fireteams (20 mechs)

Second Platoon

Platoon CO – First Lieutenant Travis (AM-3)
Platoon Sergeant – Staff Sergeant Divinar (AM-3)

Dropship Pilots
Lieutenant Buggsie

Squad One
Squad Sergeant – Fuller (AM-2)
4 Fireteams (19 mechs)

Second Squad
Squad Sergeant – Chauncy (FR-2)
4 Fireteams (21 mechs)

Third Squad
Squad Sergeant Bean (SMI-2)
5 Fireteams (25 mechs)

Fourth Squad
Squad Sergeant Kristina, 'Abs' (RR-2)
4 Fireteams (20 mechs)

FT 2-4
CPL Musel (AM-2)
PFC Bitty (K1R-M)
PFC Smitty (RR-3) (F)

Third Platoon

Platoon CO – First Lieutenant Wilson (FR-2)
Platoon Sergeant – Staff Sergeant Bookie (SMI-2)

Squad One
Squad Sergeant Char (RR-3-F)
4 Fireteams (19 mechs)

Second Squad
Squad Sergeant Mal (FR-2)
4 Fireteams (22 mechs)

Third Squad
Squad Sergeant Cory (AM-2)
4 Fireteams (19 mechs)

Fourth Squad
Squad Sergeant Lana (SMI-2)
4 Fireteams (20 mechs)

Fourth Platoon

Platoon CO – First Lieutenant Michael (AM-3)
Platoon Sergeant – Staff Sergeant Johnny (FR-2)

Squad One
Squad Sergeant Alana (RR-2-F)
4 Fireteams (19 mechs)

Second Squad

Squad Sergeant Aerin (SMI-2)
4 Fireteams (21 mechs)

Third Squad
Squad Sergeant Justin (FR-2)
4 Fireteams (19 mechs)

Fourth Squad
Squad Sergeant Val (RR-3-F)
3 Fireteams (14 mechs)

Fifth Platoon

Platoon CO – First Lieutenant Crudge (AM-3)
Platoon Sergeant – Staff Sergeant Sal (FR-2)

Squad One
Squad Sergeant Darla (RR-3-F)
4 Fireteams (19 mechs)

Second Squad
Squad Sergeant George (FR-2)
4 Fireteams (20 mechs)

Third Squad
Squad Sergeant Jessa (RR-3-F)
3 Fireteams (14 mechs)

Fourth Squad
Squad Sergeant Jynafer (RR-3-F)
3 Fireteams (13 mechs)

Sixth Platoon (Maintenance and Medical)

Platoon Commander – Lieutenant “Bondo” Carson
- Corporal Stripes (AM-2)

THE BOOKS OF AEON 14

Keep up to date with what is releasing in Aeon 14 with the free Aeon 14 Reading Guide.

The Intrepid Saga
- Book 1: Outsystem
- Book 2: A Path in the Darkness
- Book 3: Building Victoria

- The Intrepid Saga Omnibus – *Also contains Destiny Lost, book 1 of the Orion War series*

- Destiny Rising – *Special Author's Extended Edition comprised of both Outsystem and A Path in the Darkness with over 100 pages of new content.*

The Orion War
- Book 1: Destiny Lost
- Book 2: New Canaan
- Book 3: Orion Rising
- Book 4: The Scipio Alliance
- Book 5: Attack on Thebes
- Book 6: The Thousand Front War (2018)
- Book 7: Fallen Empire (2018)
- Many more following

Tales of the Orion War
- Book 1: Set the Galaxy on Fire
- Book 2: Ignite the Stars (Feb 2018)
- Book 3: Burn the Galaxy to Ash (2018)

Perilous Alliance (Age of the Orion War - with Chris J. Pike)
- Book 1: Close Proximity
- Book 2: Strike Vector
- Book 3: Collision Course
- Book 4: Impact Imminent (2018)

Rika's Marauders (Age of the Orion War)
- Prequel: Rika Mechanized
- Book 1: Rika Outcast
- Book 2: Rika Redeemed
- Book 3: Rika Triumphant
- Book 4: Rika Commander (April 2018)
- Book 5: Rika Unleashed (2018)
- More coming in 2018

Perseus Gate (Age of the Orion War)
Season 1: Orion Space
- Episode 1: The Gate at the Grey Wolf Star
- Episode 2: The World at the Edge of Space
- Episode 3: The Dance on the Moons of Serenity
- Episode 4: The Last Bastion of Star City
- Episode 5: The Toll Road Between the Stars
- Episode 6: The Final Stroll on Perseus's Arm
- Eps 1-3 Omnibus: The Trail Through the Stars
- Eps 4-6 Omnibus: The Path Amongst the Clouds

Season 2: The Inner Stars
- Episode 1: A Meeting of Bodies and Minds (Feb 2018)
- Episode 2: A Surreptitious Rescue of Friends and Foes (2018)
- More coming in 2018

The Warlord (Before the Age of the Orion War)
- Book 1: The Woman Without a World
- Book 2: The Woman Who Seized an Empire
- Book 3: The Woman Who Lost Everything (March 2018)

The Sentience Wars: Origins (With James S. Aaron)
- Book 1: Lyssa's Dream
- Book 2: Lyssa's Run
- Book 3: Lyssa's Flight (Jan 2018)
- Book 4: Lyssa's Call (2018)
- Book 5: Lyssa's Flame (2018)

Machete System Bounty Hunter (Age of the Orion War - with Zen DiPietro)
- Book 1: Hired Gun (Feb 2018)
- More coming in 2018

The Empire (Age of the Orion War)
- The Empress and the Ambassador (2018)
- Consort of the Scorpion Empress (2018)
- By the Empress's Command (2018)

Tanis Richards: Origins
- Prequel: Storming the Norse Wind (At the Helm Volume 3)
- Book 1: Shore Leave (June 2018)
- Book 2: The Command (June 2018)
- Book 3: Infiltrator (July 2018)

The Sol Dissolution
- The 242 - Venusian Uprising (The Expanding Universe 2 anthology)
- The 242 - Assault on Tarja (The Expanding Universe 3 anthology)

The Delta Team Chronicles (Expanded Orion War)
- A "Simple" Kidnapping (Pew! Pew! Volume 1)
- The Disknee World (Pew! Pew! Volume 2)
- It's Hard Being a Girl (Pew! Pew! Volume 4)
- A Fool's Gotta Feed (Pew! Pew! Volume 4)

ABOUT THE AUTHOR

Michael Cooper likes to think of himself as a jack-of-all-trades (and hopes to become master of a few). When not writing, he can be found writing software, working in his shop at his latest carpentry project, or likely reading a book.

He shares his home with a precocious young girl, his wonderful wife (who also writes), two cats, a never-ending list of things he would like to build, and ideas...

Find out what's coming next at www.aeon14.com

96020238R00166

Made in the USA
Lexington, KY
15 August 2018